VIOLET'S CHILDREN

Liverpool, 1950. They say you can choose your friends, but you can't choose your family. Yet when Violet Duffy is asked to give a home to the orphaned children of a distant relative, it is precisely the choice she must face. Can she turn her spinster life upside down and take these lost souls into her little house on Amber Street?

Abby and Will have had young lives full of tragedy. Life with Violet offers love and safety. But as they grow up, their past won't let them be and they are curious to discover life beyond Liverpool's streets.

VIOLET'S CHILDREN

VIOLET'S CHILDREN

by

MAUREEN LEE

Magna Large Print Books
Anstey,
Leicestershire

British Libarary Cataloguing in Publication Data.

A catalogue record of this book is
available from the British Library

ISBN   978-0-7505-4760-4

First published in Great Britain by Orion Books, an imprint of
The Orion Publishing Group Ltd in 2018

Cover illustration © Ildiko Neer/Arcangel by arrangement with
Arcangel Images Ltd

Maureen Lee has asserted her right to be identified as the
author of this work in accordance with the Copyright, Designs
and Patents Act 1988

Published in Large Print 2019 by arrangement with
The Orion Publishing Group Ltd

Magna Large Print is an imprint of Library Magna Books Ltd.

Printed and bound in Great Britain by
T. J. (International) Ltd., Padstow, Cornwall, PL28 8RW

Part 1

1

Liverpool, 1950

She was on her way home from work. The letter was on her knee in her navy-blue, patent-leather handbag. Violet rubbed a faint spot off the side with her gloved hand before clicking it open. There wasn't much inside: a small diary with a pencil tucked into the spine, rosary beads in a little felt pouch, her mother's cracked leather purse that she'd had ever since Violet could remember, a perfectly ironed white hanky with an embroidered corner, and a comb and hand mirror that had been in the bag when it was bought. Today, because it was Friday, there was also a wage packet containing eighteen pounds, four shillings and sixpence — and the letter. It had been in the packet with the wages and was still folded into four. Violet hadn't yet read it.

She caught her breath. The money was exactly twice her usual wage and the only reason she could think of for having been paid so much was that she'd been sacked with immediate effect, and the extra money was in lieu of a week's notice.

'You're a terrible pessimist, Violet.' Her mother's voice came to her from across the years. 'With you, the glass is always half empty, never half full.' If Mam were alive, she'd say the extra money might be a bonus, a reward for

Violet's hard work for more than three decades. 'Or perhaps they've given you a rise, luv.'

'They'd never double me wages, Mam.' Violet carried on the imaginary conversation inside her head.

'Oh, all right, maybe not,' Mam conceded, 'but they'd never sack you, either. You've been with Briggs' Motors since you was fourteen, girl, when the place was no more than a shed. Now you're secretary to the managing director and it's one of the biggest firms in Liverpool. Norman Larkin thinks the world of you. So stop being such an old misery guts and cheer up.'

The trouble with talking to a dead person was they weren't aware of the full facts. Mam had passed away only a few months before the war had ended. Unless there was a way of receiving messages in heaven, she wouldn't know that Norman Larkin had gone to meet his own maker only last year and Douglas Penny had been appointed in his place. Douglas was an ex-Royal Air Force officer with a ridiculous moustache and a dead posh voice — 'As if he had a plum in his gob,' as Violet's mam would have said. He didn't bother to hide his resentment of inheriting a secretary as old and unattractive as Violet. He was quite openly having an affair with Beryl Daly — more commonly known as the 'blonde bombshell' — who worked in the typing pool. Violet wouldn't be the least bit surprised to hear that very soon, in fact as early as next week, Beryl, with her bright yellow hair, long red fingernails and enormous bosom, had moved into the little office next to the managing director's that Violet had occupied for so long.

If the truth be known, she'd been half expecting the letter ever since Douglas Penny had been installed as managing director of Briggs' Motors. Now it had come, but she wouldn't read it until she got home, had lit the fire, made a cup of tea and was sitting in her mother's armchair with Sammy, her handsome tabby cat, both watching the fire take hold. She needed to be somewhere friendly and familiar when she learnt she'd lost her job in the only place she'd worked in her life.

'Goodnight, Miss Duffy,' said a girlish voice.

Violet looked up. Sheila Hollis, one of Briggs' Motors' telephonists, was smiling shyly at her. 'Goodnight, Sheila.' She managed to smile back. She had forgotten for the moment that she was on the works bus — surprising, really, when it was exceptionally noisy today, another conse-quence of its being Friday. There was a disjointed singsong on the top deck, and a heated argument about the comparative merits of Everton and Liverpool football teams being carried on downstairs where Violet sat. She didn't doubt that everyone on board was actively looking forward to the weekend — to the dances, the football, the shopping, or just a couple of days off work and some extra hours in bed.

'Let's hope the weather stays this nice,' Sheila said as she stood and waited for the bus to stop. It was mid-April, half past five, lovely and sunny, and unnaturally warm for the time of year — too warm for the fire she had planned. Violet decided she would light it all the same.

The windows of the bus were thick with condensation and the air full of cigarette smoke that had drifted down from upstairs. 'Goodnight, Miss Duffy,' said a different voice, a man this time speaking in a silly falsetto.

Violet didn't answer, just wondered why being Miss rather than Mrs made her the butt of so many jokes from the workers, always men. Unlike married women, spinsters of a certain age were regarded as figures of fun. She sank back into her earlier reverie, wondering about the letter, and came to only when the bus stopped by Marsh Lane Station — Bootle being its ultimate destination — and the passengers remaining got off, herself among them. Violet sighed audibly, threw back her shoulders and marched along Amber Street to the house where, forty-six years ago, she had been born.

★　★　★

Dear Miss Duffy, the letter began, *I would respectfully advise you that, due to circumstances beyond our control, your position as secretary to the managing director will be terminated as from today. Your salary for this week is enclosed with this letter, plus a further week's salary in lieu of notice.*

I would like to thank you for your long service to the company and wish you good luck in your future employment. A reference will be provided if required.

The letter was signed by Robert Hill, Personnel Manager, another newcomer to Briggs' Motors.

Violet sank back in the armchair and the letter fluttered to the floor. Sammy was perched on the back of the chair purring loudly. Her worst fears had been realised. On Monday morning, there'd be no need to set the alarm for a quarter to seven, put on the clothes that she'd left neatly folded on a chair the night before, eat her usual cornflakes, then make her way to Marsh Lane Station in order to catch the special bus to Briggs' Motors on the East Lancashire Road.

Her heart was beating so loudly and so violently, she felt sure it was about to burst out of her breast. The factory had become as much part of her existence as the place where she lived and the church where she prayed. She couldn't visualise life without it.

For a while, she wandered around the house, upstairs and down, opening drawers and looking in cupboards, without any idea why. Sammy followed her on her useless journey, rubbing himself against her legs. Apart from the unnecessary fire crackling in the grate, everywhere was unnaturally quiet. Even the Harrisons next door, who usually sounded as if they were chopping down trees, were strangely subdued, as if they'd heard about Violet's bad news and were being understanding for once.

She looked out of the window of her bedroom. According to the alarm clock it was past eight. The sinking sun was still shining and the street was full of people, mainly women sitting on their steps and children playing — the men would have filled the pubs by now. Violet sighed. She was friendly with the neighbours, but had never made a habit of sitting outside. With her job gone, she felt lost and terribly alone, even more so than when Mam died — that at least was God's will, not an act of spite or an injustice.

She sighed again, moved away from the window and opened the wardrobe that was still full of her mother's clothes. She was assailed by the smell of mothballs and began to cry, wishing with all her loudly beating heart that Mam were still alive. Mam would threaten to go to Briggs' Motors and tear the management apart, limb by limb, then stamp on their hearts. Violet was desperately in need of sympathy, even if it was in the form of murderous threats from a frail old lady who'd been too sick to leave the house towards the end. For what might have been the thousandth time in her life, she wished she had brothers and sisters, that she hadn't been an only child.

She buried her face in her mother's plaid dressing gown. 'What am I going to do, Mam?' she whispered.

'Pull yourself together, girl,' Mam would have urged. 'Don't forget the old saying, 'As one door closes, another opens.' You'll soon find another job.'

Violet rather doubted she would get one all that easily. She'd like to bet that jobs for forty-seven-year-old women didn't grow on trees. Reference or no reference, what reason could she give for having left her old job after so many years? Telling the truth would just sound like sour grapes.

She wiped her face on the dressing gown

sleeve and went downstairs. At the bottom, she caught sight of herself in the full-length mirror in the hall: a tall, thin woman, hair neatly waved, smartly dressed in a brown tweed skirt and long-sleeved blouse a slightly lighter brown, a woman sometimes described as 'handsome', though Violet would have preferred 'attractive'. Tonight, the woman looked unnaturally pale — or perhaps she always had, but hadn't cared before, or hadn't noticed. Her face was completely free of wrinkles. Why, then, did she look so old? Old and tired, Violet thought, as she viewed her face from different angles. It was entirely devoid of character, rather flat, a turned-down mouth, dead eyes. She forced herself to smile, but it was so false that it made her look slightly insane.

Her entire life had been recorded in this mirror. Her first memory was of her father carrying her downstairs and Violet, still a toddler, reaching out to touch her reflected self when they reached the hall.

'That's you, pet,' Dad had said, or something like it. It was one of the few memories of her father that she had. A dockworker, not long afterwards he'd died of a mysterious illness caught while unloading a boat laden with fruit from somewhere in Africa. The boat had been quarantined and sent back to where it came from and Mam had received a small pension from the shipping company for the rest of her life.

There'd been many more Violets in the mirror, nearly half a century of them: dressed in white with a little veil for her First Holy Communion;

9

in the sensible dark-blue frocks that Mam had made for school; at sixteen wearing stockings for the first time, suspenders pressing painfully against her thighs; wearing her one and only evening frock, navy-blue satin with cap sleeves and a sequinned collar — she was very fond of navy blue. She'd worn the frock numerous times during the war at the dances held in the factory canteen to raise funds for the war effort. Briggs' Motors had turned to making cars and spare parts for the army and the factory had buzzed with excitement.

Violet sank down on the stairs and rested her chin in her hands — the woman in the mirror did the same. She felt terrible for missing the war so much. All the men who'd died fighting, the people who'd been killed in the bombing — Bootle, so close to the docks, had been one of the main targets of Hitler's bombs. Yet Violet had felt wholly alive for the first and only time in her life, helping Norman with the company's dances, going with Norman and his wife, Betty, and Crocker, the American officer Norman had become friends with in the First World War and who was now in England for another one. She and Betty had organised fêtes in the garden of their big house in Rainford, raising money for the Spitfire Fund, Tanks for Russia Week and all sorts of other wartime charities, while her mother had joined the Women's Voluntary Service, despite being so sick, and held weekly meetings in the parlour. The house had felt empty ever since; it felt even emptier today.

She jumped up when the front-door key was dragged on its string through the letterbox; the door was opened and a woman came in.

To her relief, it was Madge McGann, and, if there was one person in the world she would like to see right now, it was her friend Madge, who lived just around the corner in Pearl Street. She looked surprised.

'Were you standing just inside the door waiting for someone to knock?' she enquired. She made her way into the living room and threw herself into a chair. 'That bloody television,' she grumbled, running her fingers through her brilliant red hair. 'I wish we'd never got it. You'll never believe it, but when I arrived home from work I found a queue waiting outside me very own door. Bob had only invited them; there's something on tonight to do with the footy and every single man in Bootle is jammed in our front parlour to watch. It's standing room only — I've run out of bloody chairs. If I don't want to watch telly and sit on the floor, the only alternative is to stand in the kitchen or sit on the bed upstairs.'

'Well, there's plenty of room to sit in *this* house,' Violet assured her. 'There's not a single chair occupied.' She went into the kitchen to put the kettle on for tea. At Christmas, Madge's husband, Bob, had won over a hundred quid on the pools and bought one of those new-fangled television sets, but Madge had decreed it a curse ever since.

'Jaysus, Vi,' Madge said, having discovered the brightly burning fire. 'It's like a hothouse in here.

11

What d'you think you are, a tomato, or something?' She lifted Sammy onto her knee. 'I advise you never to buy a telly, girl,' she said. 'You'll end up with dozens of visitors who've never been near the place before, but they haven't come to see *you*, but the bloody telly.'

'I wouldn't dream of buying one,' Violet assured her. 'Though I must say I enjoyed that *Come Dancing* programme that we watched the other night. The dresses were dead pretty.'

'Oh, it's not the telly that's at fault: it's the flaming audience. The thing is, you can't keep a telly a secret, not with that ugly aerial thing stuck on the bloody chimney for everyone to see. Mind you, Bob's told so many people we've got one, he may as well have stuck an advert in the *Liverpool Echo*.'

The kettle was rattling on the stove. Violet went out to make the tea. When she came back, Madge had removed her high-heeled black shoes and was massaging her feet. 'These shoes crucify me,' she muttered. Her legs were long and shapely and her stockings a daring smoky colour. Madge was three months older than Violet and they'd known each other since they were in the same class at infant school. At eighteen, an incredibly pretty and glamorous Madge had married Bob McGann and had gone on to have five daughters, while Violet, plainly dressed and not nearly so pretty, had ended up in Briggs' Motors as secretary to Norman Larkin, not that she'd minded.

Now all Madge's daughters were married and rapidly producing grandchildren, Madge worked as a supervisor at Scotts' Bakery, while Violet no longer had a job.

'Why do you wear shoes like that if they hurt?' she asked.

'Because they're dead glamorous and make me legs look a nicer shape.' She put the shoes back on, admiring the effect as she turned her feet one way and the other. 'It's about time you bought yourself a pair of high heels, Violet, rather than those clumpy Cuban things you're wearing now.' She gave her friend the same impatient yet affectionate look she'd been giving her for the last forty years. 'Anyroad, I'm off to the pictures in a mo and on the way home I'll call in The Butcher's for a drink. The mob round our house aren't likely to bugger off till all hours and I've no intention of hanging around until they do. I didn't tell Bob I was going,' she continued bitterly, 'so he's probably thinking I'll come bursting into the parlour any minute with a tray of ice creams hanging round me neck. If so, he's got another thing coming.'

'Are you going to the pub for a drink all by yourself?' Violet asked. The Butcher's was by Marsh Lane Station and had a bad reputation.

'I am that.' Madge crossed her long legs impatiently. 'I've no one else to go with.'

'Won't Bob mind?' Violet ignored the comment. She had no intention of going in a pub with only another woman.

'Huh!' Madge lit a cigarette and waved it around as if she were sending smoke signals. Sammy watched intently, wondering if this was a new sort of game. 'Of course he'll mind. In fact, he'd do his bloody nut if he found out, but I don't care. In fact, I'll tell him to his face. We always said once the girls got married, left home, and we didn't have to support them any more, we'd have a good time. We'd have nothing else to spend our money on except ourselves. Instead, all he does is watch television along with half the male population of Bootle, and I'm not even left with a sodden chair to sit on. I say, Vi,' she continued without a pause, 'would you like a waste-paper basket for Christmas?'

'Eh?' Violet looked at her stupidly.

Madge laughed for the first time since she'd arrived. 'There's a letter lying underneath your chair. It's from Briggs' Motors, I can see that much from here. This is the tidiest house I've ever known. You're letting the side down, girl.'

Violet reached under the chair and picked the letter up. It was hard to believe, but listening to Madge and her problem with the telly, she'd temporarily forgotten her own troubles. She hesitated a moment before handing the letter to her friend. 'You'd better read this,' she said.

'Jaysus, Violet!' Madge gasped a minute later. 'Why didn't you tell me before? Why let me jabber on and on about that stupid, soddin' telly when you had this on your mind? Now I feel dead ashamed. What are the 'circumstances beyond our control' that this creep's on about?'

Violet shrugged. 'There aren't any,' she said wearily. 'It's just an excuse to get rid of me so Douglas Penny can install Beryl Daly as his secretary.' Madge knew all about Beryl Daly, the blonde bombshell. 'Don't tell anyone, will you,

Madge? I don't want the whole world knowing I'm out of a job.'

'Jaysus!' Madge said again. She flung the letter back on the floor and stamped on it. 'The whole world should know,' she cried indignantly. 'You're a lovely person, Violet, and it's just not fair. Norman Larkin would turn in his grave if he knew what had happened. As for your mam, she'd spin like a flamin' top until she'd drilled herself out of her flamin' coffin.'

At this, Violet couldn't help but smile. 'She would indeed,' she murmured.

'If you're short of cash, I can always tide you over with a few bob a week until you get another job,' Madge offered.

'Thanks, but I'll be all right.' Violet was touched by her friend's generosity, but Briggs' Motors had paid her a good wage as secretary to the managing director, which meant that Mam had hardly needed to touch her pension. She had died with over fifty pounds in her Post Office account. It would be a long time before Violet would have to get a job for financial reasons, though the last thing she wanted was to sit at home by herself day after day. Her spirits drooped at the thought; she would far sooner be at work.

★   ★   ★

The first half of the night was full of nightmares. Violet kept waking up with a start and taking ages to fall asleep again. At about half past three she remembered the cough medicine Mam used to take that she swore worked miracles. Morphia, it was called, and it made her sleep easier than any of the pills from the doctor. There were two unopened bottles in the kitchen cupboard above the sink. She crept downstairs, took two teaspoonfuls and brought the bottle back with her to bed. Sammy appeared from nowhere and jumped onto the bed with her. She still woke up at a quarter to seven in time for work even though the alarm hadn't gone off, but at least she'd had three undisturbed hours of sleep. She remembered it was Saturday and she wouldn't have had to go to work anyway. Saturday was the day she did the housework.

Another three hours later, Violet had done the washing and it was hanging on the rack in the kitchen; the furniture in the parlour and the living room had been polished, the lino brushed, and the mats beaten in the yard. She had just made a pot of tea — she was dying for a cup — when there was a knock on the door. She could tell by the knock that it wasn't Madge, or Ernie Randolph, her other next-door neighbour, who always knocked three times, very slowly, in a doomladen way as if he were the bearer of bad news. Ena Hamilton, on the other side, who was always in a hurry, just kept knocking until the door was opened, whereupon she would ask Violet if she could borrow a cup of sugar, a drop of milk, or a penny for the gas meter. Violet would get the penny back, but never the sugar or the milk.

Her visitor was entirely unexpected. Violet found Iris Gunn, head of the typing pool at

16

Briggs' Motors, on her doorstep. Iris had never been to the house before.

'Come on in,' Violet gasped. 'You're the last person I expected to see. Would you like a cup of tea? I've just made some.' She apologised for her old frock and the fact that she smelled of furniture polish and Tide washing powder. 'Sat'days are me day for cleaning,' she explained.

'Oh, Violet, you look fine, luv, and you smell lovely and clean.' Iris grabbed her arm. 'I've just come to say how sorry I am about what's happened and what are we going to do about it?'

'Do about it?' She nudged her visitor towards a chair and sat down herself. She'd always got the impression that Iris didn't like her very much, that she looked down on her more than a bit. A tiny, delicate widow of about fifty with bouncy grey curls and the face of a middle-aged doll, she was surprisingly loud and extrovert, while Violet was quiet and retiring. They'd never been what you'd call friends, despite Violet being secretary to the managing director and Iris head of the typing pool since just before the war, the two most senior women in the firm.

'Well, there'll be hell to pay on Monday when word gets round that you've been given the push,' Iris stated angrily.

'Will there?' Violet felt dazed.

'There most certainly will.' Iris struck the arm of the chair with her small fist. 'Perhaps you don't realise just how fond people are of you, luv, and how much they hate Douglas Penny. What he's done to you is despicable: getting rid of a really hardworking, longstanding employee in favour of his girlfriend, that flighty bitch Beryl Daly. I thought she looked even more pleased with herself than usual on Friday night before we went home. It wasn't until I was on the bus that I was told what had happened.' Iris lived on the south side of Liverpool and caught a different bus from Violet. 'Ben Cousins from Wages told me — you know, the chap who lost his foot in the war. He said you'd been given a letter of dismissal. He was just as disgusted as I am and he said everyone in Wages feels the same.'

Violet was about to say, 'Do they?' in the same dazed voice, but she was making herself look a fool. 'Well, it did come as a bit of a shock,' she admitted, though it hadn't really — not a complete shock. She'd been half expecting it for months.

'I think we should all go on strike until you're reinstated,' Iris said in a fierce voice. 'After all, we've not long finished fighting for our freedom, there's a socialist government in power, and we can't have jumped-up creatures like that Penny chap flexing his upper-class muscles and throwing his poxy weight about.' She punched the arm of the chair again.

'Oh, I don't want people going on strike because of me,' Violet cried. 'Anyroad, I'm not in a union.' She hadn't thought anyone would notice that she'd left, let alone protest about it. More than two thousand people worked at Briggs' Motors. 'Everyone would lose their wages if there's a strike and I'd feel terrible about it.'

Iris winked for some reason. 'We'll just have to

see,' she said, vaguely threatening, as if the entire firm would go on strike on her behalf if it wanted to and Violet would have no say in the matter.

When Iris was about to leave, Violet asked if she would do her a favour. 'I'd like me shorthand notebook back. Would you mind getting it for me? It's got private stuff in and I don't want Beryl Daly looking at it.' There'd been times when she'd had nothing to do and had written the occasional poem or a message to herself.

Iris promised to recover it first thing Monday morning. 'I'll fetch it round one day next week.'

★   ★   ★

Saturday turned out to be a much nicer day than Violet had expected. As she was leaving, Iris mentioned she was going to the pictures that afternoon, and asked if Violet might like to join her there later. She'd almost refused — after all, Saturdays were for her housework — then Vi realised she could do it any day she liked now she had no work to go to. So, after changing into her best clothes and meeting Iris in town, they went to a matinee at The Forum, where they saw Betty Hutton and Howard Keel in *Annie Get Your Gun*.

'Wasn't the singing lovely?' Violet felt as if she'd been in another world for the last two hours.

'It was smashing,' Iris agreed. 'And that Howard Keel chap is a sight for sore eyes. I wouldn't mind being left in the dark with him for an hour or two.'

Iris was showing a side to her nature that wasn't at all what you'd expect from the head of a typing pool — not that Violet minded. She agreed, just as enthusiastically, when Iris suggested they go to Lewis's department store for afternoon tea and that they must go to the pictures again very soon.

★　★　★

In bed that night, she had different nightmares. She remembered that soon after Douglas Penny had arrived, he'd tried to get rid of the shop stewards; there were two of them for different unions. 'They're nothing but bloody communists,' he'd sneered. 'All they want to do is cause trouble.'

At the time, it was he who was causing the trouble, Violet had thought, attempting to do away with the ten-minute tea breaks, and limiting the number of times the men on the floor went to the lavatory. 'All they go for is a smoke,' he complained.

Norman Larkin had never had any trouble with the staff. They'd worked their guts out during the war and had continued to work almost as hard afterwards. Norman was a fair employer and he was well liked, whereas Douglas Penny had treated the workforce as enemies straightaway.

When word got out that the shop stewards' jobs were in danger, the entire factory had threatened to walk out. At the time, she'd wondered if she'd have the courage to join them,

20

and had been glad when Douglas Penny had been forced to withdraw his threat and she hadn't had to make a choice. She still didn't know what she would have done.

Now she imagined Iris Gunn passing her name around the factory along with the nature of her sacking until it was on a thousand pairs of lips. Just the thought of it made her shiver with embarrassment. 'Who the hell's Violet Duffy?' she further imagined people asking, then, more salaciously, 'Tell us where this blonde bombshell slapper works so we can have a decko?'

And, if there was a strike and she was reinstated, it would be even more embarrassing going back. She buried her head in the pillow and groaned out loud.

After a while, she sat up, took two spoonfuls of morphia and fell asleep straightaway. Next morning, she woke up feeling a bit muggy, remembered it was Sunday, and lay in bed until eleven, then leapt out, threw on her best clothes and went to midday Mass, the first time she'd gone so late since Mam had died. As it had been past midnight when she'd taken the morphia, it meant that she'd broken her fast so had to give Holy Communion a miss, another first since she couldn't remember when. It made her feel really odd all day.

★   ★   ★

On Monday, Violet found a postcard on the mat from a woman she'd never heard of who lived in the road next but one.

'Dear Miss Duffy,' it read. 'I'm very sorry you have lost your job. That Douglas Penny wants his bumps feeling. Yours faithfully, Angela Milligan (Kitchen Staff).'

She was touched at the thought of a woman she'd never met going to the trouble of buying such a pretty card — a bowl of roses — and bringing it round to the house.

As the hours passed on her first ever day of unemployment, she imagined her old office, Beryl Daly occupying her typing chair, using her typewriter — the 'W' key needed fixing, she remembered — getting used to the way the telephone worked. There'd be people who didn't know Violet had gone and be surprised to find she wasn't there.

She put on a nice frock, combed her hair, powdered her nose, not quite as carefully as if she were going to work, but determined not to let herself down and go round looking shabby.

The following morning, there were two more cards, five letters and a parcel. The postman knocked on the door with it. 'Morning, Miss Duffy,' he said cheerfully. 'Here, this is for you. It's either a book, or some very thin chocolates.'

It was a book, a slim volume entitled *Sacred Poems for Sad Occasions*. Violet read the first and it made her cry. The cards and letters similarly upset her, so full of sympathy it was almost as if she'd died. She decided she would have much preferred to have got the sack and no one known.

Later on, she went into town, saw *Annie Get Your Gun* a second time and bought a very smart summer frock in Blackler's — navy crêpe de chine with a white belt. She went home feeling pleased with herself.

'Oh, for Christ's sake take it back and change it for something that looks as if it was made in the twentieth century,' Madge said when she came that night and Violet showed her the frock. 'Have you still got the receipt?' Violet nodded. 'Then take it back on Saturday and I'll come with you.'

'All right,' Violet said meekly and burst into tears.

Madge apologised profusely and said she was the second most horrible person on earth, the first being Douglas Penny. 'It's that bloody telly,' she moaned. 'It's really getting me down and I'm taking it out on everybody.'

★   ★   ★

Iris Gunn wrote to tell her that the shop stewards considered it an inopportune time to strike, besides which, Violet didn't belong to a union, but a letter of protest had been sent to the Board of Directors. A few more cards and letters arrived objecting to her treatment, but the second week after her sacking everything had gone quiet and Violet reckoned she'd heard the last of Briggs' Motors.

Night after night, she scoured the 'Situations Vacant' column in the *Liverpool Echo*. There were adverts for office juniors, copy typists, shorthand typists, but very few for secretaries, and even then the favourite age seemed to be twenty-five. A whole week passed before there was a job advertised that she stood a chance of getting: secretary to a lecturer at a private college in the city centre. An age wasn't mentioned, but a 'mature' person was required. Violet applied in her very best writing, the grammar perfect, and sat waiting for a reply. If asked, she would name Briggs' Motors as a reference. She just hoped Douglas Penny had enough decency in him to give her a good one.

She was rejected by the college. 'We wanted someone younger,' the letter said, and she wondered at what age a person became 'mature'?

By now, Violet was beginning to panic. It was essential that she get a job. She still hadn't touched the money Mam had left, but, once she started drawing out four or five pounds a week to live on, it would quickly go down. Just imagine if she ended up in a typing pool or as a filing clerk or something really junior. Maybe she should look outside office work, consider other things: a shop, for instance. But forty-seven's awful old for someone to change their career, she thought fretfully. She preferred to work from behind a desk, not a counter. She was starting to feel old, really old, as if there were no longer a place for her in any office in Liverpool.

She lowered her sights and wrote after a job as secretary in the materials department of a well-known builders' firm. She reckoned she would have to work for a number of men, not just one as she was used to. It was a bit of a comedown, but beggars can't be choosers, she

24

told herself as she put the stamp on the letter, sealing it with her fist.

★ ★ ★

Weeks passed; some mornings, it was all she could do to drag herself out of bed and get washed and dressed. Madge often came round in the evening on her way to The Butcher's, leaving Bob and his mates in front of the television. Violet pretended everything was going swimmingly: she was writing after jobs daily, wondering which one to take. She had other visitors, neighbours and women friends to whom she gave the same impression. A letter had come from the builders: she was overqualified for the job and, anyway, they'd wanted someone younger. She'd had several similar letters since.

Her social life had come to an end as most of her interests had involved Briggs' Motors. The Dramatic Society, for instance — not that she'd ever acted, and wouldn't have had the nerve, but she'd helped with the costumes and the set and enjoyed being a prompt. She was on the Sports' Day, Christmas Party and May Day Outing committees. The company was associated with several charities and Violet had helped organise them all.

But now life as she had known it had come to an end and Violet felt more wretched by the day. Had it not been for morphia, she doubted whether she would have slept a wink. It was the only thing left that she could rely on — that and Sammy. At least she could tell him the truth.

The man came at four o'clock one day at the end of July. The weather that month had been very changeable with lots of rain — it had rained on 15 July, St Swithin's Day, which, according to legend, meant it would rain non-stop for the next forty days. So far, the irritating prediction had come true and Violet had felt like tearing her hair out.

Her visitor was a small, tubby man with a round red face, twinkly brown eyes — and a Hitler moustache! Why on earth hadn't someone told him? It was actually worse than Douglas Penny's. Violet was glad he'd come so late when she felt more or less alert, had remembered to comb her hair and was wearing a neatly ironed frock.

'Yes?' she enquired.

The man smiled and the moustache stretched about half an inch either side. She wondered whether he wanted to sell her insurance: he had a cardboard file under his arm. Oh, and that must be his car outside, one of those nice, sturdy Morris Minors. It was the only car in the street and already a subject of interest to several small boys.

'My name is Edwin Powell. Am I speaking to Miss Violet Duffy?' he enquired in a soft voice with a Welsh accent. She had the strangest feeling that he'd come about something really serious.

'You are indeed,' she said, nodding gravely.

'May I please come in? I have news of vast

importance to convey to you.'

'I suppose you better had,' Violet said with a shrug.

2

'If you wouldn't mind,' Edwin Powell said when they were seated in the parlour, 'I need to see proof of identity.'

'What on earth for?' Violet enquired, startled.

He looked slightly embarrassed, as well he might, she thought, asking such an impertinent question of a complete stranger. 'I'll explain once I know for sure you're Violet Duffy. Your old wartime Identity Card will do, or your passport.'

'I haven't got a passport.' The furthest place from Liverpool Violet had ever been was Blackpool — or perhaps Rhyl was further; she'd gone in a charabanc with Mam a few times on bank holidays. She took her Identity Card out of the sideboard drawer; he examined it and nodded, though it didn't have Violet's photo on it and could have belonged to any old body.

'That'll do, thank you.' He cleared his throat. 'Have you ever met your cousin, Mary?'

Violet was even more startled. 'I didn't know I *had* a cousin Mary.' Mam had had two sisters who'd never married and had lived together in a house near Penny Lane. They'd died in the same month as each other not long after Mam herself. Her father's brother, Albert, had gone to live in Canada after the First World War and as far as she knew hadn't come back.

'It would seem you had an uncle called Albert,' Edwin Powell said.

Violet acknowledged this with a little nod. 'He went to live in Canada in nineteen eighteen. Me, I never set eyes on him.'

Her visitor removed a sheet of paper out of his file and began to read from it. 'He died in nineteen thirty-five, leaving behind a wife called Clara and a daughter, Mary, who was sixteen years old at the time.'

'Well, I never!' Violet marvelled. 'I'd heard about Albert from Mam, but she didn't know he'd been married. Is Clara trying to get in touch with us?' She was rather pleased at the idea, having always felt unusually deprived of relatives.

'I'm afraid not, Miss Duffy,' the man said gravely, 'and neither, I'm sad to say, is Mary. Both are dead. Clara died in her fifties just before the war began and poor Mary passed away in her sleep earlier this month. She was only thirty-one and had suffered from a weak heart all her life.'

'Why, that's awful! Oh, I wish I'd known. I'd have gone to see her, even if it had meant going all the way to Canada.' To think she'd had a cousin all this time — and Mam would love to have known about Aunt Clara.

'It will surprise you to know, Miss Duffy,' Edwin Powell said, 'that Mary didn't live in Canada. She came to live in this country — in Netton, a village on the outskirts of Exeter in Devon.'

'I've heard it's nice in Devon.' Violet was feeling distressed and terribly muddled. 'Why are you telling me this when it's too late for me to do anything about it?' she asked. 'Did Mary know about me?'

'It would appear not. She told her friend, Jessie Arnett, that her father had had a brother who'd lived in Liverpool, but that's all.' He looked rather self-important all of a sudden. 'It was me who managed to track you down.'

'Why?' Violet asked bluntly.

'Why?' He raised his neat eyebrows. 'Why? Because Mary had two children: a son, William, known as Will, who is ten, and a little girl of four, almost five, called Abigail, but known as Abby. Both will be placed in council care — in other words, a children's home — any day soon unless I can find a relative to take them. You, Miss Duffy, are Albert's niece, the only relative I could trace. Whether Clara had a family other than Albert and their daughter, Mary, I've no idea; I've been unable to discover anything about her background.'

'Me?' For a moment, Violet's head swam. Only the beginning of his statement had registered and she was convinced she was about to faint. 'Take two children? Of course not, I couldn't possibly.' She knew nothing about children, although she loved them. She'd loved all of Madge's girls when they were little, and was godmother to the eldest, Lucy — she'd gone off them a bit as they grew older and began to plaster their faces with makeup and took up smoking. But to look after them, however appealing, for twenty-four hours a day, feed them, play with them, put them to bed at night and wake them in the morning, nurse them

30

when they were ill . . . The little girl would have to be bathed and she'd had no experience whatsoever with boys. Would she have to bathe *him*? What would they talk to each other about? 'No, no.' She violently shook her head. 'No, I couldn't possibly.'

There was a long silence. Edwin Powell stared into the fireplace into which Violet had crumpled some fresh red tissue paper that morning to resemble flames. His face was expressionless.

Violet leapt to her feet. 'I'll make some tea.' She fled into the kitchen, where she put the kettle on, then hastily swallowed a huge mouthful of morphia to calm her nerves.

'Have you ever been in an orphanage?' Edwin Powell was in the doorway looking at her reproachfully. 'As a visitor, that is.'

'No.' How dare he follow her? And how dare he look at her like that, as if she were a truly horrible, selfish person.

'I have.' He sighed. 'They're miserable places. Not everyone who works there is kind. They don't all love children.'

'What about Will and Abby's father?' How stupid of her! She'd forgotten all about the father.

'Actually it's fathers, in the plural.' He absent-mindedly lifted the boiling kettle off the stove and poured water in the waiting pot. What a nerve! Violet did her best to hide her annoyance. 'Mary, poor woman, was widowed twice. She married Will's dad, Eric Stein, in Canada, and they moved to England, settling in Devon — events around this time are a trifle unclear. He is thought to have joined the army and was later killed in a motorcycle accident in France within a year. A few years later, Mary married another soldier, a local man called Oswald Holmes. Sadly, Oswald had only been home a few months after the war ended, when he died of a fever he'd caught in India, probably malaria.' He smiled dryly. 'Poor little Abby, she was born not long after her father died. As for Will, when Mary went, it meant he'd lost his mother and two fathers.'

'That's awful,' Violet whispered. 'How is he taking it?'

'Bravely,' Edwin Powell said with a tremor in his voice. 'He's a fine young chap. His father seems to have been a strange sort of man who didn't have a proper home until he married Mary. Jessie thinks he spoke with an accent and that he might have been foreign, a gypsy perhaps. I was able to find out very little about him. Abby's dad was a different kettle of fish altogether, with quite a few relatives, some of them willing to take on Abby, particularly the grandmother, but not Will.'

'So, it's not true that both are at risk of going in a home, only Will is?'

He sighed and spread his hands a touch despairingly. 'I wasn't exactly misleading you, Miss Duffy. It's just that neither Jessie nor I want the children to be separated. If Will went into a home and Abby to her grandmother's, they might never see each other again. They love each other very much. They've already lost enough people in their young lives without losing each other. And in a home they wouldn't be together either: Will would be with the boys, Abby the girls.'

Violet put the tea things on a tray. 'Me, I don't think I'm up to it,' she muttered, 'taking on two orphaned children. I wouldn't know what to do with them.'

Edwin Powell reached for the tray. 'Let me carry that.' He followed her into the parlour. 'I assume you don't work,' he said, 'otherwise you wouldn't be at home at this time of day.'

'I'm in the throes of changing my job,' she lied. She was twisting the truth only a little bit.

'Is your health good?'

'Well, yes.' It would be even better if she could sleep at night.

'If you don't mind my asking, how are you off financially?'

'I have some savings.' She didn't say how much, but they were considerably less now than when she'd left Briggs' Motors.

'And what will happen when the savings run out?'

She didn't see that it was any of his business. 'As I said, I'm between jobs. I expect to start working again soon.' She began to pour the tea. 'But I couldn't afford to take the children, even if I wanted to,' she added. She was getting herself into a hole and wished he'd go away. He was making her feel really hard and selfish.

'You wouldn't be expected to support them out of your own pocket. You would get an allowance for each. It's a bit late now, but I didn't introduce myself properly.' He took a visiting card out of his inside pocket and held it front of her eyes. 'I represent St Jude's Bounty,' he said earnestly, 'a charity based in Exeter that provides succour in various ways in a variety of situations. We were alerted to the plight of Will and Abby and I hoped and prayed I would find a relative who would have them. The charity will be responsible for the weekly allowances, which would be two pounds and ten shillings for each child. I assume you would consider that sufficient to live on? If not, if you give me a list of expenses the charity will adjust the amount accordingly.'

Violet made a little mumbling sound as if to say she understood and sympathised with the problem, but, even if they raised the amount to ten pounds a week or even twenty, there was no way she would agree to have the children. 'Who's looking after Will and Abby now?' she asked.

'Jessie Arnett, the friend I mentioned before. Jessie loves them and would have them like a shot, but she's past seventy and crippled with arthritis. Oh, and by the way, the allowances I mentioned earlier would come to an end when each child reached the age of fourteen, but will increase should the school leaving age rise to fifteen, as has been mooted in Parliament, or if either child opted for further education. Other allowances would be granted over the years for things like holidays.'

At this, Violet became impatient. 'It's a bit much,' she said hotly, 'coming round to someone's house, quite out of the blue, expecting them to make such a big decision at a moment's notice. You should have written first, explained the situation, given me time to think about it.' She knew why he hadn't — written first, that is — and it was because he wanted to tug at her heartstrings, which was difficult in a letter. This was what was called emotional blackmail and she deeply resented being subjected to it.

'I don't expect you to make up your mind at a moment's notice, Miss Duffy,' he said mildly. 'But I have to confess I'm in a hurry, which is why I didn't write. The children know they can't stay with Jessie for ever. They desperately need to know what the future has in store for them — well, Will does; Abby is young enough to just live for the moment, though, naturally, she is badly missing her mother. After all, it's only a few weeks since she died.' He paused before adding another reason why she should take the children. 'I see you have a crucifix over the mantelpiece, Miss Duffy. I am sure you will have realised that, like yourself, the children are Catholics.'

Frankly, she was so wrought up that she hadn't thought about religion. Now she had, she wanted to point out that there were plenty of Catholic orphanages about, but that would just make her sound awkward — and from the way he'd spoken, he didn't have a very good opinion of orphanages of any sort.

'I'd need at least a week to think about it.' She ran her fingers through her hair, a sign that she was feeling excessively moidered. 'Then I'll write to you.' Oh, but that seemed most unfair on the children, Will in particular — see, she was already thinking about him as a real person, worried about hurting him, getting involved. And she knew, just knew, that at the end of the day she would say no; thinking about it would be a complete waste of time. 'Do the children know about me?'

'Of course. Will helped me look through his mother's papers. We found evidence that Albert Duffy had a brother called Reginald — your father, I assume.'

Violet nodded reluctantly, but didn't answer directly. 'Are you going back to Exeter tonight, Mr Powell?' she asked instead.

'No, in the morning. It's a long journey one way, let alone driving back the same day. I'm staying overnight in a hotel in Waterloo.'

'Then would you mind coming back in the morning? I'd like to get some toys for the children.' A doll for Abby and something for Will. She had never bought a toy for a boy before. And some sweets, of course. And she would ask for their birthdays and send them cards every year.

'I had intended leaving after breakfast, about ten o'clock.'

'That would be fine.' There was still time to rush to the shops in Strand Road before he left. 'Please call on me before you leave.'

★   ★   ★

'Where are we now?' Violet asked. It was noon the following day and she was in Edwin's car, with the sun shining brilliantly out of a cloudless blue sky, and it felt pleasantly warm. So far today it hadn't rained so perhaps the curse of St Swithin was about to be broken.

'Shropshire, approaching Shrewsbury,' Edwin replied. Earlier, he'd suggested that she call him Edwin and asked if he could call her Violet. She felt obliged to agree to both.

'The countryside is very pretty round here,' she remarked. 'And it was nice in Cheshire, too.' To think that all these places existed merely a short drive away from Bootle and she'd never been near them in her entire life.

When he'd arrived in Amber Street that morning and she told him that she'd have the children after all, he'd asked what had changed her mind.

'I'm not sure,' she told him, reluctant to admit the real reason.

'Did you talk it over with someone — a friend?' He looked curious, as well he might. Yesterday, she'd been dead set against the idea.

'Oh, no.' She'd thought about discussing it with Madge, but it was a massive decision to take, not the sort to be influenced by someone else, even if it was a friend. Once in bed, though — she couldn't possibly tell him this — she'd had one of her imaginary conversations with Mam. No, not a conversation, more like listening to a lecture — a very stern lecture.

'If you don't take those children, you'll regret it for the rest of your life,' she had imagined her mother saying — no, not merely imagined, actually heard. 'Although you didn't know they existed before today, they're still your flesh and blood; you're their auntie, girl. And didn't I always say, 'As one door closes, another opens,' and isn't that what's just happened? And don't tell me you've had no experience with children, girl, because neither had I when I had you. Most new mothers haven't. Before you know where you are, you'll love them to bits and they'll love you. When you was a little girl, you loved playing with your dollies. I always thought you'd get married and have half a dozen kids.'

So had Violet — well, not half a dozen, but two or three. However, the older she got, the more she realised that life rarely went as planned.

Mam had made it sound so easy. It had still felt easy that morning when Edwin Powell arrived and she told him she'd changed her decision. His eyes lit up and he looked so relieved that she felt awful for letting him wait so long. Now, though, the closer they got to Exeter, the more she worried whether her decision had been the right one.

'Perhaps we could stop soon for a snack,' Edwin said. 'I'm not used to driving long distances. I would really appreciate a cup of tea and a sandwich.'

Violet said that she wouldn't say no to either. Shortly afterwards, a pub came into view, all by itself in a long, leafy lane, and he slowed down and turned into the car park. The pub was called The Lamb. Edwin was a very cautious driver, unlike Norman Larkin, who'd zoomed along the roads at top speed in his far superior Morris with a much bigger engine that ran very smoothly, as well as very fast. The engine in Edwin's Morris was ear-achingly loud and the car appeared to have no suspension — Violet's bottom was painfully aware of every bump.

The Lamb was virtually empty. They seated themselves by a window and Edwin went to the bar. He returned with a huge pot of tea and two crusty rolls filled with cheese and pickle, and, giving her something else to worry about, a glass of spirit that he brought and swallowed in a single gulp; she couldn't tell whether it was whisky or brandy.

'Sorry I was so long,' he said. 'There's a public telephone in the lobby, so I telephoned Netton Post Office to ask if they'll let Jessie know we're coming so she can put you up for the night. They're sending someone round to tell her straight away.'

'Why, thank you,' Violet said politely, trying to sound grateful, as it would save staying in a hotel, but a feeling of dread had come over her and she wished she were at home feeling dead miserable, having never heard of her lost relatives.

After they'd gone about halfway, she began to doze off in little spurts, coming to from time to time to find they were passing fresh green fields, some sprinkled with sheep and baby lambs or yellow corn; trees — indescribably lovely — laden with fruit or flowers; small, sleepy villages with churches that appeared far too large for the likely congregation. She glimpsed the occasional thatched cottage or gracious old manor house usually approached by a long, winding drive. The smell of flowers drifted through the open window and she would sniff appreciatively, then quickly roll the window up when the smell changed to something obnoxious that definitely wasn't flowers. After a while, she would open it again and a slight wind would ruffle her hair.

Beside her, Edwin half mumbled, half sang war songs, putting the wrong words to the wrong tunes, or not singing any words just, 'Dum, diddy-dum, diddy-pom, pom, pom'. His voice sounded tired and she prayed he wouldn't fall asleep at the wheel.

When she was properly awake and he wasn't singing, they chatted lazily. He lived with his unmarried sister, who looked after him. 'Too well,' he said, patting his tummy. Working for St Jude's Bounty was the best job in the world. 'It's like being Father Christmas giving presents out all year round. Sometimes, it means providing furniture for a family who can't afford to buy it for themselves, or sending an invalid on convalescence for a week or two in the hope they'll feel better, giving a bike to a kid who lives a long way from school.'

Violet said it sounded wonderful and he was a very lucky man. In turn, she told him about Mam being ill and what a blow it had been when she died; how nice it was living in Amber Street, where she knew everyone and everyone knew her. She didn't say it could sometimes be a nuisance, that there were times when she preferred to keep herself to herself. When she'd got the sack from Briggs' Motors, for instance, people who hadn't known kept asking what she was doing at home.

'Me boss is on holiday,' she'd lied, 'so I thought I'd take the same weeks off as him, like.' After a fortnight had passed and she was still at home the whole time, she'd started to go in and out the back way and hope no one would notice, though she couldn't keep it up for ever.

At four, they stopped again for another snack and for Edwin to drink another glass of whisky or brandy. Afterwards, they continued with their journey. By now, Violet had become bored with the countryside and wished they'd go through a city or a big town, somewhere full of people and houses and even the occasional factory belching smoke out of a blackened chimney.

Eventually, they arrived at Chepstow, where Edwin drove the car onto a ferry and they sailed across the River Severn, much to Violet's horror. She was terrified the entire way and was relieved to drive off in a place called Aust, where they continued on their way to Exeter.

'Are we nearly there?' she asked.

'Not far,' Edwin said cheerfully. 'We'll stop for snack in a while.'

'Not another one!'

'This will be the last,' he assured her.

★ ★ ★

It was almost dark when they arrived at Jessie Arnett's house, an old cottage, with low ceilings

41

criss-crossed with black beams and an ingle-nook fireplace in which the powdery remains of a log fire still smouldered. They'd obviously kept Jessie up as she was wearing a flannel nightie underneath a heavy tweed coat and what looked like a pair of men's boots. She had lovely blue eyes in a heavily wrinkled face and, despite her age, her hair was still more black than grey. Violet could tell she'd once been a great beauty.

'Ah, there you are, luvvie.' She kissed Violet on both cheeks. 'I knew you'd come for those darling children — they've gone to bed, by the way. I just felt it in me water when Mr Powell said he'd discovered Mary had a cousin and she lived in a place called Bootle. Remember, I said as much to you, didn't I, Mr Powell?'

'You did indeed, Mrs Arnett,' Edwin acknowl-edged.

'Would you like a nice cup of cocoa and something to eat — cold chicken, maybe, or a slice of steak and kidney pie? And I've got lardy cake and fruit tarts galore — gooseberry, apple, raspberry . . . '

'Just the cocoa, please.' Violet didn't feel the faintest bit hungry. 'Then I'd like to go to bed, if you don't mind.' She found it surprising that it was possible to get so tired after sitting down all day, albeit in a motor car. When she'd got out, her legs had felt most reluctant to support her and her bottom had gone completely numb. She wasn't looking forward to returning home the same way in the same car tomorrow.

★ ★ ★

42

The sun was shining hazily through the thick lace curtains when she woke next morning. She still felt tired despite the bed being the most comfortable she'd ever slept in. The feather pillows and the eiderdown felt as light as air. At first, it took a while to take in where she was — Jessie's house, she remembered when she saw the black-beamed ceiling and white-painted walls. There was a little black iron fireplace and a picture of a vase of chrysanthemums on the wall above. The wardrobe and matching tallboy had been polished to death, as had the strange wooden box thing that she eventually recognised was a commode. It was a lovely, light, airy room smelling of lavender.

She was here to collect Will and Abby and would raise them as her own. At the age of forty-seven, she was about to become a mother — well, sort of, the children having been born to another woman who had died. Her heart turned over and once again she wished she'd never heard of her cousin Mary. Over the last two days, her thoughts had been going up and down like a yo-yo and she was beginning to get on her own nerves.

('Pull your socks up, girl,' a familiar voice in her head demanded, 'and stop bellyaching.')

According to her watch, it was only five to seven. She was about to nestle down underneath the bedclothes in the hope of falling asleep again, when she heard voices outside — children's voices. Her room overlooked the rear of the cottage. Lifting a corner of the curtain, she saw a little girl wearing a dark-brown frock covered with a frilly Victorian apron staggering down the garden carrying a rusty watering can. She wore a red ribbon in her white-blonde hair and would have made an ideal subject for a Christmas card.

A boy, much older, caught up and took the can away. 'You'll spill water all over your feet, Abby,' he chided gently.

'Will I be able to take the vegetables out me garden to Bootle?' the girl asked.

'Don't be daft. They're not nearly grown yet and they'd die on the way.' This must be Will. He was a remarkably handsome lad, very dark, very slim, with black wavy hair. His father might have been a gypsy, Edwin Powell had said. Violet had no idea whether he was tall for ten, or small.

She let the curtain fall and a wave of horror passed over her. How on earth could she expect — could *anybody* expect — the children to settle in Bootle after living all their lives in a place like this? Even if it wasn't this very house, it would have been one similar. She lifted the curtain again. The garden was at least a hundred feet long and half that wide. The bottom area was full of trees — perhaps it was an orchard. She wouldn't know, not having a clue what sort of fruit grew on what sort of tree. The nearest section was covered with grass that needed cutting and the middle consisted of row after row of what she guessed were vegetables and bushes that most probably bore fruit; she was as unfamiliar with bushes as she was with trees.

Violet's house in Bootle didn't have so much

as a window box, let alone a garden. There was only a small yard with a lavatory at the bottom. In between the lavatory and the house, a ramshackle building, supposedly a washhouse, stood unused. Will and Abby would hate it, just as they would hate the house itself with its small rooms papered with the darkly patterned wallpaper that Violet detested herself, but hadn't liked to have scraped off because Mam had chosen it an unknown number of years before, just as she, and almost certainly Violet's father, too, had chosen the ugly furniture that she detested just as much.

Really, Edwin should have given her enough time to get the house ready, she thought fretfully. He'd gone round it with her yesterday morning, checking there were enough beds. Will could have the room that had a double bed that had used to be Violet's before Mam died, they decided, while Abby would sleep in the little box room with its single bed. Mam used to call it 'the spare room', though there'd never once been a visitor who'd stayed overnight. But there'd been no suggestion of having the place decorated, made more suitable for children. She hadn't even had chance to go and get the toys she'd planned on buying.

Violet decided to get a decorator in straight-away, as soon as they were home, and she'd seriously consider getting rid of the furniture and replacing it with something lighter. She had an idea: she'd let the children choose their own wallpaper. She would love to have done that herself when she'd been a child. She could stitch new bedspreads, as well. Brighten the place up.

She rolled out of bed and began to get dressed. Jessie could be heard moving things in the kitchen and it was time her guest put in an appearance.

★ ★ ★

'Well, ducklings,' Jessie said when Will and Abby came running in from the garden, stopping dead when they saw the visitor, though they must have been expecting her to be there, 'this is Violet, who's going to look after you from now on. She'll be your mam and dad rolled into one. Introduce yourselves nicely now, like Jessie taught you.'

Abby stepped forward, curtsied, and said politely, 'How do you do, Auntie Violet?' She held out her hand. Violet took it, marvelling at how tiny it felt. The little girl showed no signs of being shy.

'I'd sooner you called me just Violet, dear.' Close up, the child's eyes were a glorious blue and her skin was like china. She reminded Violet of a doll she'd once had called Alexandra.

'That's my fault,' Jessie said. 'I thought you'd want to be called Auntie. I should've spoke to you about it first.'

'It's my fault, too — I should have told you last night.'

Abby was still clinging to Violet's hand and her bottom lip was trembling. 'You won't die, will you, Violet?'

'Goodness me, of course not,' Violet gasped, at

the same time remembering that many of the people she herself had known during her life had died unexpectedly: Norman Larkin, her old boss, for instance, had passed away in his sleep at the age of only fifty-five; then there was Mam's friend, Dorothy, who'd been knocked down by a car on Stanley Road the week before her fortieth birthday; and — oh, there were a lot of other people she could think of. In fact, there was no guarantee that Violet, or anyone else on earth, would wake up the following morning, or even Abby and Will themselves.

Will! She smiled at the boy, who was leaning against the wall, making no attempt to come forward until Jessie gave him a nudge.

'How d'you do?' he said with every sign of reluctance, making no attempt to shake her hand. His dark eyes smouldered with anger. Violet couldn't tell if the anger was with her or with his life so far. These were two seriously damaged children and she guessed Will was damaged the most and would take longer to mend.

'I'm pleased to meet you, Will.' She gave him her best smile, but the look on his face didn't change. She was wondering what to say next when there was a clattering noise and Abby ran into the hall, returning with a letter. She gave it to Jessie, who tucked it into the pocket of her overall.

The children had already had their breakfast. Will disappeared while Abby sat at the table with a mug of milk, kicking her heels on the rung of the chair, while Jessie and Violet tucked into

47

huge breakfasts of bacon, eggs, sausages and a thick slice of black pudding, followed by two mugs of tea each. Violet could scarcely move when she'd finished. Despite this, she suggested to Jessie that she would wash the dishes, then go for a little walk.

'It's so lovely around here, like a picture postcard,' she said. 'Perhaps Abby would like to come with me.'

Poor little Abby was watching her anxiously, as if worried she'd die on the spot. 'Yes, please, Violet,' she said.

'I'm afraid there isn't the time.' Jessie began to clear the table. 'Perhaps you could collect your stuff together, Violet, and leave it in the hall ready for Mr Powell when he comes. I'll get Will and Abby's bags out the parlour and put them with yours in a minute. Abby, precious, fetch Eustace downstairs, save you forgetting him.' At this, the child raced upstairs.

Violet had understood Edwin wasn't picking them up until ten o'clock. She said as much to Jessie. 'It's only just gone eight,' she pointed out.

'He's changed his mind for some reason,' Jessie said vaguely.

How could she know that? Last night, Edwin had left the house before Violet had gone to bed. Why on earth had Jessie told a lie? She went upstairs and put her nightie and the toiletries she'd brought with her in the little attache case she'd used when she'd had to take documents to and from work. On her way down, she heard someone come in the back way and guessed it was Will.

'Did you manage to speak to him, lad?' she heard Jessie ask.

'I read him the letter, Jess, and he said he'd come straightaway.'

'I knew he would. You'd best get your stuff together. You don't want to hang about a minute longer than necessary.'

There was a pause, then Will said in a ragged voice, 'I'll miss you, Jess, and I'll miss Netton and all me mates from school. I don't want to stay in Bootle with that Violet. I don't like her.'

'Ah, c'mon, lad. Give Jess a kiss. She's not bad, Violet. She's got kind eyes and a nice face.'

'I'd sooner stay here with you.' The young voice was muffled, as if it was buried in Jessie's shoulder.

'You know I'm not long for this world, Will, lad. You don't want someone else dying on you, do you, now?' the old woman said softly.

On the stairs, Violet coughed loudly and proceeded to the bottom. When she entered the kitchen, Will had gone and Violet was wiping her face with a tattered towel. 'Got summat in me eye,' she explained.

* * *

Edwin Powell arrived less than half an hour later. He'd clearly come in a hurry: his tie wasn't knotted properly and there was a spot of blood on his chin where he'd cut himself while shaving. 'Are you ready for the off?' he asked.

All five of them were standing at the front of the cottage in the midst of the children's canvas

49

holdalls, an assortment of dolls in a string bag, a collection of *Hotspur* and *Wizard* comics in another, and a toy garage that looked homemade — Violet wondered if one of the fathers had made it. Edwin and Will loaded everything into the boot of the Morris and Violet climbed into the back with Abby, who was carrying Eustace, a shabby stuffed elephant a shocking shade of pink. It meant that Will could sit in the front with Edwin, which Violet was sure he would prefer.

Had she been offered a wish, it would have been to fall asleep in about ten minutes' time and wake up outside her own front door, preferably without these children whom she'd never heard of before this week.

Jessie hovered around the car, weeping openly. It was an effort for Violet to hold back her own tears. As they drove away, it was an even greater effort not to lean forward, put her arms around Will's neck, and give him a kiss and a hug. But she knew it wouldn't be welcome and wondered if it ever would.

It wasn't until just before they were shortly to cross the River Severn on the ferry that Edwin stopped the car for a welcome break and she was able to ask what the urgency had been that morning while the children hurried ahead into the roadside café.

'A letter came for Jessie from Mrs Holmes,' he explained. 'In case you've forgotten, that's Abby's grandmother. She said she was coming to collect Abby at some time this morning, whether we liked it or not. I didn't say so before, but she's a most unpleasant woman. She only wants Abby to run round after her, fetch and carry, go on messages.'

Violet frowned. 'She has more right to Abby than I have.' She was the girl's grandmother.

'That's not true.' He tightened his lips stubbornly. 'Mary was the mother of both children and you are her cousin, a blood relative. Mrs Holmes is the mother of one of the fathers. Should it ever go to court, I am convinced a judge would prefer Abby and Will, brother and sister, be kept together.'

The children were only half-brother and half-sister, but Violet felt she was being awkward for pointing it out. 'What happens if Mrs Holmes discovers where I live?' she asked.

'Ah, there's no need to worry, Violet. She'd never do that.'

'You did,' Violet pointed out.

'Yes, but I have resources at my disposal that she hasn't.'

'I see.' She thought he was much too confident for his own good.

3

That night, Abby slept in the guest room in which a guest had never before slept and Will in Violet's old double bed. When Edwin had dropped them off at Amber Street, she'd been terrified — suddenly realising this was it, the children were her responsibility, and she didn't have a clue what to do. When they'd entered, Violet had been painfully reminded of how dull, dark and cramped her house was when compared with Jessie's cottage in Netton.

The children slept well, but they'd had a particularly tiring day yesterday, so it wasn't surprising. Violet had shown them where her own bedroom was and had left the door wide open. She was pleased when Abby came running in next morning clutching Eustace and jumped on the bed, disturbing an indignant Sammy, who jumped off and ran downstairs in a huff.

'Hello, Violet,' Abby sang.

'Good morning, pet.' Violet had thought long and hard about how to address the children. *Dear* sounded rather formal, she thought; *darling* was a bit too posh; *sweetheart* rather familiar for children she didn't know — at least not yet. But her father had called her *pet*, and it seemed to suit the situation perfectly.

Abby didn't seem to notice. 'I'm thirsty,' she announced.

Violet got up immediately, not just for Abby's

sake, but because she was worried about Will.

He was sitting up in bed, looking incredibly wretched. She could tell he'd been crying, but now he wore a tight frown, as if he was holding himself together, determined never to cry again if he could help it. It was all Violet could do not to cry herself at this unhappy little boy who had been passed from pillar to post in his short life while the people he loved had died around him.

'Hello, Will,' she said gently, longing to take him in her arms, but guessing he would be outraged if she did. 'What would you like to do today? We've got a few weeks before we have to think about school, so you can take your pick.'

His frown grew deeper. 'Dunno.' He shrugged.

'Would you like to play in the park? We could buy a ball to take with us. Or go for a ride on the ferry?' She racked her brain for more ideas. 'We could go to Strand Road and buy you both some nice new clothes and an ice cream.' She would have suggested the pictures if there was a suitable film on — she felt almost sure he and his sister had never been, but best to save the pictures for a rainy day.

'The ferry,' he said. The word almost choked him. 'I've already got clothes.'

Both his and Abby's clothes were rather shabby, as if they'd been bought second-hand, but they too could be left for another day. 'I'd like the ferry best, too,' she told him.

Edwin Powell, who had stayed overnight in the same hotel as before, came to see them first thing that morning, parking his little car outside

Violet's front door. He kissed Abby, squeezed Will's shoulder and promised to come and see them again at the earliest opportunity.

'Goodbye, Violet.' He took her hand, squeezing it tightly, finishing off with a series of pats. 'You are without doubt the nicest and the kindest woman I have ever known. It's been a pleasure meeting you and I am already looking forward to seeing you again soon.'

Violet felt as if her face were on fire and stammered something, but couldn't remember what it was after Edwin Powell and his car had gone.

⋆ ⋆ ⋆

Will looked happy for the first time when they boarded the ferry to New Brighton. He grabbed the brass handrail and ran along the side of the boat. Violet was about to warn him to be careful, but kept her mouth shut. He seemed a sensible lad and a warning would only irritate him.

Abby wasn't prepared to leave Violet's side and sat on her knee at every opportunity — on the tram into town, on the *Royal Daffodil*, where they sat on a bench on the deck. When Will tired of running around the boat, he came and sat with them and Violet described how during the war the Liverpool ferry boats had helped rescue troops from Dunkirk and bring them back to England. 'To a place called Kent,' she said and described the whole procedure.

'Big boats and little boats that only took a couple of men, all of them came to help save

British and French troops from being captured by the Germans. It was called an armada.'

'Where's Dunkirk?' Will asked.

'On the coast of France,' she told him. 'It happened during the war that ended five years ago. Do you remember much about it?'

'It's when my dad was killed, the war,' he said. 'It was near the beginning and Mam said he was riding a motorbike.'

'He must have been very brave,' Violet said.

'He was, Mam said so.' He spoke in an angry voice, as if they were having an argument. All of a sudden, he disappeared and the next she saw of him he was running around the boat again holding onto the rail.

She had thought the children would enjoy the fairground in New Brighton, but it turned out to be the first time they had had been to one. Abby was distressed at the jarring music that seemed to be coming from all different directions, and the noisy rides. Even the hobby horses, which Violet had herself been looking forward to, made her shriek with fear. It didn't help when the inevitable rain began to fall.

At this, Will demanded that they go home. 'Don't cry, Abs,' he implored, holding her hand and glaring at Violet as if she had brought them to a torture chamber or somewhere equally nasty. It was the first time she was to see how caring and possessive he was with his half-sister.

The journey home on the tram was uncomfortably quiet. Violet felt slightly in disgrace, as if she'd let the children down, and was anxious to get back into their good books, while Will stroked Abby's hair, saying, 'There, there, Abs. There, there.'

★   ★   ★

Violet wasn't all that surprised when she opened the door of the house in Amber Street to come to face with Madge McGann. 'I hope you don't mind, Vi,' she said loudly, 'but I was worried stiff when I came round yesterday and the house was empty. Then I came today and there was still no one here. I was about to panic, when that woman from next door told me you'd arrived home last night with two lovely children, but had gone out again today. I thought I'd hang about to see what was going on.'

She looked down at the exhausted children. 'And aren't they both gorgeous! I could eat the pair of them. What's your name, darlin'?' she asked Will. 'My name's Madge, by the way.'

Violet was worried Will might be annoyed at being addressed as 'darling' by such a loud-mouthed, effusive, over the top, red-haired woman, but he took a step forward, almost a smile on his face. 'William Stein,' he said, 'but everyone calls me Will.'

'Can I kiss you, Will?'

Violet cringed.

'If you like.' The words were a touch clipped, but he nevertheless turned up his face to be kissed.

With her hand still resting on Will's tousled head, Madge beamed at Abby. 'Well,' she said, 'me, I've got five daughters but not one of them is as pretty as you. And what are you called, darlin'?'

'Abby.' The little girl's eyes were shining and she gladly took hold of Madge's free hand.

'She's Abby Holmes,' Will said.

'I didn't have time to tell you I was going away.' Violet spoke at last, a touch breathlessly. 'It was only for a single night. Mr Powell came on Monday and he took me down to Exeter first thing the next morning and we came back yesterday.'

Madge led the children into the living room, where all three managed to squeeze into the same armchair. Sammy jumped onto the back and began to play with Madge's hair. Within seconds, Abby had fallen asleep. 'I'd put her down for a little nap if I were you, Vi. Here.' She lifted the little girl into Violet's arms, and she carried her upstairs and put her to bed. When Violet came down again, the front door was closing and Will was no longer there.

'I gave him a tanner, sent him in the direction of Marsh Lane, and told him to buy hisself something,' Madge said.

'Oh, but . . . ' Violet bit her lip; it seemed an irresponsible thing to do.

'He'll be all right, luv,' Madge soothed. 'Knowing you, you'll worry yourself to death and then what will the poor kids do? I told him there's a baker's on one corner of Amber Street and a laundry on the other so's he won't get lost. They're lovely kids, Violet. I'd be interested to know exactly how you came by them?'

'Well, it appears that all this time I've had a

cousin called Mary,' Violet began. 'She's the daughter of me Uncle Albert, who went to live in Canada, where he married a woman called Clara. They had Mary about nineteen twenty and she came back to this country.' She told her friend the whole story, of how Mary and both her husbands had died and it was really important that the children were got out of the way before Abby's grandmother got her hands on the little girl and poor Will was sent to an orphanage all on his own.

'It sounds like a fairy story,' Madge remarked. 'Like 'Babes in the Wood' or something. And you took them, Vi, just like that. Made up your mind in an instant, as it were.' She looked admiringly at Violet. 'Me, I'd've run a mile.'

'Oh, but Madge, you'd be so much better at it than me,' Violet cried. 'Look at the way they took to you just now. You hardly had to say a word and they were dead charmed. I haven't a notion of what to say to them.'

Madge shook her head violently. 'Oh, but you've tons more patience. Me, I'd be cracking their heads together in no time — just like I did with me girls. Me, I'm dead short-tempered. They'll grow to love you, you'll see, whereas with me we'd all hate each other in no time.'

While Madge was exaggerating, to a certain extent what she said was true. She had been strict and bad-tempered with her daughters and there were times when Violet would wince when she watched them being slapped, though the next minute their mother was drowning them in kisses. Even nowadays, there were periods when one or other of the girls wasn't speaking to her mother.

Will was out for a worryingly long time and returned home with half a dozen tattered copies of a comic called *The Magnet* he'd bought from Les's second-hand shop for a ha'penny each, along with some old copies of *Comic Cuts* for Abby at the same price.

Madge was impressed. 'I thought he'd come back laden with sweets,' she marvelled. 'And that *Magnet* comic isn't full of pictures like the others. It has pages in it full of words, like a book. You must be dead clever, Will.'

Will mumbled something that might have been, 'I like reading,' in reply and went upstairs to read the comics on his own. Sammy must have wondered what was going on and followed.

'Well, I'll be off.' Madge got to her feet. 'I'll see you tomorrer, girl. Is it all right if I bring the kids some presents?'

'Of course. Why on earth would I not want you to bring them presents?'

'Some women might think I was wanting to take over, make them like me more than they like you. But not you, Vi.' She landed a playful punch on Violet's arm. 'You're much too nice for that.'

★ ★ ★

'What on earth am I going to do with them tomorrow?' Violet wondered in a panic after her friend had gone. She could take them for a walk along the Docky — the road that ran all the way into the centre of Liverpool, passing the docks on the way. It was usually full of all sorts of different traffic, from the most modern cars and lorries to handcarts being pushed along by a solitary worker or being pulled by a giant carthorse. It was probably the most interesting road on earth. Then there was the seashore, North Park, the big shops in town, the cinema on the days when it rained. And they could walk along the Docky more than once; she herself had done it hundreds of times.

And, before she knew it, it would be September, time for the children to start school. They would go to St Anne's, the school she had gone to herself, which was run by nuns. It was only a few streets away, so close to the heavily bombed docks that it had been closed down during the war for safety's sake.

Violet recalled her own first day at St Anne's. She had returned home for her dinner, returned home later for tea, and had put on her coat for the third time, when Mam, screaming with laughter, had told her she was done for the day.

'You only go to school twice a day, luv,' she said. 'You're not expected to go every few hours for the rest of your life.'

Will and Abby would need special clothes for school — sensible clothes such as a navy-blue skirt and grey shorts, lace-up shoes. Not that all the children would be dressed that way — their families wouldn't be able to afford it. Too many men were without jobs.

Violet plucked the arm of her mother's chair, wondering how many times Mam's arm had rested on the flowered cretonne, the colour by now faded badly. It was more than forty years since she had been sent to the same school wearing everything brand new. In those days, some children quite literally wore rags; they came without shoes or underwear, and were badly in need of a good wash and a good meal at the same time.

But those days had gone. Now there was a National Health Service brought in by the Labour Government headed by Prime Minister Clement Attlee. There was still poverty, but nothing like it used to be.

'Phew!' She felt dead tired. It had been an exhausting day — not just physically so, but mentally, too. She could really do with a little snooze. She crept upstairs and found Abby fast asleep, as expected, and Will lying beside her on the bed, his arm around her waist, sleeping peacefully. Sammy was draped over a tangle of legs, dead to the world. The comics were on the floor.

Violet stared at the children. They looked so helpless, so vulnerable, lying together, unaware of anything. The weight of responsibility was overwhelming. She closed the door gently and hurried downstairs, where she sat in her mother's chair and cried and cried until she, too, was fast asleep.

4

September inevitably came and it was time for the children to go to school — Abby for the first time. Violet had asked Will whether he had liked school back in Netton and he had just shrugged, muttering, 'It was all right.'

'In a year,' she told him, 'once you're eleven, you'll transfer to senior school.'

'OK,' he said indifferently.

Despite her questioning, she had been unable to discover his feelings about school, about anything, as it happened. He was really difficult to get to know, she thought despondently. Maybe she was doing it all wrong. Every day there were new challenges with the children, but she'd, got used to their noise and activity at home, so it would feel strange to have them out at school all day.

Madge had said there was no need to tell the school to expect two new pupils. 'Just turn up with them, Vi,' she said. 'That's what I did, one by one, with me girls. The headmistress nowadays is called Sister Xavier.'

But Violet wasn't prepared just to turn up. She had written a letter to Sister Xavier, giving details of the children, and advising her to expect them the day school opened for the autumn term. 'Or is it the winter term?' she asked Madge worriedly. 'There's four seasons, but only three terms.'

'Oh, for Christ's sake, Violet!' Madge snorted. 'The woman'll know what you mean.'

She didn't receive a reply to her letter, so, on the day the new term started, she dressed Abby in her new blue frock — Will dressed himself in his new shirt and shorts — and self-consciously led them both into St Anne's, an old, single-storey building close to the docks. There were a few obviously new parents like herself and the sound of dozens and dozens of shrill voices was deafening.

A pretty, rosy-cheeked young nun introduced herself as Sister Joan and asked their names. After consulting a clutch of papers, she told Will he was in the top class. 'Number 5.' She pointed along the corridor. 'It's taken by Mr Kirkpatrick. He's our only male teacher.' Turning to Abby, she said, 'And you're in Class 1. I shall be taking that class later.'

She smiled at Violet. 'I read your letter and was surprised at the assortment of names. All three of you have different surnames, yet you are a family. What were they now?' She put her finger to her chin and thought. 'I remember. You are Violet Duffy, this handsome young man is William Stein and this dear little girl is Abigail Holmes.'

'I'm their auntie,' Violet felt obliged to explain. 'They had different fathers and they, and their mother, are dead.'

'How absolutely awful.' For some reason, Sister Joan made the Sign of the Cross while guiding Abby into a nearby room crammed with desks and already occupied by numerous children.

'Say ta-ta to your auntie, there's a good girl,' the nun said.

Abby looked at Violet, panic-stricken. But before Violet could so much as open her mouth to speak, the door had closed and she was standing outside. Will had disappeared. She was alone. And what could she have said, anyroad, other than 'Ta-ta, pet' to nobody in particular.

'Are you all right?' A young woman with a toddler in a pushchair was looking at her sympathetically. 'My Greta has just started and I didn't manage to give her one last kiss.' She sniffed violently. 'I feel as if I want to die.' The toddler, a boy, was struggling to be lifted out.

His mother wiped her nose on the sleeve of her cardigan. 'Keep still, Greg. We'll soon be home.' She and Violet left the school together. 'We came out in such a rush, he left his teddy bear behind. Look!' She grabbed Violet's hand. 'You want to die, too. I can tell. Come back with us, please, and we can have a cuppa, then die together.'

'All right,' Violet said reluctantly, though she wasn't exactly looking forward to returning home to a silent house, unable to get Abby's panic-stricken face out of her mind and wishing she'd managed to speak to Will before he'd been despatched to Class 5 in such a hurry. Sister Joan had seemed a nice young woman, but she'd been a bit too brusque for Violet's liking and this other woman seemed a touch insane.

'I live in Rimrose Road directly opposite the tram terminus,' her new friend was saying. She was unusually attractive with jet-black hair cut in a thick fringe. Her impish face was covered in freckles. 'Oh, and my name is Carol Cooper, this is Greg in the pram and Greta's gone to school, but I've already told you that, haven't I?'

'I'm Violet Duffy — Greg is an unusual name, isn't it? I've never heard it before.' Violet felt flustered, unsure what she was up to. Why was she about to have a cup of tea with a woman she'd never seen before that morning?

'Greg is short for Gregory,' Carol Cooper explained. 'Did you see that film *The Keys of the Kingdom* with Gregory Peck? He is, without doubt, the most handsome man in the entire world. He is utterly, utterly gorgeous. I would go to bed with him in an instant should he ever ask — though I don't suppose he will,' she went on sadly. 'I can't think of a single reason why Gregory Peck would want to come to Bootle.'

'He might, if he knew how much you fancied him,' Violet said, surprising herself, for she was ever so slightly shocked at Carol's loudly expressed wish to sleep with a complete stranger merely because she liked the look of him. 'I suppose Greta's called after Greta Garbo?' Everybody had heard of the beautiful actress who spoke with a Russian accent.

'Oh, she is,' Carol assured her. 'Pete — that's me husband — is mad about her. He thinks she's the bee's knees.' They had arrived at a semi-detached house with a small front garden. The front door was painted bright red.

'That's the first red door I've ever seen,' Violet marvelled. 'I've seen maroon, but never such a vivid red.'

'I hate maroon doors,' Carol said with feeling. 'And I hate black ones and dark-green ones, and all those other miserable colours. I swore if I ever had a front door of me own, then it would be a nice cheerful red.' She gave the door an affectionate pat when she opened it and they went inside. Greg had shown his disgust at being told to shut up by falling asleep in the pushchair.

'Well, it's that all right,' Violet said, following. 'Cheerful.'

It turned out that Carol Cooper was as cheerful as her door. She declared herself devastated that Greta had started school, but was affected in such a theatrical way that it hardly seemed to matter.

'I shall probably have more children,' she reckoned. 'One by one, they will all go to school, go to work, get married, and the time will come when there will just be me and Pete. He's in the Royal Navy, by the way. Do you have a husband, Violet? I noticed you're not wearing a ring.'

Violet felt obliged to describe the situation that existed between her, Abby and Will. 'I'm their auntie. The thing is, I didn't realise I had a cousin — their mother — until a few months ago.'

'Gosh,' Carol marvelled. 'Isn't life fascinating? Sometimes, it's more fascinating than a film.'

Violet felt bound to agree. She remembered losing her job only a few more months ago. It could also be fascinatingly awful too, but she wasn't prepared to go into that right now.

Greg had been left in his pushchair in the hallway. He woke up and loudly demanded his teddy, who turned out to be under the table, a hand-knitted animal more or less shaped like a bear that had become undone in several places. Greg grabbed it and a few more stitches slipped.

'One of these days Teddy will end up a ball of wool and Greg will never forgive me,' Carol remarked. 'I'm useless with a needle.'

'Have you got a crochet hook and I'll try and mend it — I mean him?' Violet offered. She felt sure Greg regarded his bear as real.

'There's a box of stuff I inherited from my mother-in-law in the sideboard. It was she who knitted Teddy, who originally belonged to Pete, so he's getting on a bit.' She rooted through the sideboard cupboard and handed Violet a rusty biscuit tin without a lid jammed full of sewing items, from a darning mushroom to several crochet hooks, knitting needles, thimbles and scraps of lace, then went into the kitchen to make the tea.

Greg must have realised his favourite toy required medical attention and didn't protest when he was handed to Violet. Indeed, he climbed onto the settee beside her to watch.

'I love him,' he declared with utter sincerity. 'Will you make him better for me?' He was a dear little boy with tight curly hair and a face more freckled than his mother's.

'I'll do my best,' Violet promised.

She picked up numerous dropped stitches and knotted the loose ends together. It took a surprisingly short time to mend the shabby bear and return him without a single loose thread to his owner. The little boy cradled the toy joyfully and kissed him better.

'You didn't hurt him, did you?' he asked.

'No, pet. He didn't feel a thing,' Violet assured him. She never realised, then, that she had just made a friend for life.

Dishes were rattling in the kitchen. 'Do you take sugar, Violet?' Carol shouted.

'No, thank you.' Like most people, Violet had given it up during the war. She returned to contemplating the walls, having been aware when entering Carol's house how bright everywhere was. The walls in this room were distempered the palest of green, a faint mint shade, yet there was also an embossed pattern there.

'How did you get your walls like that?' she asked when her new friend came in with a tray of tea and Nice biscuits.

'I just distempered over the old wallpaper,' Carol said. 'Along with miserable coloured doors, I can't stand dark wallpaper with ghastly patterns, either. I've done up the entire house,' she went on. 'You can come and look in the parlour and upstairs in a minute.'

'I'd love to.' She'd done nothing about her own dead miserable house, much as she had intended to. The wallpaper there was embossed like Carol's. She began to think about colours.

★   ★   ★

By the time Violet returned home, it was almost eleven and in an hour's time Will and Abby would be back for their lunch. They had agreed

68

that on weekdays they would want only a snack and have a proper meal when they came home for good at half past three.

When the war started in 1939, food rationing had been brought in and, despite the conflict ending five years ago, there were still items of food available only on the production of a ration book. It wasn't until a few months before, in May, that canned and dried fruit became freely available, along with chocolate biscuits, jellies and mincemeat. Petrol could at last be bought for those who had a car, but sugar and butter, two of the most popular foods, were still rationed.

At least beans on toast was readily available and Violet busied herself in the kitchen, spreading four chocolate biscuits on a plate, two for each child, then emptying a tin of Heinz beans into a pan.

At ten to twelve, she removed her pinny and went to collect Abby and Will from school.

She wasn't surprised, nor did she mind, when Will refused to walk home with her. 'I'm too old,' he hissed, and went ahead to let himself in. When she and Abby went in minutes later and she asked him how he'd got on at school, he said, 'S'all right.' It seemed to be his stock answer, accompanied by a shrug, whatever the question was.

Abby had enjoyed herself. 'Sister Joan read us stories and we had to draw a cat. She said we can bring our pictures back home with us this avvy. What does that mean, Violet?'

'Avvy means afternoon, pet.'

The beans eaten, Will insisted he was perfectly

capable of taking Abby back to school and bringing her home when it was over. 'Grown-ups only come on the first day,' he argued. 'People will only think you're daft if you keep on collecting us.'

'Will!' She was shocked and he looked uncomfortable, but only a little bit. Would she really look daft?

'It's true,' he insisted. 'You could come back with us just this once and see.'

'I believe you,' Violet muttered. She didn't want to let people think she was being overprotective.

That night, the children in bed, Violet wrote to Edwin Powell:

Abby seems to have enjoyed her first day at school. I have her drawing of a cat attached to a cupboard in the kitchen with a drawing pin. All Will says is that it was all right. Whether he's speaking the truth or not, I wouldn't know.

The boy didn't smile much and she didn't think she had ever seen him laugh. She badly wanted him to be happy. Although he had a much stronger personality than his sister, Violet considered him to be more at risk from the outside world, more sensitive.

★   ★   ★

There was a knock on the door on Friday morning not long after the children had left for school. Still unused to visitors, Violet was surprised to find Carol Cooper and Greg standing there.

'How did you know where I lived?' Violet enquired as Carol hoisted the pushchair into the hall. She had been hoping to see the girl and her lovely son again — and, of course, Greta — but hadn't liked to go round to the house in Rimrose Road unannounced. Carol might not want to become friendly with a much older woman.

'You told me the other day,' Carol said. 'I thought it would be nice if my Greta and your Abby became friends, that's if they decide to like each other. As I don't have a man around most of the time and you don't have a man at all — I hope you don't mind me pointing that out — I'm inviting you and the children to tea on Sunday afternoon. And are you taking them to Sunday School?'

'I hadn't thought about Sunday School.' Violet thought about it now. 'I shall take Abby,' she said eventually, 'but ask Will first if he wants to go.' She would never make Will go anywhere that he didn't want to. 'Anyroad, I'm not sure what they get up to these days at Sunday School. All I remember from going there myself was pressing lots of flowers. I used to give them to me mam — there might even be a few still around the house in the form of lavender bags.'

'I'll see you about half past three, then, Vi,' Carol said, preparing to leave.

'Surely, having come all this way, you'd like to stay for a cuppa?' Violet protested.

'Of course I would. I thought you'd never ask.

Just in case you're out of it, I've brought me own sugar. I know, most people gave it up during the war, but I never managed it. Got no will power at all, that's me.'

★   ★   ★

Edwin Powell arrived on Saturday at midday. Vi was having to get used to unexpected guests — a far cry from the quiet old days when no one rang the doorbell from one week to the next.

'We were just about to go to Southport on the train,' Violet exclaimed when she opened the door.

'I'll take you in the car instead,' Edwin announced.

He had been driving since two o'clock that morning and had stopped only once for a cup of tea. 'And a meat pie.' He sounded excited, as if it had been a big adventure. The roadside café was being used by lorry drivers and he'd stood beneath a canvas awning to eat and drink. 'It was pitch-dark outside, but there were some sort of hanging lamps to see by, oil, perhaps. I'm not really sure. I'm not a very technical person, you see. Oh, and the meat pie was delicious.' He rubbed his tummy in a flurry of delight.

He seemed exceptionally pleased to see the children. Jessie had sent a chocolate sponge cake, half a dozen scones and a two-pound jar of homemade strawberry jam. 'She misses them badly,' Edwin said.

'And they miss her,' Violet told him. Actually, she didn't think Abby did any more. She seemed

72

to have settled happily in Bootle more easily than her brother. As for Will, he didn't appear to be either happy or settled, but nor did he seem to be unhappy, either.

★ ★ ★

In Southport, they went to the pictures to see *Snow White and the Seven Dwarfs*, a lovely, animated production of the old children's story. The children were almost struck dumb with the wonder of it. Will's eyes shone for the first time.

'Is it true?' Abby wanted to know. 'Did it really happen?' She wanted to meet the dwarfs if it were possible.

'It's just a story. My mother used to read it to me,' Violet told them afterwards when they were in a café having tea.

Will wanted to know why Violet couldn't have read the story for herself.

Violet laughed. 'Like you, Will, like everyone, I wasn't born able to read. Someone had to teach me and it was between me mother and school. Who was it taught you?'

The boy creased his brow. 'I think it was me dad.'

But Edwin pointed out that there was no record of Will's dad having lived in Netton. 'Jessie said your mother arrived without him. By then, your dad had died or been killed in the war. No one knows. It must have been your mother, lad, who taught you to read.'

Will shrugged. 'Maybe it was.' He had ceased to be interested.

★　★　★

Edwin stayed overnight in his usual hotel in Waterloo. The following morning he collected Violet and the children and took them back to Waterloo, where they formed teams and played football on the sands, men against women. It took ages to choose. Edwin tried to insist on playing the other three on his own, but Violet refused, saying it wouldn't be fair. Abby began to cry, she didn't know why, and Will just began to kick the football about without saying anything, and the others joined in. The sides just fell into place naturally. Having never played football before, Violet discovered she was quite good at it and definitely better than Edwin. The women won, only because the men, in other words Will, were too polite to let them lose.

Afterwards, Edwin bought them an ice cream each and suggested they have lunch. 'Though I think around here you call it dinner.' In a low voice, he added, 'I must tell you this. Mrs Holmes, Abby's grandmother, came to the AGM of St Jude's Bounty last week. AGM stands for Annual — '

'General Meeting,' Violet chipped in. 'I used to be a secretary, remember?' She'd written the agendas, taken minutes, typed them.

'Oh, yes, I had forgotten,' Edwin said humbly. 'Anyway, she made a big, noisy fuss. As soon as she'd gone, I told the Board about her attitude to Will and they recommended I ignore her.'

Violet nodded her agreement. 'I intend to do the same if she ever shows her face here,' she

74

confirmed. 'As for lunch, you must let me pay. You're paying for far too much.'

'Whatever I pay is part of my expenses. If I let you pay, Violet, it would be most dishonest of me.' He looked at her pathetically. 'I'm longing for a cup of tea.'

Before they went anywhere, she insisted they find a place where she could tidy herself up a bit. Her hair must be a mess, her face felt hot and there was sand in her stockings — understandably, seeing that she had removed her shoes.

'My hotel's not far away,' Edwin remarked. 'Let's go there. In fact, it's a good place for us to have a meal.'

'You look pretty.' Will put his hand over his mouth as if he'd spoken out of turn.

'Thank you, Will,' Violet said quietly, hiding her astonishment.

'He's right, you know.' Edwin eyed her with admiration. 'Fancy him noticing.'

Not to be outdone, Abby clasped both Violet's hands. 'Your hair's all fluffy, Violet, and your cheeks are pink.'

It was only about ten minutes later that Violet was examining her reflection in the mirror in the ladies' room in Edwin's hotel. Rather than pretty, she thought she must look the opposite. Her face was bright red and shiny and her hair was indeed fluffy, as if she'd been dragged through a hedge backwards — she remembered Mam had used to say something like that when Violet hadn't looked remotely as bad as she did now. She combed the fluff until it was flat and splashed her face, though it looked even redder when she patted it dry. It would have been nice to have changed her frock, except it wasn't possible, and she felt annoyed with herself for letting such a little bit of admiration unsettle her.

They had fish and chips for lunch — served posh with a slice of lemon and a tiny bowl of sauce tartare. Will was fascinated. He ate the sauce separately in one go and seemed to like it. Violet didn't say anything and Edwin didn't appear to notice. He was discussing the headlines in that morning's *Sunday Times* — it had been on the passenger seat when she'd climbed into the car. She had folded it and slid it into the pocket inside the door.

The meal over, he ordered a pot of tea for him and Violet and lemonade for the children. 'I see the London dockers are threatening to go on strike again,' he said chattily when the waitress had gone.

'What's wrong with that?' Violet retorted. She had noticed that headline in particular.

'It's an antisocial practice, striking,' he said, slowly and loudly, as if he thought he was telling her something she didn't know.

'It's the only way a man has to protest against being treated unfairly by an employer,' she replied, just as slowly and just as loudly.

There was a horrified silence. 'You *approve* of strikes?'

'Very much so. My father was a docker. In Liverpool before the war, they were treated abominably. The men had to gather outside the dock gates looking for work and were picked out individually by the foreman.' Violet could feel herself getting hot again. 'Favouritism was rife, so were bribes. If a man wasn't chosen, he didn't work that day. He could end up not working all week, not earning a penny to feed his family.'

'But that's terrible.' He looked very much taken aback. 'I can understand your feelings,' he said, nodding.

Violet didn't care whether he understood or not. 'My father died in agony after inhaling a poisonous substance. I was eight at the time. If it hadn't been for the dockers' union, me and Mam would have been left penniless. As it was, she was in receipt of a pension for life.'

Edwin didn't speak for a while. 'We won't let this come between us, will we? I mean our different opinions on politics and the like?'

'Of course not.' Why should it in anyway affect their relationship? She was impressed with the way he ran the charity and thought so much of the children; that was all that mattered. 'The garden would be very dull if all the roses were red,' she said. Another of Mam's favourite sayings — she'd used to say it in the same prissy voice.

At half past two, he dropped them off outside the house in Amber Street, leaving her and the children with enough time to have a good wash and change their clothes before going to Carol Cooper's house for tea. Violet had forgotten all about Sunday School.

⋆ ⋆ ⋆

The following Wednesday, Iris Gunn, head of the typing pool at Briggs' Motors, came to see her after tea. The woman stood on the pavement staring at her long and hard before saying hesitantly, 'Is it you, Violet?'

Violet grinned. 'Have I turned into a pumpkin or something? Of course, it is, eejit!'

'But you look so different!' The woman's eyes popped. 'I didn't recognise you. You never used to wear your hair loose like that. It suits you — makes you look much younger.' She shook her head in astonishment. 'Blimey, girl, those two kids have done you the world of good.'

Violet hadn't had a chance to see Iris since the children had come to live with her, although she'd sent her friend a note telling her the news. But she hadn't realised what a different figure she cut now — although, now Iris mentioned it, she did feel younger somehow, even if she was twice as tired most evenings than after a day at Briggs' Motors. She put her hand up to her hair. She was unaware her hair was loose, though it was a long time since she'd been to a hairdresser's and it was definitely in need of a trim. She patted her head. 'It needs a good seeing-to. Would you like to come in, luv?'

'You've missed some really hilarious events at work, Vi,' Iris said when both women were settled in the living room and the kettle was on for tea. 'You'll never guess what happened last night.'

'Douglas Penny and Beryl Daly were found lying naked underneath his desk.' Violet made a wild and completely ludicrous guess.

'How the hell did you know that?' Iris looked at her in astonishment. 'I mean, it only happened

78

less than twenty-four hours ago. The news must have really taken off if it's reached you already.'

Violet burst out laughing. 'It was only a guess. You mean it actually happened?' She could hardly believe it.

'It did that.' Iris began to giggle until tears ran down her cheeks. 'The Chairman of Directors arrived after hours. Beryl, the blonde bombshell, had been informed he was coming, but had forgotten to tell Douglas — she's a perfectly hopeless secretary. Anyroad, they were under his desk joined together in what I think is known as the coital position when the Chairman burst in. Of course, you know what Briggs' Motors is like. Rumours have been flying about all day. One says they're still joined together, as they froze in fright and haven't been able to separate themselves since.'

'I feel awful for finding it so funny. I mean, it must have been horrible for them — well, for Beryl, poor girl. It was bound to be him who made a pass at her in the first place.' She really didn't give a damn about Douglas Penny. 'Thanks for coming all this way to tell me, Iris.'

'I couldn't wait, Violet. It won't surprise you to know that both the lovebirds have been given the sack. The Chairman is in the process of appointing someone temporary to take Douglas Penny's place and approached me in the typing pool to recommend a replacement for Beryl. He actually mentioned your name, but I hope you don't mind, I said I was pretty sure you wouldn't be interested, thanks very much. I expect there was a time when you'd have been over the moon at getting your old job back, most probably with increased wages. You'd be perfect, but I told the Chairman in the politest way possible to stuff his job.'

Violet smiled — Iris was quite right. After all the heartache over losing her job, she knew now she never wanted to set foot in that office again — and, more importantly, she didn't miss it one bit.

The kettle boiled and Violet went to make the tea. Almost straightaway, Iris appeared at the kitchen door. 'Oh, Violet!' she cried happily. 'I'm so pleased at the way things have turned out for you. There's nothing more important in this world than children. It's what we women were put on earth for, not work for bloody creeps like Douglas Penny at Briggs' Motors.'

'You're right about that, Iris, but I'd prefer it if you left out the *bloody*.' That was the first time in her life she'd actually said the word.

5

During the war that had ended five years before, there'd been six Christmases, each one meaner and poorer than the one before. Cake ingredients had become more difficult to find: dried fruit impossible, dates gone altogether from the shops, dried cherries just a faint memory, eggs as precious as jewels, and making your own icing out of sugar was actually against the law.

It was just as bad with presents, in particular children's toys, wrapping paper, decorations and cosmetics. Women were known to give used lipsticks as a gift, half a box of face powder, half a bottle of scent. But, since 1945, the situation had improved until now it was almost normal, though Christmas still felt especially enjoyable with such sparse, cold 'celebrations' still in people's minds. Vi had been anxious about giving the children a 'proper' Christmas, when she knew nothing about what children liked to do, but she'd surprised herself with how much she'd got carried away, making paper chains and humming carols around the house.

Violet would never forget Abby's thrilled surprise when she woke up on Christmas morning and found a giant, beautifully dressed doll sitting at the foot of her bed, though the child was confused on opening a shabby velvet box to discover a peeling pearl necklace inside.

'It's from your grandmother,' she told the girl.

When the package had arrived, she'd been shocked to realise Mrs Holmes had found out where Abby was. If she had their address, what was to stop her coming here and taking the girl? She had been tempted not to pass on the gift to Abby, but it seemed cruel to deny Abby all contact with what little family she had left.

Abby stared at the tatty jewellery but luckily was distracted by Will's excitement. He had been delighted to find *Gulliver's Travels* on the floor beside him along with *The Adventure Book for Boys*, a Parker junior fountain pen and a bottle of black ink.

'I hope you're watching,' she said privately to her own mother when she and the children sat down to Christmas dinner — chicken, sprouts, peas, sage-and-onion stuffing and gravy — all wearing exceptionally attractive paper hats that Violet had made. They ate in the parlour, where the fire was lit, coal no longer in short supply. 'I've never been so happy in me life before,' she sang inside her head.

Knowing her mother as she did, Violet couldn't help but issue herself with dire warnings on her behalf. 'It won't last, girl,' Mam cautioned. 'No one stays happy all their life. Just be prepared, that's all. Be prepared for whatever's round the corner. It might be good, or it might be bad. Who knows?' she finished ominously.

Violet shook her head and resolved to ignore her mother until Christmas was over. She and the children played games in the afternoon when Carol Cooper came with Greg and Greta.

Lieutenant Cooper was at sea and his wife and children had been invited to tea with the Duffys.

Carol had made a delicious trifle for afters. The meal over, they played more games and, at about half past six, everyone fell asleep. When they woke, the children were as pleased as punch to find that it was snowing.

'The perfect end to a perfect day,' Carol breathed. All four children were dead excited and there were already a few outside playing snowballs in the dark. Violet couldn't help but recall how much her mother had hated snow. 'It only looks nice for five minutes,' she would complain, 'and then it becomes as pure as the driven slush.' She giggled. 'Groucho Marx said that.'

She'd adored the Marx Brothers; they'd shared the same sense of humour.

There was something else — it wasn't exactly a present but it had arrived the week before Christmas and Violet decided to regard it as such — and that was a telephone. Edwin Powell considered it a necessity for some reason. It was connected in the parlour as the hall was too narrow for a table to hold it, so it went on the bookcase next to the fireplace, gleaming black and terrifically modern.

Will was fascinated by the dial. Violet hoped it didn't matter if the dial was used while the receiver remained in its cradle because Will did this numerous times a day.

'I bet this is the first telephone in our street,' he boasted.

'No, it's not,' Violet told him. 'Number 3, the

Dunns, have had one for years. Their Edna married a Yank and went to live in California. Him — her husband, like — paid for a phone so she and her mam could speak to each other whenever they felt like it.'

It turned out that Edna and her mam felt like it only on Christmas Day and each other's birthdays.

Their own phone had rung just after they'd finished tea on Boxing Day, frightening everybody out of their skin. It was Lieutenant Peter Cooper calling from a telephone box on the northernmost point of Scotland. He spent a good half-hour chatting to his wife and family until he'd used up every penny of the change he had been collecting for weeks.

★   ★   ★

A few days before Will and Abby were due back at school, Mr Fitzpatrick, Will's form teacher, came to see Violet.

'I wasn't expecting you.' She had been scrubbing the back yard and was wearing one of her mother's ancient flowered overalls and an even more ancient georgette scarf as a turban. She was annoyed he'd arrived without notice, but wouldn't have dreamed of showing it.

'It's about your son, Will,' her visitor said.

Violet didn't disabuse him of her relationship with Will — the teacher was probably aware of it, anyway. 'Is he doing all right?' she enquired.

'All right?' The poor man had hardly any chin at all. Violet's annoyance gave way to pity. It

84

must have been hard, growing up with a face so malformed, though he had such a lovely, sweet smile that after a while his lack of a chin didn't seem to matter.

'More than all right,' she was told with some enthusiasm. 'He's an exceptionally clever lad. In fact, we are thinking of letting him sit the Eleven-Plus examination in June if you are agreeable.'

'Of course, I am,' Violet gasped. 'It'd be the gear if he passed.'

'I think that's very likely. The main reason I ask is because passing this exam can incur a great deal of expense for the parents. A grant is available from the government, but it won't be enough to buy all the uniform, books and sports equipment required at a secondary school.'

'A secondary school!' Violet breathed. She imagined Will in uniform: a cap and blazer, shirt and tie — possibly striped — a satchel, which she would insist should be leather. And how fortunate she'd got him a genuine fountain pen for Christmas!

Mr Fitzpatrick was speaking. 'I'm sure you will encourage your son, Mrs Stein,' he said, 'but at the same time I trust you not to pressurise the lad.' He smiled and, if it hadn't been for the smile, Violet would have given him the sharp edge of her tongue. She wouldn't have dreamt of pressurising her 'son'. Oh, how she loved to hear those words! She didn't care that the teacher had got her name wrong.

'He will get only encouragement from me,' she assured him.

Violet felt exceptionally pleased with herself a few days later after she had written a long, chatty letter telling Edwin Powell what a wonderful Christmas they'd had, how many presents Abby and Will had received, the pearls from Mrs Holmes that had never been near an oyster. A lot had come from the staff of Briggs' Motors who'd heard about her change of fortune after being sacked from the firm. She'd received more than fifty Christmas cards — years ago, when it was just her and Mam, they would have been surprised to receive as many as ten. She tried hard not to smile too much as, the letter written and ready to post, she went from room to room putting away the children's clothes, bringing the dirty ones downstairs to wash on Monday. If Mam had been there she'd have told her to wipe the grin off her face. 'You're riding for a fall, girl. The Good Lord doesn't like people who look like the cat that ate the cream. It's not holy.' Whatever mood Violet was in, Mam would insist she experience the opposite.

The children came home for dinner. Will was also looking unusually happy with life. He didn't mention the scholarship, but Violet reckoned he'd been told he would be sitting it in June. Abby, usually the happiest of the three, was rather downcast. It turned out Sister Joan wasn't in today — she had a bad cold — and the class was being taken by Sister St Clare, a nun she had never seen before.

'I had Sister St Clare when I went to St

Anne's,' Violet told her, but didn't mention how horrid she'd found the woman, who'd been elderly then and must be a good hundred by now.

'I don't like her, no one does,' Abby said despondently.

'Let's hope Sister Joan is better by tomorrow.' Violet saw the little girl off to school again with a kiss, but the kiss didn't help much. She returned at half past three clutching Will's hand and in tears.

Violet, who'd been watching from the window, followed the pair down the hall into the living room. 'What's happened?' she enquired, full of concern.

It was Will who answered. 'That nun, that Sister St Clare, she hit our Abby with the cane,' he said tightly.

'What?' Violet could hardly believe her ears.

'Show Violet your hand, Abs,' Will told his sister, and the girl slowly unfolded her small fist. There was an angry red weal on her palm.

Violet gasped. Now she could scarcely believe her eyes. That someone could cane a five-year-old child, particularly such a gentle little creature as Abby, was beyond her comprehension.

'Why did she hit you, pet?' she asked gently. She knelt and took the child into her arms.

It was Will who answered again. 'The needle, the sort you sew with, pricked her finger and she cried out, that's all. For some reason, Sister St Clare thought she was being naughty and hit her with the cane.'

Violet didn't say anything. She placed Abby on

a chair beside the table and indicated to Will to sit on another. In the kitchen, she poured two glasses of milk and cut two slices of the fruit cake she'd made that morning and suggested the children drink the milk and eat the cake while she was gone.

'I'll probably be more than a few minutes,' she said. 'More like half an hour. I've made scouse for tea and we'll have it later.'

She checked the fire had enough coal — otherwise Will might remove the fireguard and pile on more, something he had a habit of doing — put on her coat and a smart hat rather than a headscarf and headed through the now dark streets for St Anne's school. It was a lovely night, not really cold for January. The street lights cast sharp shadows on the pavements. There was no sign yet of the moon. Every bit of snow had by now melted. The war was still recent enough to remind her of the dreaded blackout and she appreciated the lamplight and the bright windows of the shops.

The school building looked deserted, but there were lights on inside and the main door was closed, but unlocked. Faint sounds of activity could be heard when she went inside, subdued voices.

She had never so far met the headmistress, Sister Xavier, but knew where she could be found: in an office at the back of the building. She hurried towards it and banged on the door.

'Later,' a woman called. 'I'm busy now.'

In response, Violet threw open the door with such violence that it shot back, threatening to hit her in the face until she stopped it with her foot.

The nun behind the desk looked surprised at first, though it was quickly followed by anger. She was in the course of writing in a ledger and laid down the pen to demand, 'Who are you?'

'I'm Violet Duffy, and my children are at this school.' Violet half expected fire to come spurting from her nostrils.

'Yes?' The short word had probably never before been uttered in such an icily cold and questioning voice.

'Today, my little girl, my Abby, was caned by Sister St Clare for having the temerity to pierce her finger with a needle and daring to utter a cry of pain.' Gosh that sounded . . . Violet gave up trying to think how it sounded. Instead, she took a huge, deep breath and continued to complain in a voice she scarcely recognised as her own. 'I was taught by the same sister when I attended this school more than forty years ago. She was not fit to be in charge of young children then and apparently even less so now.'

Sister Xavier bit her lip and didn't reply for quite a few seconds. 'That was frightfully irresponsible of her, but hardly worth such a fuss,' she said in what she perhaps thought was a reasonable tone. 'There is certainly no need for this . . . this sort of exhibition.' She waved a long, elegant hand dismissively towards Violet. She was a beautiful woman with fine features and a lovely, thrilling voice.

'There is every need for it,' Violet almost roared. 'Do you honestly think an elderly woman beating a five-year-old child with a cane is reasonable behaviour, most particularly in a *convent?* In a convent, people would expect the nuns to be gentle and kind. Furthermore, she actually used the cane in the place where the child had pricked her finger!'

The nun swallowed. 'I promise Sister St Clare won't do it again. Perhaps it's time she was withdrawn from classroom duties,' she conceded.

Violet nodded furiously. 'More than time,' she remarked through gritted teeth. 'Long past time,' she emphasised.

'I feel sure your daughter won't suffer any long-term consequences from the incident.'

'I jolly well hope not.' Violet could think of nothing more to say. She supposed she could have insisted on a proper apology, but reckoned she'd already shaken the sister up enough. She turned to leave, when the woman spoke.

'We have met before. Do you not remember? Your name was Duffy then — Violet Duffy. I can't help but wonder how you have come by a daughter without changing your name. I do believe you have a son, too, in the top class.'

'Are you suggesting I am an unmarried mother?' Violet threw back her shoulders and pretended to be outraged. 'Were you as tactless when we knew each other then as you are now?' Violet couldn't recall having seen the woman before.

'I'm not usually tactless with anyone, Miss Duffy, but I make an exception with you, who seem to think it's all right to come storming into my office in such an unholy rage.' The woman got to her feet and came towards the door. Violet hoped she didn't intend to give her a smack. She prepared to hit her back, but instead the woman said, 'We met at dancing class. You used to come with your mother.'

'Saturday mornings at the Crane Theatre in Hanover Street, ballet and tap,' Violet recalled aloud. Her mother had got the idea of her daughter having a career on the stage. Violet had never forgotten her pathetic attempts to dance. She was the worst in the class, plodding heavily across the stage like a cart-horse. She'd lasted only a single term. On the day the second term started, she had managed to convey how much she hated the lessons by pretending to have hysterics for the first and only time and scaring the life out of her mother.

'I never liked you,' Sister Xavier reminisced.

'I still don't like you,' Violet responded. She opened the door to leave and closed it quickly behind her before the other woman could speak.

She walked home quickly feeling exuberant beneath the now starry sky; there was still no sign of a moon. She'd got the better of a nun, one of those remote, excessively holy beings who normally made her feel very small, inferior and full of sin. She trusted the woman wouldn't dream of treating Abby unfairly after the recent row. Well, if she did, there'd be hell to pay!

★ ★ ★

Abby and Will were playing cards when she arrived. The little girl seemed to have forgotten the reason why Violet had gone out, but Will

91

looked at her questioningly.

'Me and the headmistress had a long discussion,' Violet told him. 'The nun concerned won't be put charge of children again.'

He nodded gravely. 'That's good,' he said. 'Thank you, Violet.'

'For goodness' sake, Will, there's no need to thank me. It's my job to look after you and your sister, make sure neither of you come to any harm. I know I'm not a real parent, but I shall try to fulfil that role as best as I can.' That sounded awfully pompous, but it conveyed how she felt.

Madge came later after both children had gone to bed. She screamed with laughter when Violet described her encounter with Sister Xavier. 'Can't you remember her being at that dancing class with you?' she asked. 'Rack your brains, Vi.'

Violet screwed up her eyes as she peered back into the past. 'I went there once,' Madge recalled. 'The class put on a little show and your mam took me to watch. I think you fell over a few times.'

'Did I really?' Violet frowned in an effort to remember what had happened. 'I know I was hopeless. We were all about thirteen and I was the tallest apart from this other girl who was taller, but she was beautifully slender and suited being tall, whereas I looked like a clumsy elephant.'

'What was her name — the tall girl?' Madge asked.

Violet thought hard. 'It was a posh name

— she never came with her mother like me and the other girls, but with a woman in uniform. I always assumed she was a governess or a nurse; and her name, the girl, not the governess, was — Penelope!' she cried triumphantly. 'Penelope Cousins. I remember now quite distinctly. She was ever such a good dancer, particularly ballet.' She'd been so lithe and shapely and moved with exquisite grace. 'I'm surprised she didn't become a professional dancer,' she said. She was positive now that Penelope Cousins and Sister Xavier were the same person.

Her friend shrugged. 'Perhaps she did.'

'Become a professional dancer? In that case, I wonder why she gave it up to become a nun. Is it an achievement or a failure to end up in a convent rather than on the stage?' she said.

'Who knows?' Madge yawned, before saying, right out of the blue. 'I wish you had a telly, Vi.'

Violet stared at her in astonishment. 'I thought you hated televisions.'

'Not as much as I used to. I've discovered there's some interesting stuff on, but I wouldn't want to watch it in our house.' She made a ghastly face. 'We still have a small crowd every bloody night and they bawl with laughter if there's anything funny on, and wouldn't dream of keeping their yappers shut if it's serious and talk right through it. Luckily, there's more and more folk buying their own sets, so we don't draw the same big crowds. It's about time you got one, girl.' She gave Violet an encouraging nudge. 'There's some grand kids' programmes on. Abby and Will would love it. And you and me could watch *Come Dancing*. Remember the dead gorgeous frocks they wear. They take up yards and yards of material, usually net. It's not on until after the kids have gone to bed.'

Violet liked watching people dance, even though she was hopeless at it herself. Mind you, it was easier when you were being propped up by a man than doing it alone.

Madge had barely closed the front door when Will appeared in his pyjamas. Violet wasn't surprised. He didn't seem to need sleep like other children. She'd got used to going to bed herself at ten or eleven o'clock and finding him wide awake either reading or doing his homework. It seemed unreasonable to make him put the light out and leave him to lie there, wide awake.

'Are we going to get a telly, Vi?' He looked quite animated.

She smiled. 'Have you been eavesdropping?'

'What does that mean?'

'Listening to what me and Madge were saying.'

'You talk so loud I couldn't help but listen,' he said. 'And, if I can't help but listen, then I can't help but hear,' he added logically.

'Oh, all right, pet.' She and Madge must be more careful what they spoke about in future — and censor Madge's language. 'I suppose a television would be nice, but we couldn't possibly afford it. Why, do you fancy one, Will?'

'Oh, yes.' He came into the room and sat down. Violet decided it was the perfect time for a cuppa and went to put the kettle on. 'There's

94

programmes on about science, Vi,' he said excitedly, 'and news programmes and quizzes where they ask people questions. And there's football matches and *Children's Hour* with *Andy Pandy* and *Muffin the Mule* that our Abby would really enjoy.' He sighed longingly. 'I'd really love it if we had a television, Vi.'

'So would I, pet, but . . . ' Violet remembered there was the money Mam had saved from her father's pension that was still in the Post Office, untouched. Well, it wouldn't remain untouched much longer. She'd find out how much a television cost and get one, if it could be afforded. 'We'll just have to see,' she said.

The boy's eyes lit up. He must have recognised the tone of hope in her voice.

Violet very quickly discovered she didn't have nearly enough in the Post Office to pay for a television. Without having thought about them before, now she thought of little else and yearned for a set herself. Until now, Madge had put her completely off the idea. She remembered the day when the Boat Race between Oxford and Cambridge universities had been on. It was a Saturday and there'd been a queue in the street outside Madge's house waiting to go in and watch it.

'Don't they realise what the bloody boat race is?' Madge roared at Violet when the race was actually taking place. 'It's upper-class twits from the top universities racing each other. They don't know their arses from their elbows and hardly one of 'em will do a useful day's work in their entire lives — I mean the rowers. As for our lot, they'll never row a bleedin' boat if they live to be a hundred, unless it's in a park or something. You should've seen them urging them on, shouting 'Oxford' or 'Cambridge'. I mean, who gives a toss which side wins?'

Violet's mam would have felt the same. Well, in memory of her mother, the boat race would never be viewed on the Duffys' television — when it came, if ever.

★　★　★

Violet was seated at the kitchen table on a chilly February morning trying to work out how much she would have to pay weekly if she bought the longed-for television on hire purchase — an idea that would have horrified her mother, who had considered buying anything on tick a sign of acute irresponsibility — when there was a knock on the door. It must be a stranger, otherwise anyone local would have let themselves in.

A rather harassed, middle-aged man was standing outside. 'Miss Violet Duffy?' he enquired.

'Yes?' Violet said crisply.

'Just a minute.' He gestured towards the car parked behind him. 'She's in,' he called, and a woman in the passenger seat opened the door and climbed out.

'This is my mother, Mrs Holmes,' he said to Violet.

Afterwards, Violet was surprised that she didn't immediately recognise the woman from her name instead of staring at her foolishly while she struggled to get out of the car with the help of her son, and limped towards the house using a walking stick with the clear intention of coming in. She paused and glared balefully at a bemused Violet, saying in a grating voice, 'I'm Abigail's grandmother.'

Even if Violet hadn't then remembered what a low opinion Edwin Powell had of this woman, she wouldn't have liked her. She had no other option but to stand back holding the door open while the woman brushed past and made her way down the hall. She was small and stout with exceptionally tiny eyes and a severely set mouth, and she smelled of mothballs. Her expression was stern and unfriendly. Violet's brain worked overtime wondering whether to direct her into the parlour, which was freezing cold, or into the kitchen, which was verging on shabby and not exactly tidy, but lovely and warm.

'You'd better go into the back room,' she said. 'As I wasn't expecting you, there's no fire lit in the front.'

The man spoke. 'I said to let Miss Duffy know beforehand we were coming, Ma. It's not on, arriving out of the blue like this.'

Mrs Holmes gave her son a disgusted look when she settled herself in Violet's chair in front of the fire. 'If she'd known to expect us, she might have got that Mr Powell here to argue on her behalf or had all her answers rehearsed.'

'I can argue for myself, Mrs Holmes,' Violet said primly. 'And why should I need to have my answers rehearsed?'

'Because I know what your lot are like. You'd

lie at the drop of a hat to keep dear little Abby, my granddaughter, to yourself.'

'Lord Almighty, Ma,' her son said despairingly. 'I'm not going to listen to this. I'll go and wait in the car.' He left the house and the sound of the car door being slammed could be heard from indoors.

'What do you mean, 'your lot'?' Violet had meanwhile asked politely, having decided not to take Mrs Holmes seriously.

'You bloody Duffys is what I mean. Mary was a Duffy, weren't she, before she married that Stein chap, the boy's dad?'

'In what way did she lie?'

'She never told Oswald, my son, that Stein was a German, that Ossie was actually taking on a bloody Nazi's kid by marrying his mother.' Her small eyes turned to slits. 'I bet you didn't know that, did you, Miss Duffy?'

Violet had gone cold. Will was half German! She hadn't known that, but what did that matter? Just because his father was German, it didn't make him a Nazi. She managed to laugh casually and shrug. 'Of course, I knew. Anyroad, he'd joined the British Army, hadn't he? He was killed fighting in our war.' He might well have had British or Canadian nationality. She'd not yet sat down and decided she wasn't prepared to tolerate another minute of this woman in her house.

'Look,' she said, 'I'd sooner you left. Will and Abby are happy living here. They enjoy going to school and have made friends. There is no way on earth that I would give them up in favour of

98

you or anybody else. I think of them and love them as if they were *my* children.' She was feeling very emotional and worried she might cry.

'Except they're *not* your children, *Miss* Duffy.' Mrs Holmes was getting awkwardly to her feet — Violet didn't move to help. 'You can have the boy, by all means, but I am Abby's grandmother and have a far better claim on her than you. I also live in a much bigger house with a garden in a far superior road to this, this *slum*.' She had managed to reach the hall and was making her way towards the front door. Violet squeezed past and opened it to let her out.

'Another thing,' the woman said, pausing on the pavement. 'I've got plenty of money. I know where you live, I shall be taking you to court. Let some judge decide on who's the right person to raise my son's daughter — his mother, or some strange woman who hadn't even known that Abby existed.'

Her son had got out of the car and opened the passenger door. While his mother was getting in, he came and put a brown envelope in Violet's hand. 'This was our Ossie and Mary's,' he said. 'Ma tried to cash it, but it wasn't allowed. It belongs to the kids. That Edwin Powell bloke will know how to get it for you. I'm sure you'll spend it wisely, Miss Duffy.' He shook Violet's hand. 'Good luck. I'm sorry about today, but she's my mother and I couldn't very well refuse to bring her.'

★ ★ ★

The envelope turned out to contain a Westminster bank account book showing a balance of eighty-two pounds, five and sixpence — not quite enough for a television, but well on the way.

Violet made a pot of tea and drank the lot. She longed to telephone Edwin Powell and tell him about her visitor, but the children would be home for their dinner in a minute; she'd call him this afternoon.

They appeared, Will holding Abby's hand, and she wished she were like Madge and could bring herself to kiss and cuddle them as she longed to. They didn't seem to mind when it was Madge, but how would they feel about Violet doing the same thing? Her mother hadn't been a demonstrative woman and she'd raised her daughter to be the same. If they were my own kids, Violet thought, I'd have the confidence to kiss and cuddle them to death. I'd be the most demonstrative woman on earth.

'I think on Saturday we'll all go into town and buy a television,' she said when they had finished their vegetable soup and bread and margarine.

'Honest?' Will breathed. The single word held such passion that Violet was given no doubt how much he was pleased. For Violet it was as good as a big, sloppy kiss — well almost.

'Is Andy Pandy coming to live here?' Abby asked.

'Yes, Abs,' Will told her. 'We'll have our very own Andy Pandy from now on. Which room will we put it in, Vi?'

'I don't know.' Violet had been facing the same

dilemma most of the afternoon. 'This room's warmer — mind you, that only matters in the winter. But the front room is nicer.'

'I prefer this room.' Will stuffed his hands in his pockets and gazed around him. 'This is the nicest room I've ever been in,' he said with a happy sigh. 'I'd like it if we had the telly in here, Vi, if you don't mind.'

Abby agreed. 'I'd like it here, too.'

'Then in here it will be,' Violet cried gaily. None of the rooms had so far seen a lick of the distemper they'd been promised — there never seemed to be a convenient time to have decorating done. She gritted her teeth and determined it would be done soon.

She saw them off to school at a quarter to one, then collapsed in a chair. She'd promised the children that on Saturday, after they'd bought the television, they'd treat themselves to afternoon tea.

It gave her enormous satisfaction to see them so excited, but they hadn't been gone for long before she began to worry about Mrs Holmes, Abby's grandmother. Edwin Powell had once sworn she stood no chance of gaining control of the little girl — but he'd also sworn that Mrs Holmes would never find out where Violet and the children lived. If the woman could do the second, then there was always the chance she could do the first. The best thing to do was telephone Edwin Powell, tell him about Mrs Holmes and the money, and see what he had to say about her visit. She took ten deep breaths before lifting the receiver so she wouldn't sound hysterical when she and Edwin spoke.

'But,' she was saying hysterically ten minutes later when she was on the telephone to Exeter, 'she seems to have plenty of money — she came in a *car* — and she claims to have a much nicer house. She — '

'Violet, dear Violet,' he interrupted. '*She doesn't want Will*,' he said patiently. 'In court, she wouldn't have a leg to stand on. Even if it reached court, there isn't a judge in the land who would split the children, not when they're so happy with you.'

She wanted to say she didn't trust judges, but then she'd never met one in her life, though had read some funny old judgments in the newspaper. By now, she had calmed down a little and told Edwin about the television. 'Will, in particular, would love one. The money had belonged to Mary, his and Abby's mother, and their dad — his brother gave it me.' The brother had been nice and she was sorry she didn't know his name.

'There you go, then,' Edwin said, which Violet didn't think made any sense at all, nor did she remotely guess what he meant when he went on to say, 'I've got a surprise for you.'

'What is it?' she enquired.

'I'm moving to Liverpool — well, Waterloo, near the hotel that I stay in. I've rented a little bungalow with a nice garden. You'll love it, I'm sure. I managed to persuade the commissioners of the charity I work for, St Jude's Bounty, to open a branch in Liverpool with me running it; it will be our North West branch. Of course, St

Jude's know all about Will and Abby and are delighted with the result of my investigations.'

Violet was stunned as well as extremely pleased. It would be a relief to have him on hand whenever she came across a problem with the children. 'When will you be moving?' she asked.

'Just before Easter, hopefully. I need to buy a whole houseful of furniture — the house in Exeter's is my sister's, you see, and she's getting married in March. I shall move out while she and her new husband are on honeymoon.' He sighed happily. 'As you might imagine, I'm as pleased as punch about everything.'

'I bet you are. I look forward to your arrival,' Violet said, 'and I'm sure the children will too.'

'That makes four of us.'

⋆ ⋆ ⋆

They wore their best clothes when they went into town to buy the television. It was a Phillips model from the electrical department in T. J. Hughes's basement and came with the promise it would be delivered the following Tuesday. It cost one hundred and twenty-seven pounds, ten shillings and sixpence. Violet put the money she'd received from Oswald Holmes's brother down as a deposit and arranged to pay the rest at the time of delivery using most of the money in the Post Office.

They left in a state of high excitement, had afternoon tea in Owen Owen's restaurant, then went to see a film called *Francis* about a talking mule. When the mule said to Donald O'Connor, who starred in the film, 'If I'd known you were coming, I'd've baked a cake,' Will laughed so much he nearly disappeared beneath his seat, causing the people nearby to join in. It took ages for the laughter to stop. Violet had never known the boy be so demonstrably happy and, in contrast to everyone else, she was almost in tears.

★   ★   ★

It was twenty past eleven according to the illuminated alarm clock beside the bed. Vi was wide awake worrying about something or other, when she heard the key being drawn through the letter box, the door was unlocked, and someone came in.

Violet sat up, heart thumping. She felt frightened, naturally, but she was in Amber Street, surrounded by hundreds of people and was unlikely to be harmed. In fact, it had happened before: a drunk had forgotten which house he lived in and had entered one that wasn't his own. It was usually followed by screaming, the drunk being the person most frightened.

Violet didn't scream. She got out of bed and went quietly downstairs, not wanting to disturb Will and Abby. The low light on the landing was left permanently on and she could see someone sitting on the bottom stair.

'Who's that?' she whispered.

Madge got to her feet. 'It's me, Vi.' She limped into the living room.

Violet followed and turned on the light. 'Jaysus Christ, Madge! Who did that to you?' Her friend's lovely face was bloody and swollen and her left eye a circle of black. 'Sit down, luv. I'll just get some warm water and bathe it.' She went into the kitchen, adding extra water for tea while she was at it.

'Have you seen a policeman?' she asked while cleaning her friend's face with a damp flannel.

Madge shook her head, wincing as she did so. 'Any copper worth his salt would tell me I had it coming. Me husband did it, who else?'

'Bob?' Violet sniffed disdainfully. 'That's very foolish of him, I must say. What was his excuse?' Up until tonight, she'd always considered Bob McGann to be a soft old thing who wouldn't hurt a fly.

'His reason was finding me upstairs in The Butcher's with another fella,' Madge said tiredly. 'Can I stay here tonight, Vi?'

'Of course you can, girl. You can sleep with me. I'll make us a drink in a minute, soon as I've cleaned you up.'

'Oh, Violet, you're such a lovely friend.' She began to cry. 'Other folk, they'd only start blaming me, telling me it was all I deserved.'

'Some might say that,' Violet told her. 'But I don't hold with this sort of violence. Bob's twice the size of you. He should be ashamed of himself, no matter what you've been up to.' She patted Madge's face dry and dabbed iodine on the cuts.

Madge jumped. 'Bloody hell! That didn't half sting.'

The kettle had boiled. Violet went into the kitchen and returned with two mugs of tea and also the morphia, which she kept hidden in the top cupboard, out of reach of the children.

'Would you like some of this?' She showed Madge the bottle.

'Bloody hell, girl!' Madge's bruised eyes popped. 'Didn't your mam used to take that?'

'Yes. It really helps you sleep. This is the last bottle. I'll have to buy more soon.' She hardly took it nowadays, but still had the odd night when she found it impossible to sleep.

Despite her various injuries, for some reason Madge giggled. 'You'll have a job. It's been banned from the shops for ages. It's got morphine in, you idiot. You're a bloody druggie, Violet Duffy. You'd be thrown in prison if the bobbies found out.'

'Honest?' Just then, Violet didn't exactly care, though she might in the morning.

'Honest. Give us a mouthful, though. It's just what I need right now.' Violet handed her the bottle.

For a few minutes, the women sat nursing the drinks, the only sound Madge's hoarse breathing, until the clock in the parlour struck half eleven.

'You don't understand,' Madge said suddenly.

'What don't I understand?'

'Needs, desires. You've never experienced making love to a man, so you don't miss it.'

'Don't I?' Violet said lightly.

'No, Vi. Honest, you don't know what it's like. Months ago, when I was virtually barred from me very own house on account of that bloody telly, I called in The Butcher's. I knew it had a reputation, that it was where the prostitutes went. But I didn't care. I needed a bit of excitement in me life.' Her bloodied lips curved in a slight smile. 'I needed a bloody good shag!' Violet didn't say anything. 'I supposed you're shocked,' Madge added.

'Why should I be?' Violet shrugged.

Her friend laughed. 'Because, like I said, you don't know what it's like, do you, girl? I mean, what you've never had you never miss — isn't that what they say?'

'I don't know what they say, Madge,' Violet said quietly. 'I think I'm more shocked at Bob than anything.'

*   *   *

'Can you remember what he was like when we first met?' Time was passing. The Town Hall clock chimed midnight, though the rest of the streets were mostly silent. The women had transferred to the armchairs in front of the fire, where a heap of grey ash gave off slight warmth.

'I remember well.' Violet nodded.

'He was dead gorgeous.' Madge's eyes clouded with memories. 'Lovely and slim, always sunburnt from being outdoors playing footy. He had a smile that could take your breath away. Everybody loved him, me most of all.' She smiled, so sweetly that, despite her injuries, for the moment she reminded Violet strongly of the pretty young girl she'd once been.

107

'I remember being really impressed with his teeth, so big and white and even.' She was speaking softly, almost whispering, probably tired after the beating she'd suffered from the no-longer-gorgeous Bob. She grimaced. 'Nowadays, Bob's teeth grin at me from inside a one-pound jam jar on top of the bedside cabinet — both sets, top and bottom. The lovely white ones have turned brown and the rotten ones had to be taken out. It was the ciggies and the beer what done it.' There were tears in her voice.

'Oh, Madge,' Violet said gently, 'go to bed, luv. I'll be up in a mo. I'll just finish me tea, then wash these few dishes. Do you want to borrow a nightie?'

'No, ta, Vi, I'll sleep in me petticoat. I'll see you in the morning, eh?'

Madge limped upstairs. Minutes later, Violet heard the springs of the bed creak. After a while, she stood, sighed, and took her mug, and Madge's, into the kitchen, ran water into them, then put them upside down on the draining board. She emptied the last of the morphia down the sink, feeling sad.

Madge was apparently fast asleep, only the top of her head visible above the bedclothes.

'Madge,' Violet said loudly. She repeated the name, even louder, when the head didn't move.

'Eh? Wassa matter?' A bemused Madge appeared from beneath the clothes. 'Violet, what's wrong?'

'You know that stuff that you were on about before?'

'What part? That morphia stuff?'

'The part when you said what you never have you never miss.'

'Ye-es,' Madge said hesitantly. 'What about it?'

'Well, as it happens, I *did* have it, and I *do* miss it.' Violet angrily folded her arms. 'I just didn't feel the need to confide my private business in you and the world in general.'

'Who was it?' Despite her injuries, Madge struggled out of bed and sat on its edge. Her eyes shone with curiosity. 'C'mon, Vi. And when did it happen?'

'It's not funny,' Violet snapped.

'I don't think it's funny, girl. I think it's marvellous. I'm just aching to know who it was.'

Violet didn't speak for a good half-minute. 'Remember all those dances and concerts I used to go to during the war with Norman Larkin and his wife?' she said eventually.

'Yea,' Madge nodded furiously. Then her face cleared. 'And that American, that really gear Yank — what was his name? Cracker.'

'Crocker,' Violet supplied.

'Crocker. That's it. Was it him?' She didn't wait for Violet's reply. 'Oh, you're a dark horse, Violet Duffy. I never dreamt the pair of you were having it off.' She climbed back into bed and Violet got in the other side, irritated that there'd been so few men in her life — just the one in fact — that Madge had guessed who it was straightaway — big, brawny Crocker with his crew-cut hair and wicked grin.

Madge adjusted her pillow so she could lean against it, ready for a cosy heart-to-heart. 'I wonder what your mam would have said if she'd

109

known what you were up to?'

'Lord knows.' Violet left her own pillow where it was and lay down. She had no intention of spending half the night discussing her one and only affair. Madge would want to be told every single little detail. And Mam had known. Of course she had. Nothing had been said, but there'd been a twinkle in her eyes next morning when Violet came home and claimed she'd spent the night at the Larkins'.

'As long as you enjoyed yourself, girl,' she would say. Although she didn't exactly wink, she might as well have. Any reluctance Violet might have had about sleeping with a married man was negated by her mother's acceptance of it.

Madge stayed for five days. Violet didn't mind, but was glad when her friend took herself home to a hugely apologetic Bob, who nevertheless remained as mad as hell with her. Somehow or other the pair would have to sort out their very large differences but Violet would be keeping a close eye on Madge to make sure Bob didn't lay a finger on her friend again.

★ ★ ★

Edwin Powell telephoned to invite them to tea in his new house in Blundellsands the following Sunday, and Violet was reminded of what she had been worrying about the night Madge had let herself in and given her reason for even more worry.

The last time she and Edwin had spoken on the phone — it was when Violet had called to tell him about Mrs Holmes's visit — Edwin Powell had said something that rather alarmed her: he'd called her 'dear'. And exactly why did he expect her to 'love' his bungalow in Waterloo? What did it matter whether she loved it or not? Did he regard her as a future tenant?

Did he want her for his wife?

Violet did not feel inferior to other women because she wasn't married. She put down her lack of a husband not to the fact that she hadn't met a man who wanted to marry her (Crocker had told her from the start that he had a wife back in Boston, USA, so the subject of marriage had never been raised). The need to have a ring on the third finger of their left hand was so strong in some women that they married any old body. She'd known women at Briggs' Motors who'd married men they made no pretentions of being in love with merely to get 'Mrs' rather than 'Miss' in front of their names.

Edwin Powell was a genuinely nice person, but Violet didn't feel remotely attracted to him. He was too small, for one thing, and she found his moustache, so similar to Hitler's, quite repellent. Furthermore, he wasn't a socialist. Mam would turn in her grave if her daughter married a man who didn't vote Labour — as would her father, who'd been dead for so long that Violet no longer thought about his reaction to her movements. Mind you, she had had no idea what Crocker's politics were. The last thing to interest people during the war years was people's voting intentions.

'Don't worry,' she assured her deceased

111

parents. 'If Edwin Powell proposes, I'll turn him down.'

★ ★ ★

The bungalow was sweet. *Sweet* was not a word much used in Liverpool except when people referred to sweets such as toffees, dolly mixtures and the like. *Sweet* was just a bit too posh to describe people and things, a bit yucky, but, when she first saw Edwin's bungalow in Blundellsands, *sweet* was the first word that came to mind. Bright-red brick, it had a chocolate-coloured front door with a white-painted gate, a pebble path leading to it, a bay window on each side and a green-tiled roof.

'Oh, isn't it sweet!' Violet trilled. 'It's like something out of a Grimms' fairy tale.'

'Come and see round the back,' Edwin said. 'There's a surprise for you children.'

There were already daffodils growing in the borders of the small back garden, but on the miniature lawn stood two swings, a big one and a little one.

'I suppose you can tell which is which,' Edwin said with a rather self-satisfied smile on his face. 'The big one is for Will here, and the small one for . . . ?' He paused and raised his eye-brows.

'Me,' Abby called excitedly. 'The small one is for Abby.' She climbed onto the swing and Violet began to push her.

Will didn't appear nearly so impressed. He casually strolled around to the larger swing, sat

112

on it, and pushed himself with his heels.

'And now a really big surprise for you, Violet.'

He was standing there, such a nice chap, red-faced and so anxious to please. What am I going to tell him? she thought anxiously.

But Edwin was going towards the back door, which he opened. 'Darling,' he called.

A young woman appeared, about twenty-five years old, as pretty as a picture with long, black, wavy hair tied back with a yellow ribbon to match her smart yellow linen frock.

'Darling!' he said again and, taking the woman's hand, he led her into the garden. 'This is Violet, who I've told you so much about, and this is Will and this is Abby. Everyone, let me introduce you to my wife, Barbara.' He grinned widely. 'We only got married yesterday and this is our honeymoon.' He patted her bottom playfully and she giggled. She works in the hotel where I've been staying all this time. It's only just round the corner.'

★   ★   ★

'It's a strange thing,' Carol Cooper said when Violet and Abby turned up that afternoon — they were going to Sunday School, which Will refused to have anything to do with — and she was told what had happened, 'but I always thought that Edwin person had a bit of a crush on you.'

'Really?' Violet laughed, as if the idea had never entered her head. 'I'm much too old for him — old enough to be his mother.'

113

'He's thirty-something and you're forty-something. There's not a big difference,' Carol argued. 'You wouldn't have looked exactly odd together.'

'I would have *felt* odd,' Violet argued back. 'He's not at all my type.' She actually shuddered at the thought. If he'd patted her bottom the way he'd done Barbara's, she'd have told him where to go — and it wasn't somewhere very pleasant. She felt nothing but relief at the way things had turned out.

At this point Carol announced that, after her husband's week-long presence in January, she was pregnant with their third child. 'He, or she, will be due about the end of September.' She smiled joyfully. 'I don't know which I want more, a boy or a girl.'

They discussed the merits of boys versus girls until Carol said she really didn't care. 'I'll love my baby with all my heart, no matter what sex it is.' She regarded both her children fondly.

'I'd feel the same.' Violet nodded, though she weren't being truthful. No one would ever know, but there was something about Will that touched her heart just that bit more than did Abby. Abby would have quickly accepted almost anyone who had taken over the role of mother as long as they were kind to her, but Will was far more particular. After nearly a year, Violet still wasn't sure what his feelings were for her, but she yearned for him to love her more than anything on earth.

★ ★ ★

The television produced one unpleasant consequence when Abby began to bring her friend, Doreen Flynn, home from school to watch the children's programmes. The Flynns were a notoriously violent family consisting of eleven children, all boys apart from Doreen, who lived together in a house in Amethyst Street. Two of the boys were in prison and Mr Flynn was in and out by the minute. Violet managed to put up with Doreen by forcing herself to feel desperately sorry for the girl — or the 'poor girl', as she was wont to think of her. The 'poor girl' was permanently in need of a good wash. She smelled dirty, as did her clothes, had no manners and hadn't been taught how to eat properly or wash her hands after she had used the lavatory. Why on earth couldn't Abby have made a best friend out of Greta Cooper, a much nicer little girl whose mother Violet was best friends with? But, although the two girls got on well, they showed no sign of wanting to spend more time in each other's company.

Violet introduced Doreen to soap and water. She bought a nice new face flannel and told the girl it was hers, which she supposed was the reason why the flannel disappeared after only a few days and was never seen again. She never said 'please' or 'thank you' when given food, which she stuffed into her mouth, sometimes using her fingers. The child looked half starved. Violet would ask God for His forgiveness whenever she had bad thoughts about Doreen, such as when she suggested Abby bring her friend to tea only occasionally rather than every

115

day. 'We don't always have enough food to go round, pet,' she said, quite truthfully. Not only that, although it was six years since the war had ended, quite a few foods were still rationed, including sugar, meat and cheese. Abby took no notice.

Will's attitude to his sister's friend was surprisingly benign. Violet suspected Doreen had a crush on him and he felt a touch flattered. He taught her how to do basic arithmetic and write her name.

'Perhaps you'll become a teacher when you grow up,' Violet suggested, but Will said he had no idea what he wanted to be. 'It depends whether or not there's a war on.'

'I don't think I want to know what you'd be if there was a war on,' Violet said, horrified. If he joined one of the forces, there was always the chance he'd be killed, like his father. She couldn't remember whether it was the war that had not long ended, or the one before, that had been touted as 'the war to end all wars'.

'I'd like to go in the army like me dad,' Will said, merely confirming her fears.

But, Doreen's presence aside, everybody loved the television — or 'the telly', as the children called it. Violet's favourite was *Come Dancing* — Madge always came round when it was on and the two women kept a bottle of sherry to sip while they were watching the glamorous women in their glorious clothes and the stiff, haughty faces of their male partners, who looked as if they had a bad smell beneath their noses, according to Madge, who couldn't stop giggling.

Abby was mad about *Andy Pandy* and *Muffin the Mule* and anything to do with animals. As for Will, he watched just about everything, though his favourite programme of all was *Kaleidoscope*, featuring Memory Man, Collector's Corner, Be Your Own Detective and Word Play, the section he liked most.

'Words are dead interesting,' he told Violet. 'I mean, *rough* is pronounced *ruff*, yet *bough* is pronounced *bow* and *cough* is *coff*.'

Violet tried to think of other examples and from then on they frequently discussed words. 'The other day,' the boy said seriously, as if conveying a secret, 'the teacher, Mr Fitzpatrick, said the rule is *i* before *e* except before *c* — like in *ceiling*, but I remembered lots of words where *e* comes before *i* and the word doesn't begin with *c*. *Beige*, for example — that's a colour,' he said, as if Violet didn't know. 'And *deign* and *feign* — I found them in the dictionary,' he said happily, 'and told Mr Fitzpatrick about them and other words.'

'I bet he was pleased with you.' Most teachers would rather resent being proved wrong, but she remembered Mr Fitzpatrick and felt sure he wouldn't mind.

'Oh, he didn't,' Will confirmed. 'He said he was impressed.'

Violet was impressed too.

Sammy sat on the top of the set looking down at the screen, stretching out his paw to catch the ball when a football match was on or if billiards was being played.

All in all, the television had a powerful and

117

supremely entertaining effect on Violet, her small family and her cat. She reckoned the time would come when virtually every house in the country, or even the world, would have a set, but Madge said that was daft.

'It's just a five-minute wonder,' she claimed. 'Couple of years and people will have forgotten they'd existed.'

★ ★ ★

Will was studying diligently for the Eleven-Plus examination in June. There were no specific books for him to read, but Violet gave him spelling tests and made up sums to do. Four other children in the class were taking the same exam, three boys and a girl. Some days, they stayed on for extra lessons after school had finished.

Violet went in late one afternoon with an umbrella for Will after a rainstorm had erupted, hoping he wouldn't take umbrage at her idea of not wanting him to get soaking wet. Mr Fitzpatrick discovered her in the corridor and invited her into the classroom.

'This,' the teacher said, waving an arm at the five children who were bent diligently over their exercise books in an unusually quiet classroom, the only sound the scratching of pen on paper, 'is what teaching is all about: working with kids who genuinely want to learn, to get on in life, use their brain.' He sighed blissfully. 'This is my favourite time of the year — exam time.'

The year was racing by. Not long after, Abby wore the white satin dress that Violet and Madge had made between them when she took part in the May Day procession around Bootle. Tiny silk rosebuds had been sewn around the neck and on the edge of the little puffed sleeves. It was a beautiful day, the sun a perfect circle in a spectacularly blue sky, the air fresh and salty.

'You're as pretty as a picture,' Madge exclaimed when the little girl was ready to join the parade. This was the Sunday when the Catholic children of Bootle walked the streets in a procession to profess their love for Our Lady.

Abby's job was to hold a ribbon along with seven other little girls, similarly dressed, all holding a similar ribbon while plaiting it neatly around a Maypole held by boy wearing a white shirt and black trousers. They got themselves in a terrible tangle. It was mainly the fault of Greta Cooper, Carol's little girl, who revealed herself as left-footed as well as left-handed and kept going the wrong way. They kept bumping into each other, so the plait looked nothing like a plait and more a tangle.

They sang, 'O Mary, we crown thee with blossoms today, Queen of the Angels and Queen of the May.'

As a child, Violet had taken part in the same procession, though her own role had never been more onerous than carrying a prayer book containing a white rose while singing hymns, including 'Queen of the May', once her favourite hymn, though as she grew older, it was overtaken by 'Faith of Our Fathers', which had such stirring words as 'We will be true to thee till death,' sung with such fervour.

She had imagined watching her own children doing something similar in the future, but had eventually given up on the idea. However, now it really was happening, though with another woman's children. Violet said a little prayer for her cousin Mary, whose sad fate had been to miss this wonderful sight.

★ ★ ★

The results of the Eleven-Plus came in July on the last day of the summer term. Will arrived home with a letter and a big grin on his face. 'I've passed,' he announced. 'It says so in the letter. Mr Plunkett said we weren't to open it, which is why he told us first, so we wouldn't be 'tempted',' he said.

Violet longed to throw her arms around his neck, but there was still a distance between them. She contented herself with a brief hug which he didn't seem to mind.

Weeks later, another letter arrived, this time from the Ministry of Education in London saying that William Stein would be attending St Peter's College in Liverpool. Attached was a list of the items of uniform he would require as well as other things such as a cricket bat, a geometry set and a selection of books. There would be a government allowance to help towards the cost.

Will was disappointed to find the school played rugby rather than soccer in the winter months. 'I'm quite good at footie,' he said despondendy.

Violet had never known anyone who played rugby, but had seen bits on the television and it was a rather violent sport. Will hadn't grown an inch since coming to Liverpool. Feeling worried, she imagined him being picked up and thrown around like the ball.

She shared her worries with Edwin Powell, who was no help at all. 'I hated rugby, too, when I was at school — least I hated the look of it.' He shuddered delicately. 'Fortunately, I suffered from asthma as a child and never had to take part in any sort of games. I was able to spend the time in the Art Department drawing.'

'Well, you're not much help.' Violet felt annoyed. 'I'm sure Will would far sooner be left to do something like that.' Using his brain, rather than risking having it damaged by the horrible studded boots that had to be worn.

Edwin shook his head. 'He won't be given the opportunity, Violet, dear. He runs like the wind. They'll definitely want him in the team.'

★   ★   ★

It seemed odd in the midst of a brilliant summer to spend their time in Passmore & Edwards in Sandy Road, Waterloo, buying stout winter shoes, pullovers and a gabardine mac along with a cap and blazer as well as two heavy woollen rugby shirts — a pale-blue one for home games

121

and black one for when St Peter's rugby team played away.

Will looked horrified. 'They play away!' It meant the school was really serious about the game. 'They might be in a league.' It wasn't something they did for only a couple of hours one afternoon a week.

'It looks like it, pet.' Violet began to wish he hadn't passed the blinking Eleven-Plus and that he was going to senior school in Bootle along with most of the other boys in his class and where they played football. Instead, Will was about to attend an elite establishment such as St Peter's, which was miles away in the centre of Liverpool. In order to get there on time, he would have to leave the house at about a quarter past eight to catch a tram, whereas the local senior school was a mere few minutes' walk away.

Madge insisted there was no need for her to worry. 'As far as boys are concerned, as long as they're good at sport they'll be dead popular, you'll see.'

Violet prayed that would be the case. She had come to realise that there was a definite disadvantage to having children. Although she wouldn't want life to be one iota different, sometimes she looked back on her old one as being blissfully trouble-free. On reflection, even losing her job in such a cruel way didn't seem all that worrying compared with how she felt now about Will starting a new school. She would have found another job eventually — she could have taken in a lodger if a job hadn't turned up. She would have managed — somehow. But how would she manage if the boy was unhappy at St Peter's? Would she just storm into the place and confront the headmaster, Dr Edward McDowd, as she'd done Sister Xavier?

Violet frowned and chewed her lip. Well, yes, she would if it came to it; doctor or no doctor, she definitely would.

Part 2

6

1955

Will had settled into St Peter's College without a hitch and, as the years went by, he surpassed even his teachers' expectations, though Violet remained ready to face up to Dr McDowd should any problems arise. Abby was halfway through her years at school, doing rather better than Violet had expected, and Will was even wondering which university to attend when his time at school came to an end. St Jude's Bounty would support him while he remained in education, so money wouldn't be a problem, and, although Vi would miss him terribly, this would be made up for by knowing he was doing so wonderfully well.

On two occasions during this period, inspectors from the charity came to Bootle to check on the children's progress at school. One, a man, had apparently written a book on the Spanish Inquisition, which meant most of his questions for the children seemed to be about their knowledge of history, rather than arithmetic or grammar. Fortunately, Mr Fitzpatrick had taught William well and the inspector's book had even been part of the curriculum in the top form. He answered every question correctly, even adding a few questions of his own, and the inspector was extremely impressed.

★　★　★

Violet had experienced only a few big surprises in her life. The first she could think of was receiving the letter giving her notice that she was being sacked from Briggs' Motors, the job she had loved so much. But it hadn't been a *total* surprise, not really, because she'd vaguely suspected it might happen for a long time.

Then there was Edwin Powell turning up out of the blue to tell her about Will and Abby. Now that had been a real shock, but truly wonderful news all the same.

Nothing, though, prepared her for the arrival of the man who knocked on her door one afternoon early in October.

A lamb stew was bubbling on the stove and she was in the throes of demolishing a stack of ironing, her thoughts miles away, concentrating on when she could get back to the Agatha Christie book she was reading, and on Abby, who was desperate to have her lovely blonde curls cut off because everyone else in her class had short hair. Violet was praying she would go off the idea. 'Once those pretty curls have gone, it'll take years to grow them back again,' she assured her.

'I'll never want to grow them back,' Abby argued.

'Just wait a few more weeks before you have it cut. Don't forget, you won't be able to have it in bunches any more, or plaits.'

Abby said grudgingly that she'd think about it. She must have thought about it hard, because she never mentioned it again.

Now that Will was out of the house for longer, Violet had more time for his sister, who had announced she wanted to be a nurse when she grew up. She felt ashamed for not listening before, having taken for granted that she hadn't much of interest to say. Will, she'd assumed, was the one with the conversation and the brain. Now she realised Abby had her own gifts, if she only took the time to notice them.

She was thinking about buying a nurse's costume for Abby's Christmas present, when there was a loud knock on the door. After smoothing her pinafore and her hair, Violet went to answer it.

'Jaysus, Mary and Joseph!' she gasped, stumbling backwards when she saw the broad-shouldered man with crew-cut grey hair, wearing a Humphrey Bogart mackintosh and a hat tipped over his right eye. 'Crocker!'

'Hi, babe.' Crocker stepped into the hall, his huge form almost touching both sides as well as the ceiling. He took off his hat, gave her a semi-hug, saying, 'Is it all right for me to have come?'

'Of course.' It wasn't, really. Not without some warning. But why on earth had he come?

He explained some time later when they were sitting in the parlour. He had removed his mac revealing a well-cut grey suit, a dazzling white shirt and a darker-grey tie with yellow spots. He accepted a cup of tea, as well as a glass of brandy after Violet remembered there was an elderly bottle in the sideboard cupboard. No, brandy doesn't go off, he informed her.

'My wife died last year,' he said in his rusty, gravelly voice. 'There's no need to be sorry,' he cut in when Violet began to offer her sympathies. 'We hadn't been a proper couple in a long time. I told you that during the war, remember? It was having Ben that put her off that side of things for ever.' Ben was his son, their only child. 'Nora swore she'd never have another baby — it hurt too much.'

'I remember you saying.' It had been at one of the dances. An American army band was playing 'In the Mood' and 'String of Pearls'. She couldn't remember the name of the composer, though did recall that he'd died towards the end of the war — drowned, disappeared, his body never discovered. Glenn something? She shook her head and brought herself back to the present.

Crocker had never been to the house before. Her mother might have been tolerant of what her daughter did when she was out, but under her own roof was a different matter. Violet was finding it hard to believe he was there now, sitting in her mother's chair, slightly broader, a bit more grizzled, his voice a touch huskier. She tried to imagine what Mam would say if she knew about the visitor, but for the first time ever she was unable to think of imaginary words to put into her deceased mother's mouth.

'I called Betty,' Crocker said, 'to ask how you were.'

'Betty?' Violet felt confused.

'Betty Larkin, good old Norman's wife.'

'Oh, yes, of course.' Betty still lived in Rainford, but the two women had never met since Norman's death. They exchanged the occasional letter and sent each other Christmas cards, but that was all. Violet often wondered why they never bothered to meet again, but perhaps memories of the dances, the music and the atmosphere, were too precious to risk spoiling, what with one of the protagonists deceased and another on the far side of the ocean. Her visitor took a silver cigarette case out of his breast pocket. He opened it and offered it to Violet. 'She told me life had thrown some surprises at you — but she wouldn't say anything more. Suggested it was down to you to tell me the rest — and so here I am.'

Violet had noticed his gaze moving to her left hand — no doubt looking for a wedding ring. She took a deep breath and began with Edwin's visit to her door.

'Jeez, that's quite a tale,' Crocker said as she brought him up to date. 'No husband ever snapped you up, but you're a mother just the same. These kids of yours. Are they around?'

'Will and Abby? They're both at school. They'll be back in a few hours.'

It sounded so formal, so polite. During the war, at the parties and the dances, all they'd done was laugh. Their times in bed together had been full of fun rather than passion. Everything was a joke, though he'd told her many times that he loved her. She had taken for granted he didn't truly mean it — not that he was lying, but it was the thing to say under the highly dramatic

131

circumstances when life, love and death became intertwined. Also, at that particular moment in time it was genuinely meant, as surely as if it was sworn on a bible. Sometimes, she was so moved she would tell him that she loved him back. It had been casual and romantic and at the same time terribly intense.

But why was he here? she wondered again.

'I suppose you're wondering why I'm here,' he said as if reading her mind. His dark-blue eyes glinted and she was relieved to see he was grinning.

'Yes.' It seemed an inadequate response. Violet tried to relax. She grinned back, but it felt fake and unnatural. 'It's nice to see you,' she forced herself to say.

'And you too, Violet, more than nice.' He sipped the brandy. 'We were all Catholics,' he announced, as if she didn't know — he, she, Nora. 'I couldn't divorce her and marry you, but now she's gone and I can do what I want with my life. I just wondered how things stood. I hadn't known about the kids, naturally, but now I do and, for me, it doesn't change a thing.' He shifted in his seat. 'So how d'you feel about all three o'yis coming back with me to Boston?' He paused and then, noticing the confusion in Violet's eyes, he carried on. 'I think you know I don't mean just for a visit. I'm serious. I was hoping we could make a life together out there, as a family. We could get married there, or here, whatever you like.' He looked at her almost shyly. 'You're the only woman I've ever wanted, Vi. There's not a day

132

passed since I got back home that I haven't thought about you, girl.'

He drained his glass, seized the bottle, and poured more. She realised he was nervous and waved her hand, as if to indicate he was to stay quiet while she thought.

Never in a million years would she take Will and Abby to Boston. Their young lives had already been disrupted enough. She wished, though only briefly, that Nora had died years ago, before her precious children had entered her life. She visualised the war ending and living in Boston with Crocker — perhaps Ben, his son, would have lived with them. She caught her breath. It would have been paradise.

'I've retired from the army,' he ventured now. 'I've opened an aeronautical design office.' That's right, in private life he'd been an engineer, something to do with aeroplanes.

'Could you run your office from Liverpool?' she asked. She knew the answer before she'd finished asking the question.

He half smiled and shook his head. 'No chance, honey. I've got connections to the military. I need to operate on US soil.'

'Of course.' Violet sighed. It was out of the question, all of it. Their chance had come too late. 'I'm sorry, Crocker.' She sighed again; she had to stop all this, before they both lost themselves to dreams of what might have been. 'You've had a wasted journey.'

'I've seen you again,' he said. 'So it's not been wasted for me. And I'd like to see the kids. Let's go out somewhere later — to dinner — all four of us in this great, big, wonderful city of yours. You know — ' he paused and smiled sadly — 'there's never been anyone else, only you.'

She thought about dinner and shook her head. 'I'd sooner not. They'll wonder who you are, why you're here, and I can't tell them — not everything.' Crocker and her children came from two entirely different worlds and she'd rather neither of them met.

He looked disappointed, let down. Violet wondered if she should apologise for her lack of enthusiasm. He'd offered her a new life altogether in a new country full of promise. Most women would have jumped at the chance. A part of her wanted to tell him how right it felt seeing him there, sitting across from her as if he belonged here. Even after all these years, the words came easily between them, the smiles. But it wouldn't be fair to give him false hope. How would Will and Abby react if she explained the situation to them? Much better, more conducive to a happy life, was not allowing it to happen, just continue as they were, perfectly content, except for Crocker!

He was about to leave after being there less than an hour; all the way from Boston for about fifty minutes of her time.

'Shall I come with you into town?' she offered when he started to put on his coat. Despite everything, she was reluctant to see him go.

'That would be nice, kiddo.' He sighed hugely. 'But no, thank you. You're right. If it's over, I'd sooner it was over straightaway, not dragged out for another hour or so.' He opened the front door and was gone.

She was tempted to open the door and call him back, at least kiss him goodbye.

The house felt as if it had died. Violet sat in the total silence wondering if his visit had been a trick of her imagination, but he had left behind the faint aroma of the cheroots he still smoked and the tingling scent of his cologne — he was the only man she'd known who used scent. His brandy glass was on the hearth and she picked it up and drained it. The liquid almost took her breath away. She felt a rush of the old attraction, but she shook it away. There was no place for it in her life any more.

Crocker had been and gone. It turned out that no one had seen him call at the house. It didn't get back to Madge or any of her neighbours that Violet had briefly entertained a strange man. His visit had raised not so much as an eyebrow.

★   ★   ★

She was glad when Abby came home, without Doreen, and Crocker was pushed to the back of her mind. It looked as if the girls had found other friends as Doreen was rarely seen nowadays. A dozen fairy cakes were baking in the oven and Abby pleaded with her to let her ice them.

'Can I make pink icing, Violet? Please!'

'Of course, pet.' Violet removed the cakes and nudged them out of the metal tray with a knife. She took the bottle of red colouring from the cupboard, half-filled her smallest basin with icing

135

sugar, added two tablespoons of water and began to mix it with a fork. 'What was school like today?'

'Oh, we had a new teacher. She's come all the way from a place called Australia — that's on the other side of the world. It took ages on the boat. And you know what, Vi?' Abby's eyes were round with surprise. 'She's not a nun.'

'Honest?' Violet pretended amazement.

'She wears ordinary clothes like you and me. And she's got hair.'

'The nuns have hair too. It's just hidden beneath a veil.'

'I wonder what colour Sister Joan's is.'

'I reckon it's black, like her eyebrows.' Having made the icing, Violet carefully added two drops of colouring and handed the basin and fork to Abby to blend it in.

★   ★   ★

At seven o'clock, Abby went to bed and Will came out of the parlour, where he had been doing his homework. As the nights grew colder, Violet intended buying a small electric fire for the room. It wasn't worth lighting a fire, yet the place was cold without some form of heating. The boy shivered as he packed his satchel for the following day. He rarely complained about anything.

'I planned to get a little fire soon,' she told him. She'd buy it tomorrow.

He rubbed his hands together. 'Jolly good.' It was his favourite expression, only recently

136

acquired at St Peter's. 'Can I turn the television on?'

'You know you can; you don't have to ask.'

'*The Warden*'s on at nine o'clock.' *The Warden* was a dramatisation of the novel by Anthony Trollope. 'It's the third part tonight,' Will went on. 'You know the sixth form are doing the novel for their English A-level and Dr McDowd has actually advised the whole school to watch.' His eyes shone with sheer delight. 'I mean, don't you find that extraordinary, Vi, children being advised by a teacher to watch the telly? Mostly we're told off for watching too much.'

'I'll nip round and remind Madge later.' Madge's opinion of television was still not exactly favourable, but she was enjoying watching *The Warden* with Violet and Will.

They watched the news — it was the final day of the Festival of Britain in London. 'I really should have taken you,' Violet remarked. 'We never go anywhere much.'

Will nestled in his armchair. 'I don't want to go anywhere much. I like us going to New Brighton and Southport during the summer holidays and going to the pictures. And I *really* like The Palace in Marsh Lane on Saturday afternoons seeing *Deadwood Dick.*' Violet smiled. He would gallop home with his mates, Abby hot on their heels.

The boy sighed and she could have sworn it was a sigh of happiness. Upstairs, Abby coughed and the springs on the old bed squeaked as she turned over. Who needed America? she asked

137

herself. There was nowhere in the entire world she would sooner be than in her little house in Amber Street and she reckoned she could say the same for the children — *her* children.

★ ★ ★

Much to her delight, early in October, Carol Cooper gave birth to a girl, Marilyn, named after the latest film sensation, Marilyn Monroe.

'I'm so pleased,' Carol said gleefully when Violet went to see her in Bootle maternity hospital. 'If I'd had a boy, I wouldn't have known what to call him.'

'I thought you were mad on Montgomery Clift?' Violet reminded her. 'That's a nice, unusual name.'

'Oh, I am, but Montgomery is such a mouthful and everyone would have called him Monty and assume I'd called him after the famous general during the war; it would have been a lot for the lad to live up to. It sounds a bit grandiose to call a child after a general. People would expect great things of him.'

'Isn't that a good thing?' Privately, Violet thought the girl was as daft as a brush.

Carol kissed her new daughter on the tip of her little stub nose. 'All I want is for my children to be happy, not great.'

Perhaps she wasn't so daft, after all. All Violet wanted for her own children was exactly the same.

★ ★ ★

Christmas came and Will and Abby were invited to numerous parties. Violet was buying presents almost every day during December — embroidered hankies for the girls were easy to obtain, but the boys mainly gave each other books. One day Will came home with a penknife that had a number of strange attachments, one of which was for getting stones out of a horse's hoof, he told Violet.

'You won't need that often,' Violet told him. 'The last horse down Amber Street got killed in the Blitz. His stable was round the corner in Pearl Street close to Madge's house. His name was Nelson and he delivered the coal.'

'You never know where I might go where there's horses,' Will said enigmatically. 'Anyroad, it's got a blade to sharpen things and a nail file and other stuff. I'm going to start filing my nails from now rather than cutting them, just like Charles does. It's him I bought the penknife for.'

Violet thought that a rather poncy thing for a boy to do, but didn't say so. 'Who's Charles?' she asked instead.

Will became unusually animated. 'He's a few years above me in school and he lives in Southport. His mam's invited us to tea on Sunday. And you know what, Vi?' he chortled. 'He calls his mam, 'mater', just like in *The Magnet*. It's his favourite magazine, same as mine. He gets old copies from some place in London and he's going to lend me the ones I haven't already read.'

The Magnet had ceased publication years before. Violet panicked, but it wasn't anything to

139

do with the magazine. '*This* Sunday? We're invited to tea this Sunday?'

Will revealed he had a letter in his pocket and Violet demanded to read it straightaway. The boy looked surprised. 'It's nothing to get worked up about, Violet,' he said kindly.

Will had pulled a creased envelope out of his trouser pocket. Violet removed the enclosed card, trying not to crease it more.

It was an invitation to tea, in Southport, sent by the mother of Charles in Class 3, which meant he was two or three years older than Will. It all seemed rather grand and overwhelming: Mrs Sonia Hanley-Rice, who resided in The Willows, Golden Lane, Southport, requested the pleasure of Mrs Violet Stein's presence the following Sunday at the birthday of her son, Charles.

The handwriting was barely legible. There was no mention of Abby and the card also wished them a Merry Christmas.

But Will was talking about being invited to tea, not a party. And she'd been invited, too. Violet put her hand over her heart in an effort to stop it beating quite so fast. Will was looking at her oddly.

'What's wrong, Vi?'

'Nothing, pet,' she replied. She was being stupidly nervous as well as extraordinarily silly. Mrs Hanley-Rice was merely the mother of one of Will's fellow pupils. There was no reason for Violet to be impressed or overawed or in any way inferior to the woman. For many years, she'd been personal secretary to the head of one of the

140

largest companies in Liverpool. She had attended conferences, written to government ministers, typed vitally important quotations and taken the minutes of equally important meetings. And here she was, feeling totally intimidated by an invitation to afternoon tea from a woman with a hyphenated name. Mam, who couldn't stand people with hyphenated names, would have claimed the woman was a snob.

'You could call yourself Violet Plumb Duffy, if you wanted, luv.' Her maiden name had indeed been Plumb. This had been a running joke for years. At this point Mam would burst into peals of laughter that stopped only when she was in danger of choking to death. At one point she had demanded the name in full on her gravestone.

'Here lieth Beatrice Edna Plumb Duffy. Oh, what a pity I wasn't christened Victoria. Just imagine, Victoria Plumb Duffy died from being boiled to death in a piece of muslin. I wonder what I would've tasted like.'

'Oh, shut up, mam,' Violet muttered.

'Eh?' Will looked at her in surprise.

'Nothing, pet. Nothing at all.' She wondered what she would wear on Sunday. What would the other mother be dressed like? She reckoned she'd have to have something cleaned.

★ ★ ★

The Willows in Golden Lane, Southport, was an elegant, bright-red brick house down a leafy cul-de-sac on the edge of the seaside town. Violet's house, upstairs and down, would have

141

fitted in the vast lounge, which was only sparsely furnished — she assumed this was deliberate, not that the Hanley-Rices had run out of money after moving into their new house. She found she was raising her voice, worried she might not be heard. In Amber Street, everybody's knees were pressed against each other if there were more than two visitors.

A giant Christmas tree, beautifully decorated, stood in the window. The coloured lights were barely visible, but would look lovely when it was dark outside. Abby would have loved it, but she had been left in Bootle to go to Sunday School with the Coopers. Violet wasn't sure whether to be glad or sorry that Will was the only guest.

Sonia Hanley-Rice, Charles's mother, was incredibly thin. She wore tweed slacks, a cream polo-neck jersey and gold sandals with very high heels, and was expertly made up, particularly her eyes, which were rimmed with black pencil, the lashes made longer with the heavy use of mascara. She had long brown hair, rather untidy, but perhaps it was supposed to be that way. It might be the latest fashion, like not having enough furniture.

Violet, sighing inwardly, supposed it was only natural that she felt plain and unfashionable in her black-and-white check dress. She should have made more of an effort. Her shoes had the usual Cuban heels, the sort Madge hated. At least she was wearing nylon stockings — Crocker had given them to her during the war and they had remained, unopened, in a cellophane packet until this morning. She was worried about laddering them. Being reminded of Crocker didn't help. She'd been horribly rude to him — if only she could have the day again and treat his visit in a nicer, more friendly way. Perhaps she should write to him. It should be easy to find his address: they had foreign telephone directories in the city library. But, if he'd wanted her to contact him, all he'd had to do was leave his details, a business card or something.

Her hostess was speaking to her. If she wasn't careful, she'd spend tomorrow worrying about the way she'd behaved today. Mr Hanley-Rice worked in publishing and was away in Edinburgh on business, his wife was saying. His son, Charles, was going on for seventeen, and Violet wondered why on earth he and Will, nearly two years younger, had become friends. After a while, she understood they seemed to have a similar of sense of humour. At least, they giggled a lot and nudged each other from time to time as if pointing out that something immensely funny had happened that no one else had noticed.

They ate in a sectioned-off corner of the kitchen, which had a table covered with a gingham cloth with a bench each side — much cosier than the vast dining room, which would have seated twenty and cost the earth to heat, or so declared the mistress of the house. Violet considered the food a bit sparse. At least she would have provided a bigger choice of sandwich fillings had their positions been reversed. Also, she would have stuck a bit of tinned fruit in the jelly so it became a trifle. The custard tasted a tiny bit burnt. Violet was always extra careful

143

when she made custard, stirring the mixture like mad so it wouldn't stick to the pan. Did the Hanley-Rices have a cook, she wondered, or had the lady of the house burnt the custard herself?

Charles opened the French window leading to the garden and the boys went outside, Will almost a whole head smaller than the older boy. Violet prayed that he'd start growing soon. Mind you, Charles was several years older and tall for his age. He was an exceptionally handsome boy, slim and graceful, with perfect features — Carol Cooper would have compared him favourably to the film star Alan Ladd. His blond hair was a tad too long, the lock at the front that fell casually onto his forehead was bleached from the sun, probably from spending so much time on the tennis court she had glimpsed in the garden.

'What does Will want to do with his life?' her hostess asked in a bored voice. She and Violet were sitting opposite each other on the benches in the kitchen and she was smoking a black cigarette that emitted grey smoke. She looked bored. Violet got the firm impression that the idea for their visit came from Charles, not his mother.

'We've hardly talked about it,' Violet replied, 'but he said he wanted to join one of the services; his father was in the army, but he died in the first year of the war. What about Charles?' she felt bound to ask. She couldn't have been more surprised by the answer.

'Oh, he wants to be — well, he *will* be, there's no doubt about it — a singer. He should really be at a school specialising in music, but that would have to be in London and we don't want him leaving home so young.' She flicked the cigarette casually towards a beautiful jade ashtray. The ash went nowhere near it.

'I don't blame you.' Violet nodded. 'I couldn't stand the thought of Will leaving home.'

'He's our only child.' The woman's expression of boredom had changed to one of intense sorrow. 'I lost two babies after he was born and never had any more. He's very precious to me and his father. We'd wanted a big family, at least four.' She sighed deeply. 'Charles told me you have a daughter too. You must bring her with you next time you come to tea.'

'Why, thank you,' Violet said, 'but they're not my children — well, they are, but I didn't give birth to them. My cousin was their mother, but she died.'

'Do you mind me asking if you have a husband?'

'Of course I don't mind. I was — am — a spinster.' Violet wrinkled her nose. 'I don't like that word, *spinster*, it's so ugly — so is *old maid*. *Bachelor* doesn't sound nearly so unpleasant.' She sniffed expressively. 'And just *unmarried* would do.'

'I agree.' Mrs Hanley-Rice was smiling. 'I think that's a wonderful thing you did. And Will is obviously terribly fond of you.' She stretched her hands across the table to cover Violet's own and, despite her initial reserve, Violet had the strong feeling that they were about to become good friends.

Later, Charles sang 'Ave Maria' for them,

145

accompanied on the piano by his mother. His voice had not fully broken, but it still sounded beautiful in the big high-ceilinged room. The low notes had a singular warmth and the high ones were pure and even. The song finished and Violet was about to applaud when he continued to sing, this time 'Silent Night, Holy Night', followed by a modern song, 'My Funny Valentine'. Violet felt sure she'd heard it sung by Frank Sinatra.

She felt close to tears, having heard this talented young man perform at the very beginning of what would surely be a glittering career. She felt sure that one day he might become as famous as Gigli. Wait till she told Madge about him!

Mrs Hanley-Rice was about to close the piano lid, when her son burst into song again with 'Rock Around the Clock'. He pretended to have a microphone in his hand while wiggling his hips. His mother closed the lid with a bang. 'I never want to hear anything in this house by that awful young man,' she shouted. 'He can't sing and the song is dreadful. What's his name?'

'Bill Haley, Mummy darling.'

'Well, Bill Haley deserves to be shot.'

Charles blew her a kiss from across the room. 'Rightio, Mummy.' He winked at Will, who nearly fell off his chair laughing. 'I'll arrange to have it done tomorrow.'

⋆　⋆　⋆

Over the years, nothing had come of Mrs Holmes's various attempts to gain custody of

146

Abby, who remained unimpressed by her curious gifts of broken jewellery, a used handbag, a once-beautiful silk scarf with a frayed hem and other useless objects. She obviously wanted to buy the girl's affections but was too mean to part with anything of real value — or perhaps she thought Violet was raising Abby so poorly that the child would be glad of these hand-me-downs. Either way, she clearly had no idea as to what young girls really wanted. Nevertheless, Violet kept an eye out for strange cars on Amber Street, studying the drivers in case they had been sent to snatch the girl, but this would be breaking the law and she doubted if Mrs Holmes's sons would allow her to commit what was undoubtedly a crime. Anyway, once Abby understood this strange woman had no wish to meet Will, she didn't want to have anything to do with someone who didn't love her adored brother as much as she did.

On one of his regular visits, Edwin Powell told Violet, 'Sister Xavier from St Anne's School wrote a wonderful letter to the Board saying how happy Abby was there, how well she was being raised and that she and Will were a credit to you.'

'The Board of what?' Violet felt narked that there had been some sort of meeting about her family to which she'd not been invited. And, anyway, she thought Sister Xavier hated her.

'The Board of St Jude's Bounty, of course.'

'Shouldn't I have been there?'

'No, Violet. Evidence was only admissible in written form.' He could at least have told her when the Board was due to meet. 'I thought it best not to burden you with the worry.'

'Thank you,' she said tartly. She preferred to be kept in touch with the worry if it was anything to do with the children. 'And the board asked St Anne's for a reference?'

'It would seem so,' Edwin replied blandly.

Violet wanted to be annoyed, but didn't know how to. Relieved that Mrs Holmes seemed to be no closer to taking Abby from her, she changed the subject. 'How is Barbara?' His wife was five months pregnant.

He beamed. 'Well, very well. The doctor thinks she might be expecting twins.'

'Oh, that's marvellous.' She forgot her irritation with him — if only he would shave off that awful moustache.

★ ★ ★

Barbara Powell, Edwin's wife, gave birth to the twins, Marcus and Mary, in the summer of 1956 and, later in the year, Carol Cooper had another boy. Again, Violet went into the hospital to see her.

'Now I have four children, two boys and two girls,' Carol declared with a self-satisfied smile. She was sitting up in bed looking as healthy as a horse and nursing a giant baby.

'Which film star will this one be called after?' Violet asked.

'I've not yet made up me mind.' Her friend wrinkled her nose. 'What do you think of Clark Gable?'

'I think he's the gear, but he's rather ancient

and his name's a bit weird.'

Carol looked doubtful. 'I don't like his moustache.'

'It doesn't mean your baby has to have a moustache.'

Carol grinned. She held up the baby and kissed his nose. 'What do you think, darling?' The baby ignored her.

'If he was your baby, Vi, which film star would you call him after?'

Violet thought hard. Given the choice, she would sooner call him after a politician, Clement Attlee, the best prime minister the country had ever had. 'Spencer,' she said. 'After me own favourite film star: Spencer Tracy. He was me mam's favourite too. And he's a Catholic.'

Carol pretended to be sick. 'Spencer! Isn't a spencer a vest or a singlet or something?'

'Yes, girl,' Violet said patiently, 'but I've not had a baby, so I won't be calling him after a vest, will I? And, anyroad, back in Hollywood, Spencer and Clark are very good friends.' Well, they probably were. 'I'm amazed you haven't thought of Elvis Presley.'

'Of course! Fancy me forgetting about him. Elvis it is.'

> *Roses are red, violets are blue,*
> *Sugar is sweet and so are you.*

Violet didn't recognise the handwriting and wondered who on earth had written the words in her old shorthand notebook. A few years back, only a few weeks after she'd been so unceremoniously sacked, Iris Gunn had managed to retrieve it from her office at Briggs' Motors. Nowadays, she loved glancing through it and wondering who had composed the little messages in strange handwriting, left when she wasn't at her desk. The notebook was big and clumsy with thick cardboard covers and at least twice as many pages as the ones she'd had before, not easy to hold on her knee when she took down shorthand in Norman Larkin's office.

'It looks like a brick,' he'd remarked more than once and Violet had reminded him she was lucky to have managed to obtain a notebook when there was a war on and paper, like so much during that time, was hard to come by. Mam's favourite magazine, *Woman's Weekly*, had frequently been unavailable from the paper shop in Marsh Lane, where she had bought it for years.

The pages in her notebook had been written on only on one side. Violet had been using the blank sides to make odd notes and reminders on ever since it had been returned.

She looked at the little verse again, 'Roses are red . . . ' People often left messages if she wasn't at her desk when they came to see her. 'Can I see Norman late this afternoon? Jeff,' read another. There were names, telephone numbers, notes that didn't make sense. 'Tell Norm I can't make pigs fly,' read one, all interspersed with page after page of her famously neat shorthand that she could still read without a pause after all this time.

Mam had insisted she learn a proper trade

when she'd started work with Briggs' Motors as an office junior at the age of fourteen. 'You've got to learn to type, Violet. Any old body's got enough nous to file papers as long as they've got eyes in their head, but shorthand's a different kettle of fish altogether. It's a real skill. Same with typing.'

So, for three months, when she was fifteen, Violet had attended Miss Beatrice Grogan's commercial college, held in the basement of her big house in Walton Vale on five evenings a week as well as Saturday morning. Unlike at an ordinary school, the pupils' ages ranged from early teens to middle age. All were women. But, unlike when Violet had been sent to learn to dance and failed abysmally, at commercial college she was top of the class in both shorthand and typing. And, although it was nice to be the star, she would far sooner have been a star dancer.

⋆ ⋆ ⋆

Will was fascinated with 'the book', as it became known. He studied it for ages and wanted Violet to teach him how to do shorthand. 'What's that say?' he would ask, pointing to a squiggle.

'*Likelihood*,' she had told him on their most recent discussion.

'Where's the *k*?'

'There.' She pointed to a flat line in the middle of the squiggle.

'But you said *k* should be a heavy line and that's a light one,' he argued.

151

'No, I didn't, Will. If I'd written that line more heavily then it would be *g*.'

He grinned. 'And then it would be liglihood?'

'And it wouldn't make sense. Now, go away, stop tormenting me, and do something useful with yourself.'

7

In January 1957, the Cooper family moved south. Both women were devastated. Violet had come to look upon Carol as her younger sister. But Peter Cooper, having completed his service in the Royal Navy, was now captain of a cruise ship that operated from Southampton to New York.

'Couldn't he do it from Liverpool?' Violet cried.

'I only wish he could, Vi.' Carol was almost in tears when she told Violet the news. 'But Liverpool's no longer the port it was. Like the river, the Dock Road is deserted. When I was a kid, it was full of traffic. I thought it was the busiest road in the world.'

'I remember,' Violet said fondly. She'd thought the same.

The women sat in silence for a while, recalling all that had happened over the time since they had met — nothing spectacular, just pleasant and nice with hardly anything to get upset about.

'Remember when the children all started at St Anne's?' Carol reminisced. 'You came back to our house and mended Greg's teddy bear. He's loved you to death ever since and Teddy's still all in one piece.'

'And I've loved him,' Violet cried. 'We always hoped Greta and Abby would become best friends, but they never did. Abby still knocks

153

around with that Doreen Flynn.' She kept hoping the relationship would end, and it would for a while, then spring up again like a weed.

The Coopers left for Southampton and for Violet it felt as if she were losing half her real family.

★   ★   ★

Over the years, Violet had become more friendly with Sonia Hanley-Rice, Charles's mother. They met in Southport for lunch about every fortnight. It was a town Violet's mam had been fond of — posh and elegant. Mam and Violet had always worn their best clothes when they'd gone for tea on Sunday afternoons.

Poor Sonia was seriously depressed. She had never recovered from losing her babies after Charles was born. Violet did her best to cheer up the woman, but she needed professional advice. It didn't help that Charles hadn't completed his degree. He had walked out of university and successfully auditioned for a small part in a musical, *The Boyfriend*, showing in the West End of London. He'd received excellent reviews. But Sonia had always expected he would become involved in classical musical, concentrating mainly on opera.

Violet was unable to offer much in the way of genuine sympathy. She thought the lad should have his own choice when it came to music and it was best not to tell Sonia how much more she herself liked the swingy stuff — rock'n'roll, it was called.

154

It didn't seem long before Will was nearing the end of his final year taking Modern English at Birmingham University. His three years there had gone so fast. At weekends, it was so much easier for him to catch a train to London and stay with Charles in his Pimlico flat than to come all the way back to Liverpool and see Violet and Abby, which he did rarely these days. Violet understood why, but oh, she really did miss him.

Once university was over and done with, she hardly saw him at all. Instead of concentrating on his career — he'd swapped his boyhood plans of joining the army or RAF for a notion of doing charity work abroad for a few years before settling in England to teach — he got a job in the menswear department of Selfridges while moving in permanently with Charles in Pimlico.

Violet and Abby went to see him occasionally, staying in a cheap hotel, or he would come to Amber Street and wonder loudly what to do with his life. Violet had no intention of offering advice other than reminding him he'd planned on some sort of charity work. As far as she could see, he and Charles were having a great time and all she wanted for both her children was that they be happy. He'd grown, too. He still wasn't tall, but he wasn't small, either. When they were standing together, she had to look up to him. Only a bit, but enough. Sometimes, it was hard to think this was the same boy she'd first seen playing in the garden in Netton.

Abby had changed her mind a dozen times since she'd announced her ambition to be a nurse. Her latest wish was to become a designer.

'Of what?' Violet wanted to know. The girl was fifteen, and had done reasonably well at senior school. As the years passed she had lost her baby fat and had grown even prettier. The long tangled hair that once she'd wanted to cut was still as blonde and she was enviously slim and shapely. Violet was hugely flattered when people assumed she was Abby's mother.

'Clothes, jewellery, things like that,' she said in answer to Violet's question. 'I want to go to Liverpool Art College like John Lennon.'

'Who's John Lennon?'

'Oh, Vi!' Abby gasped. She tossed her head impatiently. 'How ignorant can you be? He's a member of the Beatles, isn't he?'

'Oh, yes.' The Beatles were four Liverpool lads who had recently taken the music world by storm. 'Oh, well, that's all right, then.' She was relieved that Abby had a proper ambition in mind. As to whether she'd get in the art college, they'd just have to wait and see.

★   ★   ★

A coach trip to the Victoria and Albert Museum in London had been arranged by St Anne's Senior School for pupils intending to study art in any of its various forms. Violet had no hesitation sending the necessary two pounds for Abby. The outing would take place at the end of February on a Saturday.

'I wish Greta was still here,' Abby said wistfully.

Violet was surprised. 'I didn't think you and Greta liked each other all that much.' Mind you, the two girls had got on well when the Duffys had gone to stay with the Coopers during the summer holidays.

'Me and Greta got on fine.' Abby shrugged. 'Never mind. Doreen's going, so we can sit together on the bus.'

'Where will Doreen get two pounds from?' She wished she didn't sound so waspish. Her immediate suspicion was that the money couldn't possibly have been honestly gained.

'Her dad's not long come out of prison and he gave it her.'

Violet didn't speak, only because she didn't know what to say.

On the Saturday of the outing to London, Violet found herself alone in the house in Amber Street. This was inevitable as the children grew older and could look after themselves, though it was something she was finding it hard to get used to.

She stood in the middle of the living room wondering what to do. The house felt strangely still — perhaps it was because it was about to be empty for so long. The coach had picked up the children at six o'clock that morning and wouldn't return until as late as ten o'clock that night. It wasn't yet ten in the morning and she was already bored out of her mind. As it often did in moments of calm, her mind settled on Crocker. Had she been too hasty in turning him down? The children would both be off leading their own lives soon, and she'd be alone in

Amber Street once more.

Violet ironed the few clothes, mainly Abby's, that were waiting in the basket. After they'd been put away, she picked up her knitting — she was making a highly complicated Fair Isle sleeveless pullover for Will. It required intense concentration that she didn't feel up to right now; she put it back on the shelf. Carol in Southampton was due a letter, but Violet decided to leave it until she was in a happier frame of mind.

She recalled there was a film on at The Forum in town that she really fancied — she'd read about it in the *Liverpool Echo* only the other day and the title escaped her. She dug the paper out of the pile waiting to be thrown away and looked in the films column — *All About Eve* with Bette Davis and Anne Baxter. She could go to that afternoon's matinee, but what a pity Iris Gunn was no longer around to go with. Iris's husband had died a few years ago and she'd moved to Halifax to live with her already widowed sister. When Iris was around, the women would have lunched together before they went to the cinema, where they always sat in the most expensive seats. Violet pulled a face. She really didn't fancy eating in a restaurant on her own or sitting by herself in the pictures, come to that. Part of the pleasure of the outing was the company, not just the food or the film.

Violet sighed and laid the newspaper on her knee. In a way the last ten years of her life had turned full circle and she was once more in need of a job. It was inevitable that as the children grew older they wouldn't need her so much. But, seeing how she'd had no luck finding a job when she was forty-seven, she was even less likely to get one an entire decade later. And it wasn't just the money she was after, but something to occupy her mind.

Out of interest, she turned the *Echo's* pages to the 'Situations Vacant' column. There were machinists wanted. She'd been hopeless with Mam's sewing machine, with the needle forever running away with her or even breaking. Once it had sewn her thumb to the material and there'd been blood everywhere. Reading on, she reckoned she'd be just as hopeless driving a forklift truck, cleaning windows or having anything to do with agriculture — anyway, the advert only wanted men. She didn't bother reading the office vacancies. There were plenty of jobs on offer, but she imagined the personnel officer, or whoever read her letter of application, collapsing into fits of laughter when he or she saw her age. She was going to have to think of something different. Perhaps she could take on typing for other people, she thought. She knew she hadn't lost the knack — and she could do it from home, around Abby's school hours. And, best of all, it would mean she wouldn't have the misery of scouring the 'Situations Vacant' column, which made her feel positively ancient.

She let the paper float to the floor and the flames on the fire flickered in the draught. Whenever she'd done this in the past, Sammy had leapt upon the paper and torn it to shreds. It was one of his favourite games.

'Oh, gosh!' she whispered, as the tears ran

down her cheeks. This always happened when she thought about her beautiful tabby cat. It must be five years since she'd woken up one morning and found him curled up on her bed, as cold as ice. He had died in his sleep.

The children had run into her room, alerted by her cries, and all three had lain on the bed sobbing their hearts out until it was time to get dressed and get on with their lives without Sammy.

Irritated with herself, Violet caught the bus to Waterloo with the intention of visiting Barbara and Edwin Powell and their twins, but no one answered when she pressed the doorbell of the little bungalow she still thought of as 'sweet'.

'They've gone away, dear,' a woman shouted from the next-door garden. 'I don't know where or for how long. They left early this morning in the car.'

'Thank you, I'd forgotten.' Edwin had told her only the other day. The initiator of St Jude's Bounty was about to retire and Edwin had been asked to take his place at the main office in Exeter. He would be interviewed on Monday, having spent the weekend looking at property in the area. What an idiot she was for not telephoning first!

She caught the bus back home, groaning inwardly. With Edwin gone, as seemed likely, she would lose another friend. There were only Madge and Sonia left. Sonia wasn't exactly a bundle of laughs and these days Madge was nothing at all like she used to be.

Abby was expected home from the trip to

London between half past nine and ten. Violet put water on for tea and prepared a ham sandwich; the girl was bound to be hungry. She sat in the parlour waiting for the sound of her footsteps in the street, but had to move into the living room when the parlour became too cold — after all, it was only February.

At going on for half-nine, she opened the front door to keep a lookout, though naturally it felt even colder. After a while, she put on her coat and walked to the end of the street, where she looked up and down Marsh Lane, willing the coach to appear; there were forty children and they couldn't all be delivered to their various homes at the same time. Some were probably being dropped off right now. Abby might be one of the last to get off.

She returned home, made herself tea and bit into Abby's ham sandwich, but found she could easily drink the tea but couldn't finish the sandwich.

There was a knock at the door and she rushed to open it. Why wasn't Abby using her key?

Miss Rutherford, Abby's form teacher, was outside. 'I'm sorry, Miss Duffy, I wasn't on the trip to London and I've just had a phone call. I'm afraid Abby's disappeared along with Doreen Flynn. They're not on the coach, but somewhere in London, and they can't be found.'

Miss Rutherford sat in front of the fire warming her hands. They had toured the Victoria and Albert Museum, she told Violet, and everyone had apparently enjoyed it. Then they boarded the coach to Piccadilly Circus to sit on the steps by Eros for a little while before coming home. Miss Rutherford hurried on, her voice rushed and hoarse. She hardly looked old enough to be a teacher with her attractive red hair and big green eyes. Oh, my goodness, she wore lipstick and what looked suspiciously like mascara on her long lashes! Violet took for granted she didn't paint her face like that when she was at school.

'Abby and Doreen were definitely on the coach when they were picked up at the museum,' the teacher continued shakily, 'but, due to unforgivable inefficiency on someone's part, not only did no one notice they didn't get back on the bus when the children were collected from Piccadilly Circus, it wasn't noticed they were missing until they were almost back in Liverpool.'

Violet would like to bet a hundred pounds that it was all Doreen's fault. 'What's happening now?' she asked shakily.

'The coach is touring Bootle dropping children off on the way. It should arrive any minute at the Town Hall, where the last will get off,' Miss Rutherford said, adding sensibly, 'if I were you, Miss Duffy, I would go to bed, go to sleep, and I'm sure Abby will be brought home to you in the morning, probably quite late. The police have already been informed and I gather that, once they're found, they would like the girls to be interviewed in London rather than be whisked home to Liverpool and then have to return. They'll probably have quite a tale to tell. After all, who knows what might have happened

162

to them? Oh!' She clapped her hand against her mouth. 'Oh, I'm sure nothing bad has. I'm certain they're both absolutely fine.'

Violet hoped so too. The young woman had introduced dozens of horrible ideas into her head that she would never have thought of herself. She was still wearing her coat. She fastened the buttons, tied the belt and stood up. 'Goodnight, Miss Rutherford,' she said coldly.

'Where are you going?' the teacher stammered.

'To Bootle Town Hall and then hopefully on to London. By the way, when it was eventually noticed that Abby and Doreen weren't on the bus, did anyone see where they took themselves off to in London?'

'Yes, one of the boys. Dennis Hayes. He said he saw them go down Shaftesbury Avenue. Do you know where that is?'

'I'm afraid not, no.' She'd never been to London and cursed her ignorance.

'Shaftesbury Avenue leads to Soho, which is virtually a den of vice,' the teacher said tactlessly, 'full of prostitutes, shops selling disgusting books and theatres where women dance naked — I think they're called strip joints.'

'Jaysus!' Violet said again. The longer she and Miss Rutherford were together, the worse everything got. 'What shall I do?' She ran her fingers through her hair and Miss Rutherford grasped her arm.

'Don't do anything hasty, Miss Duffy. Stay here. Go to bed. Like I said, the police in London are already looking for the girls. There's

163

nothing you can do to help.'

Violet ignored her. She ran into the street, stopping in Marsh Lane, where she'd stopped before, once again looking up and down for a coach, the coach. She wanted to speak to the other children herself.

Miss Rutherford had followed.

'Where are they? The other children?' Violet shouted.

'I've already told you, the coach is by the Town Hall, or will be any minute.' The young woman looked moidered.

A car, big and black, was gliding slowly along Marsh Lane. It stopped beside them and the passenger door opened.

'Miss Duffy,' a voice called.

Violet looked inside. Sister Xavier, the head of St Anne's junior school, was sitting on the back seat and a man dressed all in black wearing a peaked cap was behind the wheel.

'Get in, Miss Duffy,' Sister Xavier urged.

'Where are we going?' Violet asked.

'To London,' the nun replied. 'Where else?'

'I need my handbag.'

'Then fetch it quickly,' the nun commanded.

Sister Xavier was the last person Violet had expected to come to her aid. For one thing, Abby had left the junior school years back and moved to the other site where the senior school was based. But it was clear Sister Xavier felt that the teachers at the senior school weren't doing enough to track down their missing pupils. 'Besides,' she added when Violet was back in the car, 'I'm the only one who could get hold of a

164

car at this hour of night.'

'Is this car yours?' Violet asked.

'It's my brother's,' Sister Xavier replied, pointing at the driver. It turned out he wasn't just the driver of the car, but the owner of this one and another five. It was his business.

Neither woman spoke much on the way. Violet felt awkward thinking of the cross words she'd shared with Sister Xavier in her office years ago — and yet the nun had still written that letter of support to the board of St Jude's. She didn't know what to say.

There was silence for at least an hour until the nun asked how Will was. 'I shouldn't say this, but he was one of my favourite pupils. How is he getting on now he's left university? I understand he got a first-class degree. English literature, wasn't it?'

Violet nodded. 'He's just taken a conventional job for now,' she said.

'He really should have gone somewhere like Oxford or Cambridge.'

'You mean the universities?'

'Of course.' The words were spoken impatiently, as if Violet was a fool to think she meant anything else. She probably was.

The car sped smoothly through the outskirts of Birmingham, where the streets were darkly lit. Violet knew they were in the city only when she saw a sign outside a shop: 'Birmingham Tools'.

She decided not to speak again unless Sister Xavier spoke first. They were long past Birmingham when the nun produced a flask and asked Violet if she would like a cup of tea.

'Yes, please,' she said gratefully.

'Tea doesn't usually taste all that nice out of a flask, but the trick is to keep the milk separate and pour it in the cup rather than the flask. Do you mind stopping a minute, Tom?'

Her brother stopped the car, the tea was poured, and tasted excellent. They continued on their way, Tom having refused a cup.

What shall we do when we get to London? Violet asked herself. Where shall we start? Shall we go to the police station first? If so, which police station? Was there one in Soho? She recalled she had a photo of Abby in her handbag.

She found the presence of the nun calming. Although she would have liked to scream and shout and generally make a scene, she would have felt ashamed.

'I suggest we go to Shaftesbury Avenue first,' Sister Xavier said, 'where the girls apparently disappeared, speak to the first policeman we come across, and ask him if he knows what's happening.'

'This is my first visit to London,' Violet said in a small voice. 'You sound as if you've been there before.'

'I lived there for many years,' the sister replied. 'I had a flat in Soho.'

'Miss Rutherford, the teacher, said Soho was a den of vice.'

'Oh, it is,' the other woman agreed.

'Is there a convent there?' Violet asked innocently.

'No, Miss Duffy, there isn't. But there are numerous theatres. Don't forget we both attended the same dancing class. I went on to take it up professionally and I appeared in several London shows, some in Soho. I'm surprised you didn't go on to take it up professionally yourself. You were quite good at it if I remember rightly.'

Violet managed a strained smile. Was she being funny? 'I danced like an elephant,' she murmured.

'Then I'm even more surprised you weren't a great success.' She *was* being funny, and Violet felt the tension between them ease. 'Oh, look, here we are!'

'In Shaftesbury Avenue?'

'No, London.'

Shop windows were lit, there were quite a few cars about. As they drove further into the heart of the city, the shop windows became bigger and brighter, the traffic increased, there were people, lots of them, some in evening dress strolling along, lots of fur coats around, music could be heard, singing, a guitar — a man was singing to a guitar.

'This is Piccadilly Circus,' Sister Xavier announced.

'Aah!' Violet wasn't sure whether she made the sound, or just imagined it. The lights were so intense, so vivid, colourful, some flashing on and off, the steps around the statue full of people, the pavements crowded. And for years and years, while all this was going on, she'd been fast asleep in Liverpool missing all the excitement.

'And this is Shaftesbury Avenue,' the nun announced.

167

The driver braked and the car proceeded slowly along, close to the pavement. Violet peered out of the window, half expecting to see Abby and Doreen Flynn come skipping past.

'Turn left here, Tom,' Sister Xavier said to her brother. 'Then right.' The first street was almost nothing but restaurants, all open, all full of people eating at whatever unearthly time it was in the morning. The next street was gaudily bright, places with illuminated and rather suggestive signs outside, 'Strip Jacky Naked', 'Girls-Girls-Girls', 'Penny's from Heaven'. Without exception the entrances had a man outside in evening dress to welcome customers or prevent them from going further.

'Stop,' the nun commanded and the car slid to a gentle halt. 'Ask one of those gentlemen if there's been any police activity recently involving two innocent young Liverpool girls being sought or rescued from the utter depravity of their places of work. 'Strip Jacky Naked' looks the sleaziest.'

'OK.' Tom got out of the car and Violet gave him Abby's photo. He spoke to the man in question who wore an emerald-green evening suit over a bright-pink shirt. Violet couldn't hear what they were saying. He wasn't there for long when he returned and slid back behind the wheel. Turning, he said in a well-bred voice, 'The police have been around, quite a few of them, asking questions. But he didn't know if they'd found the girls yet.'

Violet's heart was hammering in her chest. But Tom was undeterred. He worked his way

168

along the street, asking doormen and even a few of the girls they saw leaving some of the bars and theatres, showing them the photo.

Eventually, he jogged back over to where Vi and Sister Xavier waited in the back of the car. This time he looked more hopeful. 'Two young girls were found in Tip Morgan's place. They've been taken to the station. The man that told me said he'd heard they'd been doped.'

'Were these girls from Liverpool?' Violet asked anxiously.

'He told me all he knew,' Tom replied.

Sister Xavier leaned forward. 'Did he tell you which police station it is?'

'Soho Square. It's only a short walk from here.'

'I know where it is. Let's go there straight-away.'

Violet and Sister Xavier came rushing into the police station only to be told by the desk sergeant that the girls had been taken to Charing Cross Hospital. 'Both of 'em were only half conscious,' he continued. 'But they were coming to by the time the ambulance arrived,' he added encouragingly, and the two women rushed out again.

It being Saturday night, with London full of drunks rather than the sick and injured, the girls were hard to find in the crowded wards of the hospital. The noise was horrendous. None of the so-called 'patients' looked damaged enough to account for their violent yells and roars and occasional raucous singing. A young woman in a white overall splattered with blood was helping with the search for Abby and Doreen. Her name was Shirley, according to the cardboard badge on her lapel. It wasn't like this every night, she assured them. Saturday was always worse than most.

Violet was full of admiration for the staff whose job it was to cope in all this bedlam. Shirley looked little more than sixteen.

'They're in here,' she cried, flinging back the curtain on a little annexe at the end of a corridor with just two beds, the occupants of which, two middle-aged women, stared at Violet and Sister Xavier blankly.

'That's not them!' the nun said loudly. 'They're much too old. We're looking for children.'

'There were children here before us, two girls,' one of the women commented. 'Though they might well be as old as us by the time they get out, and Mamie and me will be dead.'

'Do you know where they went, the children?' Violet asked.

'Outside,' the woman said. 'One of 'em wanted to be sick and she was too embarrassed to vomit in a hospital. Nice pair of kids, they were — funny accents, though.'

Sister Xavier grabbed Violet's arm. 'We'd better get outside.'

Their car was parked directly in front of the main entrance. Both left-hand doors were wide open and Tom was crouched in front of Doreen gently stroking her forehead while she was being sick in the gutter. Abby was sitting in the back, eyes half open, neither fully awake nor asleep.

170

'There you are,' Tom said, stating the obvious when the women arrived. 'I'll take these kids back in, sort them out. You two stay here, have some more tea if there's any left. I won't be long.'

He disappeared inside the hospital, a girl virtually carried on each arm.

'He's very capable,' Violet remarked. 'Exactly the right person to have on an occasion like this.' She climbed into the back of the car.

Sister Xavier was already opening the flask. 'He was very capable during the war, brave as well. He won the George Cross in Italy.'

There was a small amount of tea left. The women were sipping it when Tom returned alone, having left Abby and Doreen with a doctor who intended contacting the police again once the pair looked fit enough to be interviewed.

'At first glance, a quick examination made the doctor think the kids were both unharmed, but shaken up quite a bit,' he said authoritatively. 'He suggests we find somewhere to spend the night and return in the morning, around tennish, to collect the pair.'

With that, Tom slid behind the steering wheel and started the engine, his sister put the tea things away, and they set off.

At last the city looked as if it was closing down for the night. They drove through a miserably silent, badly lit Piccadilly Circus, which was in the process of being cleared of rubbish in preparation for the day to come, and stopped outside a grand hotel called The Ritz. Violet was

171

taken aback but Sister Xavier seemed quite at home and led the way inside. Tom disappeared and rejoined them inside in an impressive dining room, where they were served delicious meat soup with crusty bread and butter.

'It's so late, it's barely worth taking a room,' said Sister Xavier. 'If we let ourselves dawdle over this, we can sit in the lounge until it's time to contact the hospital. We might even feel like breakfast.'

A dance was being held in the next room, a ball perhaps. Through an open door Violet glimpsed satin dresses, silk-clad legs, diamante shoes. The music was old-fashioned, the men in evening dress. The orchestra was playing a Viennese waltz.

Yet again, Violet was reminded that, apart from the war years while she'd been asleep in her little house in Bootle, in other parts of the country people had been dancing the night away and having a marvellous time. Despite that, right now, the house in Bootle was the place she'd prefer to be than anywhere else.

★ ★ ★

It was five hours later and the women were back in the hospital. The girls lay in adjacent beds, both awake, both pale. Violet bent over Abby, who blinked tiredly and managed the suggestion of a smile. 'Oh, Vi, I'm so pleased to see you,' she whispered.

'What happened, pet? Are you all right?' She really should be cross with the girl — both girls

— for causing so much trouble and upset, but they looked so worried and frightened that she couldn't bring herself to raise her voice.

Hardly anyone spoke in the car on the drive home. The radio was switched on for the entire journey, Irish folk music, very stirring and drowned out now and then by the sound of church bells because it was Sunday. It meant there were no long, noticeable silences and they didn't feel obliged to talk to each other. They stopped twice for drinks and the toilet and it was growing dark by the time they reached Liverpool. Violet and Abby were dropped off first. For some reason, Violet found it hard to get Doreen's mournful face out of her mind when the car drove away with her still inside.

Abby went to bed immediately, for which Violet was thankful, having not slept a wink the night before and anxious to get to bed herself.

★　★　★

Now it was Monday and Violet was downstairs, sipping her first cup of tea of the day, anxious for Abby to wake up so they could talk about the events of the weekend, but reluctant to disturb the girl so early. She'd agreed with Sister Xavier that Abby could be excused from school that day, partly to give Violet a chance to get to the bottom of what had happened. Initially, both girls had come up with a garbled tale of passing a brightly lit building in Soho called Theatre of Delights, where a man wearing a sequinned cloak was outside and had invited them in. They

173

didn't know why they had left Piccadilly Circus.

Violet felt ashamed that Abby and Doreen had caused such a fuss, inconvenienced so many people. Then, to crown it all, late on Sunday, Will had telephoned. The news had actually reached him — Violet had no idea how. As he was staying in London, he was angry he hadn't been approached to help.

'Charles and I don't live all that far away from where you were in London, Vi,' he'd complained. 'Why didn't you give us a call? Abby's my sister. I have a right to know if she's in trouble.' He was coming that weekend to stay with them in Bootle, only for a single night, to make sure Abby was all right.

It hadn't crossed Violet's mind to contact him. Her brain had been too focused on Abby to think about Will. It later emerged that Abby had mentioned to the police she had a brother who might be in London. A policeman had tracked him down, by which time Abby was on her way home.

She was wondering whether to wake the girl up with a cup of tea, when she heard youthful voices upstairs and groaned inwardly: Doreen! She'd actually forgotten Doreen was there, too. The girl had turned up at first light. Although Sister Xavier and her brother had delivered her to the Flynns' house the night before, Tom had driven away before it was realised that Mrs Flynn had no intention of letting her daughter back in.

'Where have you been since then?' a shocked Violet demanded to know when she had answered the tentative knock on the door at dawn.

It turned out Doreen had spent the night in St James's Church porch.

'Why on earth did your mother turn you away?' Violet asked, rather more brusquely than she'd intended.

'Because I'd stayed out all the night before,' the girl sobbed. 'She said I can't go back no more.'

'Oh, dear me!' Violet had sighed and had kept saying the same thing over and over again ever since. She had sat the girl in front of the fire, fetched a coat from the hall, and put it round her shoulders. Her own coat wasn't nearly thick enough for February. When she'd warmed up a bit, she'd taken her upstairs and put her in Will's bed.

Eventually, both girls appeared downstairs in their night-clothes — Abby's nightclothes — their feet bare. 'Oh, Doreen, your mam's a bitch,' Abby cried. 'You should have come straight to our house. Violet wouldn't have minded, would you, Vi?'

Violet shook her head. She would never have turned the girl away, but she might well have minded, if only a bit.

She still minded, more than a bit, that night when Doreen slept in Will's bed again and continued to without any suggestion of sleeping anywhere else, apart from sharing the double bed with Abby when Will came home.

★ ★ ★

175

It was Will who managed to get some sort of truth out of his sister about what had happened in London when the coach had dropped the youngsters off at Piccadilly Circus.

'Apparently, it was Doreen who fancied the look of Shaftesbury Avenue and suggested the pair go for a stroll,' Will had told Violet before he returned to London.

'I thought as much,' Violet said knowingly.

'Ah-hah!' Will held up a reproving finger. 'But it was Abby who suggested they went inside the Theatre of Delights.'

'But why?'

Will shrugged. 'She just liked the look of it. She thought it was a proper theatre, that there'd be a genuine play on or a pantomime, which was why the chap outside was wearing a 'glittery suit'.' He paused. 'Did they tell you they were given a Micky Finn?'

Violet gasped. 'No,' she said hoarsely. 'Neither of them mentioned it. Didn't the hospital notice?'

'Yes, but both girls hotly denied it. I think it was Doreen who seemed to realise all along that what they were up to was wrong, then thought it best that they lie, otherwise the school, the hospital, but most of all the police were likely to make a big deal of it and they might end up with their names in the *Bootle Herald*. I think they've learnt their lesson, though. They both realise something much worse could have happened.'

Violet was impressed with the way he was dealing with the situation. The girls hung on his every word. She wished he could be persuaded to return home for good, but he seemed to be enjoying life in the capital too much to contemplate returning to Liverpool for more than a couple of days, and, now she'd had a glimpse of London, she could understand why.

8

Violet was woken about six weeks after the incident in London by the sound of one of the girls downstairs vomiting in the kitchen sink. It was Doreen, Violet discovered when she went down to investigate.

'It must have been something you ate,' she said. Later that day, she bought a bottle of milk of magnesia and gave the girl a teaspoonful before she went to bed. Next morning, at roughly the same time, she was again woken by the sound of Doreen being sick.

The bottle of milk of magnesia had almost gone by the time Violet could bring herself to take the girl to a doctor. A horrible suspicion had entered her mind.

She took her to her own doctor, whose surgery was in one of the big, four-storey houses opposite North Park. After describing her symptoms to Dr West, Violet went to sit in his waiting room. It didn't seem right that she, who wasn't a relative, should remain in the surgery while Doreen was being examined.

Almost half an hour had passed before Dr West opened his door and asked Violet to come in. He indicated a chair in front of his desk for her to sit on. A white-faced Doreen was in an adjacent chair.

The doctor coughed. 'I have examined this young lady thoroughly,' he said quietly, 'and can find nothing physically wrong with her. The only reason for her early-morning sickness that I can find is that she's expecting a baby. Doreen is almost certainly pregnant, Miss Duffy. Her parents have to be told. She needs to be looked after. Whether she stays at school during the pregnancy is up to the authorities.' He shuffled through the papers on his desk. 'I'll give you a note to take to the hospital.'

Doreen had begun to cry, heartrending sobs that sounded as if they were tearing her apart. She fell on her knees in front of Violet and gripped both her hands. 'Oh, can I stay with you, Miss Duffy? Please say, can I stay with you? And me mam must never know. If she found out, she'd bloody kill me.'

Violet stroked the girl's hair. 'Is it true that you might be expecting a baby, Doreen, luv?' Her voice quivered. 'Are you really pregnant?' It was scarcely believable. Doreen nodded, but didn't speak. When did it happen? Violet wondered. She felt herself go cold. The day in London, the Theatre of Delights. Hadn't Will said the girls had been drugged? She went cold and actually shivered, thinking about Abby. Had they been raped? Was it possible for Abby to have been so heavily drugged that she wasn't aware of what had happened? But she would have been aware it had happened once the effects of the drug had faded.

Dr West gave her a letter, advising that she should take it, along with Doreen, to the hospital. 'I'd like her to be examined in the appropriate department and appointments made

179

for the next six months.'

'Thank you,' Violet said tiredly.

She had no intention of taking Doreen to the hospital. That was someone else's responsibility, not hers. And, while Violet was totally opposed to abortion, whoever was responsible for Doreen, or Doreen herself, might prefer that option. Neither the woman nor the girl spoke as they made their way back to Amber Street, by which time Abby was home.

'Please keep what happened today to yourself for now,' Violet whispered to a shivering Doreen when she unlocked the front door and heard the sound of the television. Abby was the only person who could have switched it on.

'I can't keep it secret from Abby,' Doreen said quietly.

Violet shrugged. 'All right, but no one else. I need to speak to someone about it before the whole world knows.'

★   ★   ★

Two hours later, Violet was in the office of Sister Xavier for only the second time since Will and Abby had started school. She didn't know who else to tell about Doreen's encounter with Dr West that afternoon.

'Pregnant!' Sister Xavier expressed her consternation by pushing back her chair and jumping to her feet. Her mouth fell open. 'Pregnant! Doreen Flynn, only fourteen, is expecting a baby?' She took a long breath. 'Do you think the recent incident in London is anything to do with it?'

Violet shrugged helplessly. 'I've no idea.'

'Does Abby show any signs of being disturbed in the same way?'

'None whatsoever.'

'I can tell by the sound of your voice you're annoyed. But wasn't it Abby who suggested they might have been given a Micky Finn?'

'She didn't suggest she'd been raped,' Violet said coldly.

There was a long pause until Sister Xavier yanked her chair forward with her foot, sat down, and said, 'What should I do?'

'Don't ask me.' Violet was surprised. 'I came here to ask you.' She was already much too involved for comfort. 'Someone has to take Doreen to the hospital to be examined and I don't think the responsibility should be mine.'

'What's her family like? Do you know the mother?'

'Her mother threw her out purely over the London thing, because she'd been out all night.' Violet lowered her voice. 'I'd sooner it didn't go beyond these four walls, but she's a terrible woman — they're a terrible family altogether. Mr Flynn only came out of prison in the new year.'

Sister Xavier chewed her bottom lip. 'Sometimes I wish I wasn't a holy person and could smoke a cigarette on the job.' She snorted inelegantly. 'Doreen Flynn is nothing to do with me, either. She's no longer at this school. She moved from junior school three years ago. Tomorrow, I will pass over the care of Doreen, poor child, to the appropriate person at the senior school. I'll give you a call, let you know what's happening. Phew!' She pretended to wipe the sweat from her brow. 'I'm about to hide myself somewhere and have a smoke.' She got to her feet and Violet did the same.

'Here's the note I was given by my doctor for the 'appropriate person' to take with them to the hospital.' She fished the note out of her handbag, but the nun waved it away.

'Keep it, Violet. You can give it to the appropriate person yourself when he or she arrives in the morning.'

Violet sniffed. She very much hoped the appropriate wasn't a 'he' — it would be entirely unsuitable.

★ ★ ★

Next day, it was Miss Rutherford of the glorious red hair who would take Doreen to the hospital. 'She's their youngest member of staff,' Sister Xavier said when she'd telephoned this information to Violet. 'It seems she's a great favourite with the girls — and the boys.'

Abby didn't seem surprised to find she was expected to go to school alone again after Violet had explained that Doreen was due at Bootle Hospital.

Half an hour later, Miss Rutherford arrived in a bright-yellow mini car to collect her charge. She was perfectly made up, and became agitated when she discovered Violet wasn't going with her and Doreen to the hospital.

182

'I won't know what to say,' she gulped. 'Sister Xavier distinctly said you would be coming too.'

Well, one of them was lying, Violet thought to herself — the nun or the teacher. Or perhaps one had got mixed up, she thought a bit more charitably. After all the upheaval, she had been planning — looking forward to, even — a dull morning darning the socks Will had left on his last visit and starting to read her new library book, an American thriller.

Miss Rutherford looked close to tears and Doreen, conscious of the fact that she was the cause of all this turmoil, only fourteen years old and burdened with the worst mother in the world, looked even closer.

Violet reached for her coat.

☆　☆　☆

The hospital doctor was much older than Dr West. This one's name was Harrison and he was unhealthily thin with straggly grey hair that looked as if it needed a good wash. He was also outrageously rude and Doreen, lying half dressed on a narrow metal bed, had been reduced to utter wretchedness.

'She's been a very naughty girl,' he snapped, 'and is definitely expecting a child. I'd say she's a good three months pregnant, possibly even four.'

'But she can't be,' Miss Rutherford objected. 'They only went to London six weeks ago.'

'What relevance does London have on the girl's pregnancy?' the man almost sneered. 'If I say she's three months pregnant or more then that is most certainly the case.'

Miss Rutherford appeared stuck for words. She looked frantically at Violet, who licked her lips and also tried to think of something to say. She had assumed, as the teacher so clearly did too, that, if Doreen was having a baby, it was linked to her experience in Soho, but Abby had denied anything bad had happened. They hadn't been persuaded to go inside the London club, but had gone of their own accord. She thought they'd been given a Micky Finn, but after a long discussion at home it had been decided it was probably just a glass of sherry, or maybe something stronger, and, as Abby had never drunk alcohol before, it had made her feel dizzy.

'Doreen,' Violet said gently, 'do you know how babies are made?'

'Course I do,' Doreen said contemptuously before bursting into tears.

Violet picked up the girl's frock, which was lying on the bed, and helped her into it followed by her shoes and socks. Dr Harrison or the nurse should have made sure she was properly dressed before the two women had been invited into the room.

'Come on, child.' Violet led the weeping girl to a chair, where she sat her down and stood behind, hands resting on her shoulders. She was suddenly aware how slight and delicate she was, neither old enough nor big enough to be expecting a baby, to have been touched in such an intimate and adult way by a man. 'Who's the father of your child, Doreen?' she asked softly. 'If it can't be someone from that London club, it must have happened before you went to London.'

Doreen licked her lips. 'If I tell you,' she whispered, 'you won't make him go back to prison, will you?'

Miss Rutherford looked shocked; Violet felt sick to her stomach. The father of Doreen's baby was her own father. The doctor had sensed the meaning of Doreen's words and his manner turned from disapproval to sympathy. 'How bloody disgusting!' he muttered. 'Is the father living at home?'

'I don't want to go home,' Doreen screamed. 'Me mam'd kill me. I want to stay with Abby.'

The doctor's eyebrows rose. 'Who is Abby?'

'My daughter,' Violet replied, not wanting to further complicate things by explaining she was in fact her niece. 'Doreen's been living with us for a while.'

'Can she go back with you?' Dr Harrison frowned. 'Only for now. I'll get something sorted out with whoever's in charge of this sort of thing. There's a nursing home in Birkdale that will probably take her.'

The nurse, who hadn't spoken so far, said, 'You're right, Doctor. Would you like me to ring them?'

'Straightaway, if you don't mind.'

Poor Doreen might as well not have spoken. She looked wildly from the nurse to the doctor. 'But I don't want to go to no home.' She stood and flung her arms around Violet. 'Please, Miss Duffy, can I stay with you and Abby?'

It was like the time Edwin Powell had come to

ask if she would take Will and Abby and Violet had felt reluctant, then kept wondering if she had done the right thing. It turned out that she had and never regretted it for a minute.

She said, 'Of course you can, pet,' wished she hadn't, but it was already too late to change her mind. She felt Doreen relax against her, knowing she was safe, if only for now, from being sent home or any other sort of home.

'Thank you, Miss,' the girl mumbled. 'Oh, thank you.'

The older woman stroked her head, saying, 'I suppose from now on you'd better start calling me Vi.'

Doreen had never called her Vi, or Violet. Perhaps she was too shy, or nervous, or in her eyes Violet ranked with a teacher, because all she got was 'Miss' for a long time.

★ ★ ★

Sister Xavier had been pleased to discover Violet was on the telephone. She called regularly, usually with the request that she visit her in her office in school — 'Whenever you have a minute.'

'I hope you don't mind coming here,' she said, in the tone of a best friend, which seemed to have happened after the trip to London, 'but, when parents see me outside, they want to discuss their children. Others want to argue with me about religion or make fun of my habit — I mean my nun's outfit, not my habit of smoking black cigarettes.'

186

The first visit was the day after Doreen had been to the hospital and confirmed pregnant. The Mother Superior's office was surprisingly luxurious, thickly carpeted, with heavy brocade curtains and beautiful furniture. There were holy pictures on the walls and a massive brass crucifix on the mantelpiece under which a fire crackled cheerfully. She smiled at her visitor, thanked her for coming, and asked, 'Does Abby know her friend is having a baby?'

Violet nodded. 'Yes, but she's promised not to tell a soul.'

'Jolly good. Miss Rutherford was sent to inform me what happened. Apparently the father is the guilty party; it was he who put his daughter in the club.'

'I'm afraid so.'

'Does Mrs Flynn know that?'

'I have no idea. I suppose I should go and see her.' Violet sighed at the thought. 'She's a difficult woman, but then you would be, living in a house with all that violence.'

'It's not your job to tell her, dear, and, if no one from the senior school will do it, then it's mine.'

'Well, look after yourself,' Violet warned. It wasn't really the nun's job either, but someone had to take care of the girl.

'I shall go tomorrow and take a weapon with me. That brass crucifix should see anyone off with a single blow. Miss Rutherford also told me you are looking after Doreen for now. That's frightfully kind of you.'

'What else could I do?' Violet spread her

hands, palms upwards, in a gesture of despair. 'There'll come a time when she'll have to leave school. She can't be quite openly having a baby in front of the other children.'

'Good gracious me, no!'

9

Madge opened the back door to Violet's knock. 'It's ages since you last came,' she grumbled.

'It's three weeks,' Violet argued. 'Not exactly ages.'

'Come on in, sit down.' Madge rolled her eyes. 'Have a cup of tea, I've got one made.'

Violet thought about it, shrugged, and stepped into her friend's kitchen. 'I'm reluctant to take part in Bob's crazy games,' she said. She went in the house and sat in what was the easiest place to escape, if Bob came in the front way or the back and she could leave the other. She didn't want them coming face to face.

It had begun, the crazy game, a few years ago, when Madge returned after being beaten black and blue for spending her evenings getting drunk and having sex in The Butcher's. Bob had made his wife a prisoner. On leaving for work, he would lock all the doors and take the keys with him.

Of course Madge could have escaped. On the very first day she climbed through a window and got a key from one of the neighbours, but decided she'd not say a word to her husband and instead played along with Bob's twisted game. Perhaps she realised this was a way out, a way of breaking her riskier habits without appearing to give in. She was even willing to give up her job for it.

After a while, she began to like her new life, she told Vi. With the circumstances being so different, Bob was willing to keep the television to themselves. There were programmes on in the afternoon that Madge enjoyed such as baking and gardening. Bob made a window box for the backyard that was presently crammed with tiny daffodils.

'We make love like savages,' Madge had whispered as if the whole of Pearl Street were listening. She was annoyed when Violet laughed. 'I bet you wish it was you.' She stuck out her tongue.

Violet might well have wished that, had someone like the Bob McDowd of old been involved, but it was the Bob of now, who kept his teeth in a mug overnight and had a potbelly. 'Oh, I do,' she lied, not wanting to hurt her old friend's feelings too much.

Madge grinned. 'Liar!'

★   ★   ★

A solution for the Doreen Flynn problem was found when Sonia Hanley-Rice learnt about her situation. Where would the girl live while she was obviously pregnant and expected to be at school?

'She can come and stay with me,' Sonia cried, clapping her hands in delight. 'At least until the baby comes. And afterwards if she likes, for as long as she likes.'

Shirley Rutherford, the young teacher who had been such a help during and after the London episode, had become attached to the women who had formed a sort of committee to assist Doreen through this difficult period of her life, along with Gail Scott, a senior nurse attached to the maternity department of Bootle Hospital, and of course Sister Xavier had been involved from the start. She was unable to attend most meetings and the women would sometimes gather in her office and bring her up to date on the situation in relation to Doreen.

It was during Easter that there was a meeting at Violet's house at which Gail Scott spoke. 'I'll get in touch with whoever's responsible for Doreen's long-term care. It won't be all that long, anyroad, she'll be fifteen in July and in another year she'll be out of care — but the baby, bless him or her, is only just beginning.'

'We'll still be keeping an eye on the baby until we're sure it's in a good home,' the nurse said.

There was a murmur of approval at this.

The girls, Abby and Doreen, were upstairs learning how to use the portable typewriter that Edwin Power had bequeathed to Violet now that he would be moving back to Exeter and be provided with a new, more sophisticated model. Violet was intending to use it to start her business but the girls kept commandeering it.

'I think I'll buy some new bedding,' Sonia was saying more or less to herself. 'Pastel-coloured — pink! It's got to be pink — with flowers. Pink with flowers. Rosebuds would look nice.' She smiled to herself. 'And a couple of pretty nightdresses. Oh, and slippers. Just to help Doreen settle in and feel at home.'

A warning light clicked on in Violet's head.

191

Perhaps Sonia having the girl would be a bad idea: she could become too fond of her, find it hard to let her go when the time came for Doreen — and her baby — to leave. Then the warning light flickered and went out. She warned herself not to put a damper on things, not to be too cautious. Doreen had had precious little love and care in her short life so far. Why deny her the comfort and affection Sonia was ready to offer?

'Don't make the baby clothes pink or blue in case it's the wrong sex,' Shirley advised. 'Yellow or lavender would look nice and white is always acceptable, then it wouldn't matter if it's a boy or a girl. In fact, my mam loves making baby clothes. She'd be pleased to make a contribution.'

'A couple of little cardies would be nice,' Gale Swift put in.

'Cardies?' Sonia enquired.

'Cardigans, dear,' Violet told her. She might try to make some mittens and booties herself.

Just then Edwin Powell arrived to say he'd brought one of the twins' old pushchairs in the car. 'It's for Doreen's baby. We ended up with a single one and a double; it was more convenient that way. We're not likely to have more children,' he told them. 'Two is enough!' He looked at Violet, 'Can I leave it with you, Vi?'

'Of course.' She could store it in the bathroom for now, though it would be very much in the way.

'I'll take it with me back to Southport,' Sonia offered.

'What happens if Doreen doesn't want to go to Southport?' Shirley Rutherford asked.

Sonia looked taken aback. 'Where else will she go?'

'She'll love the idea of Southport, of course,' Violet insisted. 'It's healthy there with a really gear beach. It'll be like a holiday for her. It's better any day than staying with strangers who might not approve of fourteen-nearly-fifteen-year-old girls who get in the club. And she can't possibly stay here with me, where everybody knows her.'

Edwin said, 'She's lucky having so many people on her side — mind you, she deserves our support. Her family sound like they come from hell. Has her father been reported to the police for what he did to his daughter, which is a monstrous crime?' His face twisted in disgust.

The women all felt torn over their promise to Doreen that admitting who the baby's father was wouldn't send him back to jail. They knew Mr Flynn had a violent streak and so had decided they wouldn't do anything to put Doreen and the baby at risk while she was under Violet's roof. But perhaps, once Doreen was safely in Southport, they could talk again about how to make sure Mr Flynn never did something so wicked again. Violet wondered aloud whether Mrs Flynn was aware it was her husband who'd put her daughter in the club but their speculation was soon cut short when Abby and Doreen came downstairs.

'Would you like us to make some tea? Abby offered. 'And do we have any biscuits?'

'We've loads of tea and plenty of biscuits.' Violet got to her feet. 'Biscuits are in the tin. I was going to do some baking tomorrow — shortbread.'

'Are you allowed to bake on Good Friday?' Abby enquired.

'Since when have you not been allowed to bake on Good Friday?' Gail Scott raised her eyebrows. She was a tiny woman with jet-black hair who looked faintly Chinese.

'Well,' Abby said, 'Father Garrett used to look very cross when he came round on Sundays and found Violet in the kitchen — though I don't know how she was supposed to make the dinner without working.'

'As Father Garrett is no longer with us, and it's not Sunday tomorrow but Good Friday, I don't think there's any need to worry,' Gail Scott said.

In the kitchen, Violet nodded confirmation as she checked that the newly acquired mugs were clinically clean and spread them on the draining board. It had been a different priest in Mam's day: Father Gallagher, who'd arrive at the house each Sunday already as drunk as a lord and leave even drunker. Mam would chortle, knowing that at some point in the blessing of the small town of Bootle, the good father would break down altogether and have to be carried home.

★ ★ ★

Since the 'London incident', as those involved referred to it — it sounded like a film, Abby said

194

— Violet had longed to return for a proper visit. She resented the fact that it had taken something positively dangerous to happen for her to have seen the capital city for the first time at the age of fifty-seven. Despite the worry of the 'incident', London had both charmed and intrigued her. She longed to go again and experience the city in the daytime, when the shops were open and there were ordinary people about.

Will booked her a room in an inexpensive hotel close to Charles's flat.

'When are you going to find a proper job — a position, I think you'd call it rather than a job?' she asked him on her first day when they had lunch together in a restaurant called The Happy Egg.

He laughed. 'I can assure you, Vi, that working as a sales assistant in Selfridges store can definitely be classified as a proper job. A lot of men would be envious — ideal working conditions, decent salary, good prospects.' His brown eyes twinkled — he could not possibly be more handsome; she could not possibly be more proud, but she was shocked at his words.

'But these men, the envious ones, won't have an honours degree in nineteenth-century English literature,' she argued.

'I know, Vi, but I've plenty of time to find a better job.' He patted her knee. 'I'm only just twenty-one.'

'Even so . . . ' She shrugged, but didn't continue. He returned to work and she wandered, enchanted, along Oxford and Regent Streets, arriving at Piccadilly Circus, where she joined the tourists sitting on the steps around the statue of Eros. This was where Abby and Doreen and the other pupils had sat on the fateful day of the 'incident'. It looked very different in daylight. She stayed for a while, then got up to look for Shaftesbury Avenue and the places where the girls had been given alcohol. But the places were closed and they looked shabby and run down in the bright afternoon sunshine.

That night, Will took her to see Charles in his latest performance. He had moved on from *The Boyfriend*, and had what Will said was the junior lead in a musical called *Firefly*.

His name was on posters outside the theatre in Leicester Square where *Firefly* was being staged. 'Charles Rice' — third from the top. He had got rid of the 'Hanley' and his mother was extremely annoyed about it. Violet had seen little of him in all the years he and Will had been friends. He had never been to Bootle and she'd met him only rarely at the house in Southport. She was therefore surprised when he danced onto the stage in the theatre in London and was greeted with a round of enthusiastic applause from the audience as well as a few cheers. He seemed to be illuminated by a brighter spotlight than the other actors; his smile glittered and his voice had a warm, deep resonance all of its own. She had to concede he was even better looking than Will, who was merely quietly handsome, whereas Charles was like a lamp that was permanently switched on.

'He's fantastic,' she whispered to Will, sitting beside her.

'Isn't he just!' Will had glowed at the reception his friend had received, particularly from Violet.

★ ★ ★

Her second visit to London was in May. Since her last stay in the city, life in Liverpool had been more than usually eventful. A fit, healthy and heavily pregnant Doreen had moved in with Sonia in Southport and was delighted with the pretty nightwear and bedding. The pair got on well — the mother needed a child and the child a mother.

Edwin and Barbara Powell and their twins had left Liverpool for Exeter and a new chapter in their lives had begun. Violet felt highly emotional. It was due to Edwin that she'd been tracked down and presented with two wonderful children who had completely changed the course of her life. She regarded it as nothing but a miracle. Perhaps Mam was up in heaven keeping an eye out for her.

A sad thing, though inevitable, was that Jessie Arnett died. She was well into her eighties. Violet went alone on a coach to the funeral; Will had a job to go to, Abby a school. But the church was packed. Jessie had dozens of relatives and had been well loved in Netton, the village in which she'd been born. The funeral turned out to be not such a sad affair, but more a celebration of a life well lived and holding a special place in people's hearts.

During her second time in London, Violet saw the sights from the top deck of a bus along with other tourists, mainly from America. Just being around their accents brought Crocker to mind, but Vi pushed the thoughts away — she'd been the one to turn him down and she couldn't turn the clock back. She focused on the landmarks around her instead. Although it was fascinating to see the Houses of Parliament, Westminster Abbey and other old buildings and monuments that told the history of London, it was the crowds in Trafalgar Square and Hyde Park, the buskers, the speakers and the hecklers, and the shoppers that she found the most fascinating. She was angry with herself for leaving it so late to discover what the capital of the country into which she had been born was really like; angry to have spent so much time in bed when the other half of the population was dancing the nights away, probably in Liverpool as well as all the other major cities!

She had asked Will if she could see Charles in *Firefly* again because she had enjoyed it so much. 'I can't get it out of my mind,' she confessed. 'Mind you, I've never seen a West End show before.' They might not all be as good as Charles's.

Will said that wouldn't be a problem. 'I'll leave you a ticket at the stage door. I need to speak to Charles before he goes on tonight, but he'll be dead flattered when he knows you admired him enough to want to see him again.'

Violet laughed. 'He has hundreds, perhaps thousands, of admirers and I'm sure I'm the least important of them all.' Gosh, that sounded stilted, and as if she were a bit of a toady.

The West End was packed by the time the theatres were due to open, though there was plenty of entertainment in the streets outside for people who couldn't afford to buy a ticket. Will had told Violet to call at the theatre where someone called Pete, who could be found just inside the stage door, would have a ticket for her.

Violet walked slowly through the narrow streets, breathing in the atmosphere, the throbbing noise, the heady smell of foreign cigarettes and strange perfumes that assaulted her nostrils. She came to Charles's theatre. The stage door was down a dark, narrow passage that was oddly quiet compared with the street it led from. She collected her ticket from Pete, who was terribly old and sported a white beard.

'Be careful in there, dearie, if you're trying to get through to the front of house,' he warned. 'It's not all that well lit.'

For some reason the light bulbs backstage were blue, and Violet stumbled here and there. Pete called, wanting to know if she was all right. 'I'm fine,' she assured him. She could hear voices, men's voices, and made her way towards them. Why hadn't Will left her ticket outside at one of the booths where they were sold? Perhaps the staff were too busy to cope with such requests, she reasoned. An orchestra was tuning up and playing snatches of *Firefly*'s score, and somewhere quite far away women were screaming with laughter.

She was near enough to the voices now to recognise they belonged to Will and Charles, and could understand some of what they were saying. Charles was speaking. 'For fuck's sake, Will, why the hell won't you tell me the chappy's name you're going out with?' His beautiful voice was thick with anger. Violet froze. She had heard the word beginning with F before only in the workshop of Briggs' Motors and that was when the person who said it didn't know she was within hearing.

'So you can have the poor sod tracked down and beaten up or something?' Will said mildly.

'As if I would, my darling boy.' The anger had turned to humour.

'You threatened to have your agent beaten up when he invited me to lunch. He only wanted to arrange a birthday party for you.' Will sighed impatiently. 'The 'chappy', as you put it, who asked me out is a reporter and wants to grill me on what you were like at school. I've turned him down if you want to know.'

Violet turned and was hurrying out of the theatre. Pete was in deep conversation with a woman and hardly noticed her rush past. She dashed back round to the main street and presented the ticket at the box office and was let in with a smile from the woman in the kiosk. She made her way to her seat but Violet couldn't make sense of what had happened. Perhaps Will had intended she should overhear their conversation.

★ ★ ★

From that day on, she knew that life would never be the same again. The words Will and Charles

200

had just exchanged could only mean one thing: they were homosexuals, lovers, and the relationship had surely been formed when they were at school. Will hadn't looked for a job in keeping with having a first-class degree because he wanted to live with Charles.

Violet stayed in London for the five days as she had planned, though she longed to return to Liverpool the next day. She behaved naturally, not wanting Will to know she had discovered he wasn't just Charles's friend. There were other names for people like him and his 'friend': queers, queens, fairies, pansies, and names that were really offensive. Until then, Violet had never knowingly met a homosexual in her life.

On the night, in the theatre, after hearing Will and Charles's conversation, sitting in the balcony, she had felt herself go cold when she remembered that men who indulged in sex were regarded as criminals and could be sent to prison. It had happened to Oscar Wilde, the famous writer, though that was in the last century.

The journey home to Liverpool seemed to take twice as long as it actually did. The morning train was half empty and she found it hard not to burst into tears and cry her heart out the entire way. Was Will happy with his way of life? Did he not realise it was actually against the law, a criminal act? Did he not realise just how much she loved him and wanted him to be happy?

When Violet reached her house in Amber Street, it was empty, as expected. It was half-term and Abby was staying with Sonia and

Doreen in Southport. She sighed. She had meant to go tomorrow to see them, but she might not if she couldn't stop thinking about Will. She sighed again. They would be expecting her and would only worry if she didn't turn up. One of them would telephone and she would feel awful.

The other day, she had considered going more often to London, where everywhere seemed brighter than Liverpool, more alive, more exciting. But now she never wanted to go near the place again.

If only Madge were still her old self! There was nothing she would like more than to sit with Madge puffing away like a chimney with a ciggie stuck in her mouth, Violet sipping something cheap and alcoholic while they had a good old chinwag.

But those days were over. It felt as if everything had changed. Well, no, not everything. Violet picked up the telephone and dialled a number.

★　★　★

'I thought you might have a holiday yourself at half-term,' she said as she arrived in the nun's office a short while later.

'Half-term's when I get more work done than any other time.' Sister Xavier inhaled delicately on a black cigarette.

'Why isn't the smoke black?' Violet asked.

'Don't ask me, dear. I know nothing about science. Why does the sun look the same size as the moon when it's so much bigger?'

Violet thought it obvious. 'Because the sun's much further away than the moon,' she said.

'How clever you are, Vi,' the nun said, chuckling. 'So very practical. Now, why did you want to see me so urgently? What's wrong?'

'Please don't laugh. It's deadly serious.' Violet eyed the inch of whisky in a glass on the other side of Sister Xavier's desk.

The other woman noticed the look. 'Get yourself stuck into that,' she said, sliding the glass over to Violet.

'In a minute.' Whisky made her cough. She picked up the glass, then, aware she was doing things in the wrong order, lowered it again and began, 'I thought I'd missed my chance of having children.'

She started with describing the day, ten years ago, when Edwin Powell turned up to tell her about Will and Abby and finished with the moment when she'd overheard Will and Charles's conversation in the theatre. She reached for the whisky, drank it in a single go, and sank back in the chair, breathless. 'That's it!'

There was silence for a few minutes until the other woman said sympathetically, 'Oh dear, Violet. It's not the end of the world. Charles and Will are still the same people you've always known.'

'Yes, but what they're doing is a crime,' Violet cried. 'And, anyroad, it makes me sick to think about it.' Right then, it felt like the worst thing she'd ever known, worse than Mam and Dad dying, worse than getting that awful letter from

203

Briggs' Motors all those years ago. How could Will, such a nice, gentle little boy, turn out to be the way he had?

The nun said softly, 'One of the nicest, sweetest men I've ever known was homosexual — still is, always will be. He went to prison and wrote a book about it — I'll lend you my copy; he signed it for me personally.'

Violet regarded her with astonishment. 'But you're a nun, a bride of Christ,' she said a trifle portentously. 'How can you approve of someone with such low morals?'

'Who decided it was immoral for men to have sex with another man? The police? The Church? Members of Parliament?' The Sister shrugged her shoulders in an exaggerated fashion. 'Men and women can do it so why not men and men? Who are they harming?'

Violet shrugged back. She had no idea.

'Say if someone decided we weren't allowed to sneeze?' the other woman argued.

'But no one can help sneezing,' Violet argued back.

'I think that proves my point. You've come to the wrong person.' Sister Xavier got to her feet. 'I was on the London stage for more than half my adult life. Some of the sights I saw, the people I met, and the things that happened to me and to those I knew, would make you blanch.'

'Why did you become a nun?' Violet enquired. It was moving from one extreme to another, from a theatre to a convent.

'It was the only way I could think of avoiding a broken heart.'

'Was he married?'

Sister Xavier's eyes twinkled, but her smile was sad. 'No, Violet, but she was.'

When she got back to her own house, Abby was there. She hugged and kissed Violet warmly. 'I know I went away too, but we've all missed you badly,' she cried. 'None of us want you ever to go away again, but that would be really mean of us. But at least don't go away for ages. Please, Vi.'

Violet promptly burst into tears.

★ ★ ★

It was a lovely summer. Violet knew she should have felt like the happiest woman in the world when she and Sonia, Abby and Doreen strolled along the flat golden sands of Southport in their bare feet, water squeezing between their toes as they followed the receding tide. They spent all their coppers daily on the games machines on the pier, never once making a profit. Still, Violet couldn't escape an uneasy feeling — but worry was the price you paid for raising children, she told herself.

Violet reckoned Doreen was the happiest. This wasn't how she had expected her summer to be: living in a beautiful house, wearing pretty clothes, eating delicious food and being made a fuss of by two women and her best friend, Abby. Other summers she'd spent in Bootle and in all her life no one had thought to take her for a ride on the ferry or buy her an ice cream or push her on the swings in the park.

Of course, the most significant thing of all was that she was having a baby. If it was a girl, she swore she was going to call her Goldilocks, while a boy would be Jack and have a beanstalk.

10

Doreen's baby was a boy, Jack, though he arrived without the beanstalk. Because of the odd circumstances, he was born in Bootle Maternity Hospital, not Southport, where his young mother had lived throughout most of her pregnancy. Mrs Flynn turned up not long after the birth and looked bitterly through the window of the ward at her beautiful, healthy grandson, knowing he wouldn't be nearly so bonny had his mother been left under her own mother's care.

Sister Gail had alerted Violet to the imminent birth as soon as Doreen was admitted. Sonia Hanley-Rice and Shirley Rutherford were on their way; Sister Xavier had been advised.

After the nun arrived, Mrs Flynn, unnoticed, turned her back on the women who were so much more fortunate than herself and returned to her own unhappy home.

Doreen celebrated her fifteenth birthday and Jack thrived. Mother and son spent half their lives in Southport with Sonia Hanley-Rice and her husband, and the other half in Bootle with Violet and Abby. Will turned up with surprising frequency, always on a Sunday after buying a day return on the train. He had long conversations with the baby and was the first person for Jack to treat with a smile. Violet recalled Will helping Doreen with her schoolwork when she was a scruffy little girl. She was no beauty, but she had a nice face, lovely thick chestnut hair and a kind nature. Violet thought how strange life could be, full of surprises, not all of them pleasant, but some full of magic.

★ ★ ★

Violet returned from Mass on a Sunday early in March to find the telephone ringing. Although it wasn't possible, there seemed to be a touch of panic in the ring. She ran to answer. It was Sonia calling from Southport.

'Violet,' she said urgently, 'Jack's gone. He was in his pram in the back garden and someone took him! Doreen was about to take him for a walk. She seems to know who's responsible. She doesn't seem all that worried.'

'Did they take the pram too?'

'Yes. Shall — '

'I'll be there as soon as I can.' Violet slammed down the receiver, looked for her coat and realised she still had it on. She rushed out of the house, came to her senses and rushed back in, where she grabbed the phone again and telephoned the number Sister Xavier had given her 'for emergencies'. Despite being unable to imagine an emergency involving herself and the nun, which was perhaps foolish considering their history, Violet had written the number in her diary.

'Jack's been stolen,' she said hoarsely as soon as her call was answered. 'Is your brother around? I have to get to Southport.'

'No, Tom's in Paris, but he's not the only

person with a car. Hold on, I'll be with you in five minutes.'

Sister Xavier didn't exactly come zooming into Amber Street, but, shortly afterwards, a black Morris Minor screeched to a halt in front of Violet's house. The driver leaned across, opened the passenger door and said grittily, 'Get in, Vi.' Sister Xavier set off with a squeal of tyres.

'I nearly phoned for a taxi,' Violet said. 'I've never done that before. It's the sort of thing they do in the films. Like, 'Follow that car.''

'You don't sound very worried.' The car swerved round a corner. 'How old is Jack now?'

'He's five and a half months. I'm not exactly worried. It seems Doreen knows who's taken him,' Violet said.

'Then why haven't you called the police? I take it no one has.'

'It's never been discussed. We don't want the police involved,' Violet said sensibly. 'Once they are, we might lose control of the situation. Someone with a bit of authority might decide Doreen isn't fit enough or old enough to be in charge of such a young baby.'

'She's got Sonia and Sonia's husband,' the other woman suggested. 'And there's other people. There's us.'

'Some folk might say Sonia's depression makes her an unsuitable guardian, even though we know she dotes on that girl and the baby. And her husband is fond of a drink — or that's what they'd say if he was ever at home long enough between business trips,' Violet pointed out. 'We know these people and they wouldn't hurt a fly, but Doreen was raped by her own father. It's a perfect case for social workers and the police. They'd leap upon it if they had cause to intervene. Once they did, Jack would be taken away and given to strangers to look after, while they sorted all of us out.'

'Us?'

'You're part of it.'

They were outside Liverpool by now, speeding through Sea-forth, Waterloo, Formby, Birkdale, approaching Southport. Now and then the Irish Sea became visible, like churning grey cement. It looked hard and unbreakable.

The car stopped. Violet breathed a sigh of relief.

'Where to now?' her companion asked.

'Stop when you see a telephone box and I'll ring Sonia to see if Doreen's called to say Jack's been found,' Violet instructed.

'There's a box directly across the road,' the nun pointed out. 'Do you need coppers?

'No ta, I've got enough.' Violet opened the car door and ran to the phone box. Barely a minute later she ran back to the car and threw herself inside. 'Drive to the station,' she demanded. 'There's a snack bar and Doreen and Jack are there with the supposed kidnapper.'

Sister Xavier turned on the engine and set off. 'Who is it?' she asked. 'The kidnapper?'

'Jack's granny,' Violet told her. 'Mrs Flynn.'

★   ★   ★

The nun went off in the car to find somewhere to park and Violet went into the snack bar, which

210

was on the platform from where the trains ran to Liverpool. Doreen looked mightily relieved to see her. She was sitting at a table next to her mother, who had a firm hold on Jack's pram. The baby, who had been showered with love from the day of his birth, was smiling delightedly at the world.

'She follows me everywhere,' Doreen said in a low voice to Violet. 'I daren't leave Jack anywhere by himself again, not even Sonia's garden.' The room reminded Violet of the picture, *Brief Encounter*, with Trevor Howard and Celia Johnson, most of which was set in a station waiting room. She and Madge had gone to see it just after the war and both had cried their eyes out. It was so sad. Just thinking about it now made Violet want to cry. In the real world, this snack bar was very similar to the one in the film: there were half a dozen round wooden tables and an assortment of chairs that didn't match. The only other people present were an elderly couple with a pot of tea between them and a plate of assorted cakes.

Sister Xavier arrived and made the thumbs-up sign — she'd found somewhere to park the car. Mrs Flynn looked up and her face fell when she saw who it was.

She let go of the pram. 'I'd best be going,' she muttered. Violet had thought she might have put up a fight or even offered an apology — she had, after all, just stolen a baby — but she didn't say another word.

The sister spoke. 'Don't go,' she urged. 'Sit down and have a cup of tea with us.' Better Mrs

211

Flynn view them as friends rather than enemies. She waved at the young woman behind the counter. 'A pot of tea for four, please,' she called, 'and sandwiches, scones and jam.'

'Yes, madam.' The girl virtually curtsied. This was, after all, a real live nun in full regalia, in her snack bar. The tray, when it arrived, was laden with extra items such as mustard, pickle, jam and honey. There were paper doilies on the plates. The cutlery had been given an extra polish.

Mrs Flynn ate her fill of the food provided, then informed them again that she'd best be going. She stood.

'Stay!' Sister Xavier commanded. 'I'll give you a lift back to Bootle in the car. We haven't yet finished our food.'

'Thank you,' the woman whispered.' She meekly sat down and stared at her feet.

A train came in. Violet could see through the open doorway that it was for Liverpool. She nearly jumped out of her skin when Mrs Flynn shot through the door and jumped onto the train, leaving the pram with the baby in it behind.

★ ★ ★

'I thought it was much later,' Violet said to herself when she arrived back at her own house and saw it had only just gone five o'clock. She wished she'd eaten more of the food that Sister Xavier had bought in the station café — she really fancied a ham sarnie now, though hadn't then. There was plenty of bread in the larder, and a meat and potato pie, but she wouldn't normally buy ham unless she was expecting visitors.

She wondered whether to expect Abby home for tea. Or had she turned up in Southport after Violet had left? Life was very confusing at the moment. Who was sleeping where? There'd been no sign of Will today. Young people seemed to see no need to let people know where they were. They would just turn up and expect food and a bed that night. What was she going to do with the pie? Have it for tea tomorrow?

Violet poured a glass of milk and took two digestive biscuits from the packet. It had been Mam's favourite snack, though in those days the biscuits had been bought loose and in winter the milk had been warmed to dip them in. As soon as she'd finished eating, she left the house and walked around the corner to Pearl Street, where she knocked on Madge McGann's front door.

Madge opened the door almost immediately and her eyes widened when she saw who it was. 'Violet Duffy!' she said in surprise. 'I've been round your house a few times recently since Bob stopped keeping tabs on me, but didn't like letting meself in, not like in the old days!'

'I've done the same,' Violet assured her. 'Is Bob here?'

'No, he's playing billiards in the working men's club in Strand Road. What's brought you here, Violet? Come in, anyroad.' She winked. 'Or is it Bob you've come to see?'

'I've come to ask a question.' Violet grinned.

213

'And it's you I want to ask, not flippin' Bob.' She followed Madge towards the kitchen and stood in the doorway while her old friend put on the kettle and spread the crockery on a tray.

Madge looked at her curiously. 'What've you been up to today? It's ages since we had a cup of tea together.'

'I've been to Southport. There was a bit of an emergency. And didn't Bob discourage you from having visitors? That's the only reason I didn't come.'

'Bob doesn't give a damn what I do any more.' Madge shrugged.

'You must tell me about that in a minute. The reason I thought of you was the waiting room on Southport Station looked just like the one in *Brief Encounter*. We both really loved that film.'

'Is that why you went to Southport, just to look at the station? This is all very mystifying, Vi.'

'Oh, I'm sorry.' Violet was impatient with herself. 'To cut a long story short, Mrs Flynn stole her own grandson. He's a beautiful baby — Jack, he's called. I expect she looks at him and wonders why none of hers looked like that.'

Madge looked predictably shocked. She shook her head sadly. 'All she had to do was look after them proper. After all, they all had the same father.'

'Precisely,' Violet said indignantly. 'She follows Doreen around, wants to hold him — Jack, that is. She's a flamin' nuisance if the truth be told.' But she couldn't help but feel sorry for the woman. Imagine being married to a brute like Doreen's father.

She stayed with Madge for almost an hour and a half. Madge confessed that Bob was having a relationship with a woman from the canteen at work but Madge didn't give a toss. And she certainly wasn't going to mope around, locked in her own home waiting for him.

With *Brief Encounter* to remind them, they decided to go to the pictures in town during the coming week. 'To a matinee!' Violet said. 'We can have afternoon tea before we've seen it or afterwards. We'll decide on the day.'

★　★　★

Back home, there was a shout from upstairs when Violet opened the door.

'Vi, it's me. I'm upstairs.'

It was Abby. She came running down. 'Where is everyone?' She wore trousers. Violet didn't mind tailored trousers, but couldn't stand the sort made out of denim. It seemed all young women were wearing them. She nevertheless smiled. 'You look like you're going to play tennis,' she said. Abby's shoes were like plimsolls except they were white. She'd put whitener on them that morning and they almost sparkled.

It wasn't like Abby not to return Violet's smile. 'Where is Will?' she demanded irritably.

'He didn't turn up today, luv,' Violet told her. 'Perhaps he was busy with something.'

'But he promised he'd come,' Abby insisted.

Violet felt helpless. 'I'm afraid I've no idea why he hasn't.' She rolled her eyes and made a funny face. Abby made a face back and started to laugh.

'I'm sorry, Vi. I just really miss him. I rushed home from the club so we wouldn't lose a minute together.' The girl attended a senior Sunday club at the church where they had quizzes, danced and played games all with some connection to religion — even told jokes! One of the priests played the guitar. Abby loved it but always cut short her time there if she knew Will was coming to visit.

'I'll make you the best cup of tea in the world,' Abby said, holding her hands together meekly, 'in the hope you'll forgive me for being so horrible.'

'You haven't been horrible, Abby,' Violet said. 'Tell you what, though, make some tea, and I'll tell you what happened in Southport this morning.'

'You've been to Southport?'

'Yes. Actually it was more like midday than morning.'

Violet sank into a chair, suddenly aware of how exhausted she felt. She was blinking tiredly when Abby put a mug on the table beside her.

'Wake up and sit up, Vi,' she said, 'otherwise it might spill over you.'

Violet managed to stay awake long enough to drink the tea, but must have fallen asleep straight afterwards because all of a sudden she was being woken up by the sound of the telephone ringing in the parlour. Abby had disappeared, but not to answer the telephone because it was still ringing when she herself picked up the receiver.

'Hello,' she cried briskly. She didn't want whoever was at the other end of the line to know they'd just woken her up out of a very deep sleep. The person was in a call box and she heard the pennies being inserted.

'Did I wake you up, Vi? I'm sorry,' said Will.

'I wasn't asleep,' Violet lied.

'Really!' he said sarcastically.

She knew he didn't believe her and wondered why she found sleeping during the daytime so shameful that she had to lie about it. 'Where are you?' she asked and was amazed when he said, 'I'm in a phone box on Lime Street Station about to catch the London train.'

'Where have you been all day?' She was even more amazed at his reply.

'Southport,' he said surprisingly. 'The train from London was really late, so I thought I'd go there first and come back to Bootle later, but there wasn't time in the end, so I've come straight here to get the train back down south. I tried to call you several times to tell you this, but there was no one in. Anyroad, Doreen said you'd already been there — Southport, that is.'

'That's right,' she said. 'And I was at Madge's later.'

'Have you two made up?' He sounded amused. He'd found her relationship with Madge funny for some reason, though he knew nothing about the beating she'd had from Bob or her behaviour in The Butcher's.

'We never really fell out,' she said a little crisply. He was getting on her nerves. 'Out of interest, why did you go to Southport and not come here?' she asked, feeling rather hurt.

'Well, it's been a lovely day and I really fancied going for a walk along the promenade in Southport rather than be in Bootle. I must have just missed you — they told me what had happened with Doreen's mum.' He paused. 'And I think they needed a nice walk in the fresh air to take their mind off all the worry, though it was rather windy.' He sighed pleasurably. 'Jack loved it, though. The wind actually blew the pram off course a few times. It's a good job I was there. Doreen couldn't have kept control of it by herself.'

Abby had crept into the parlour. She sat on the settee and for some reason glared at Violet.

Will was feeding more coppers into the box. He didn't answer her last question. 'I called to ask you a favour, Vi.'

There wasn't anything in the world she wouldn't do for him. 'Go ahead,' she said.

'Can I come and live at home for a while?'

Her heart leapt at the idea. 'Of course, luv. When would this be?' She was pleased he still thought of Bootle as 'home'.

'Soon. I've given in my notice at Selfridges, I'm living in a dead cheap hotel in London and have been applying to schools all over the country for a job as a teacher.'

'Oh, Will, I'm so pleased!' She wished he were there in the flesh so she could give him a hug. 'What's happening with Charles?' She felt obliged to ask. If she didn't talk about him, Will might realise it was embarrassment that prevented her from mentioning his name.

'Charles is looking for a new place to live,' Will told her. 'He needs somewhere bigger so he can hold parties more in fitting with his status as a successful actor.'

Violet couldn't help but wonder if there was more to it than that — Will didn't sound heartbroken, but what would she do if she questioned him further and he told her the truth? She wouldn't know what to say. Sister Xavier's words had stuck with her, and while she loved Will regardless of the company he kept, she still didn't have the words to talk about it.

They said goodbye and rang off. Violet looked at Abby and sighed happily. 'He'll be home in a few days. He's not sure for how long.'

Abby said, 'I heard what he was saying.'

Violet got to her feet. 'I'll make some more tea. Oh, and did you hear he's given up the job in that posh shop? He's looking for something more appropriate for a person with a degree from a first-class university.'

Abby trailed after her into the kitchen. 'I don't understand,' she said. 'Did he go to Southport instead of coming here and end up going for a walk with Doreen and Jack?'

'Well, yes.' Violet nodded. She looked curiously at the girl, who sounded angry. 'Does that bother you, luv?'

Abby was clearly still in a bad mood. 'Yes, it does. He promised to come here, to Bootle; this is his home, not Southport. He's being awfully rude.'

'Rude!' Violet laughed. 'He's twenty-two, Abby, well old enough to make up his own mind

219

where he spends his Sundays. Besides which, isn't he coaching Doreen to take an O-level? Remember, he used to help with her schoolwork when she was little.'

'Don't we come first? We're his family.'

'No, girl.' Violet shook her head. 'It's a really kind thing that he's doing. I expect he took for granted we'd approve. And after all the drama of Mrs Flynn snatching Jack, they deserved a nice walk and a bit of sunshine.'

There was silence for a while. Violet was a bit shocked at Abby's attitude. Then more than a bit when she burst out with, 'I hate that Doreen.'

Violet was astounded by her words. 'But you've always been such good friends! You used to bring her home with you in your very first year at school.'

'Well I wish I bloody hadn't.'

'Abby!' Violet wanted to cry. They'd had arguments before, usually about being allowed to go and see a film or watch a programme on television, which sometimes got quite heated, but never this heated. Nobody had sworn before, and certainly not Abby.

Abby flushed and looked embarrassed. 'I'm sorry,' she muttered. 'And I didn't mean to swear.'

'I didn't know you could swear,' Violet said dryly. She wondered why she was in the kitchen and recalled it was with the intention of making tea. Hadn't Abby had promised to make some? At that moment she really felt like a cup and remembered Abby had woken her with a drink when Will telephoned. Gosh, she marvelled, that was only minutes ago, yet felt like ages. She felt dreadfully confused and her head was beginning to ache.

Years later, looking back, Violet decided that was the night when everything changed. She and the children were no longer a close, tightly knit family, but were breaking apart. They were growing up. Will seemed more concerned with Doreen than with Abby. She was cross with him in a way she'd never been before. Violet was worried about taking sides. She supposed this was the way with most families. She'd just have to get used to it, that was all.

⋆ ⋆ ⋆

Much later the same night, Violet woke and found Abby sitting cross-legged at the foot of her bed.

'You're ever so kind, Vi,' she said quietly. 'I'm sorry I swore.'

Violet half sat up. 'It's all right, Abby. It wasn't a very bad swearword, was it? There's worse.'

Abby ignored the question. 'I want to tell you something,' she said.

'What, luv?' Violet asked encouragingly when the girl seemed disinclined to continue.

'When we came to live here, I loved Will so much it really hurt — it literally hurt my heart.' She placed her hand on her chest in the place that she assumed her heart was. She sighed so deeply that the bed actually creaked.

'Oh, Abby.' Violet leaned across and lightly squeezed the girl's shoulders. You both truly loved each other. He looked after you and you depended on him for everything. It was wonderful seeing you together.' It was also just a little bit sad that closeness had faded recently.

Abby smiled rather wistfully. 'I'm so glad we ended up living with you, Vi. We couldn't have wished for anyone nicer. You more than made up for all that had happened before.'

Violet couldn't think of what to say, but it seemed Abby hadn't finished. 'I used to think that when we grew up, Will and I would get married.'

'You couldn't possibly, luv.' Violet froze. 'You're brother and sister — well, half-brother and -sister. It's called incest and it's a sin and a crime. Mr Flynn committed it when he raped Doreen, his daughter.'

'Why is it against the law?' Abby asked bluntly. 'I can understand with Mr Flynn, but not me and Will, even if we were proper brother and sister.'

'You and Will share the same blood group, that's why. You both had the same mother,' Violet said. 'As for what Mr Flynn did, it's despicable — your parents are meant to love and care for you, not bring you hurt and shame.' She knew birth defects could be passed on if children were the result of an incestuous relationship — privately, she'd fretted about Doreen's baby until the day he was born, healthy and happy. But she didn't want to worry Abby with that. 'I can never replace your mother, but I think of you and Will as my children — I hope you know that. We may not be a big family — heaven knows, you two

222

have lost so much in that way — but we're family nonetheless, and that is a special thing, a truly special thing.'

Abby had a faraway look in her eye and seemed to be deep in thought. The girl must be exhausted.

'Why don't you go back to bed, Abby?' Violet lay down herself. 'You've got school tomorrow — I'll take meself to Southport and ask Sonia if anything interesting happened with Will yesterday afternoon.'

Abby very slowly uncrossed her legs and climbed off the bed, so slowly that she could have been an old, old woman. 'Night, Vi,' she said tiredly.

'Goodnight, luv, hope the bugs don't bite.'

Abby's feet could be heard making their way along the landing to her bedroom, still slowly.

Next morning, her bed was empty. She had gone and not a single solitary soul knew where.

11

The train had reached its destination; it was time to get off. Abby's legs had gone numb after sitting still for so long. The train had just dawdled along. She assumed it took its time so as not to arrive in London until the city had woken up and the buses and the underground trains were running.

She dragged her suitcase off the rack. It wasn't her suitcase, but belonged to the whole family, until somebody, almost certainly Charles, had given Will a real leather one for his twenty-first, so now the old case belonged only to Vi and Abby.

Abby caught her breath. What would Vi do if she suddenly needed to go somewhere urgent and the family suitcase couldn't be found? She would turn the house upside down, empty the cupboard under the stairs, look beneath the beds. But she wouldn't find it. Perhaps at some point it would occur to her that Abby had taken it. And what would happen then?

Her eyes filled with tears; they poured down her cheeks. She felt awful. She knew it wasn't really the suitcase she was crying about. She'd been gone only a few hours and she felt terrible already. But she knew she had to hold her nerve.

She got off the train. A young man helped with the suitcase and slapped something on the side, a sticker of some sort. She handed her ticket to the collector at the barrier, emerging onto the mainly empty concourse, wondering what to do next. First of all, she had a good look around in case there was any sign of Will, possibly sitting on a bench somewhere. After all, it was only a matter of hours since he had travelled to London on an earlier train. She wasn't surprised that Will was nowhere to be seen. She gave up looking for him and more sensibly headed for the restaurant, a huge, high-ceilinged room with just five customers, and ordered a pot of tea, two rounds of toast and jam off a bright-eyed waitress with ringlets. She wore a too-big white apron and a white cap.

'Phew!' she muttered after she'd sat down and was waiting eagerly for the food.

She hadn't done any planning on the train. She was waiting until her feet were on the London concrete before she decided what to do next. Now her feet were in the proper place and she had to make up her mind whether to leave the precious suitcase in Left Luggage or book into a hotel and leave it there. Or should she turn round and go home?

'Hello, dear.' A woman sat next to her at the table. 'You're a stranger to London, aren't you? Have you got somewhere to stay, luv?' She was a woman of about fifty wearing too much makeup and a revolting fur coat that looked as if it had been made out of half a dozen different animals, mainly cats, though a curly dog could well have been involved. 'You look lost,' she remarked, patting Abby's hand. Her gloves badly needed mending. 'I know a place where you can stay, dear. It's safe, perfect for a young woman who's in London on her own.'

Abby hadn't spoken so far, but recalled that when she'd come to London with the school, the girls in particular had been lectured by one of the teachers about having anything to do with strangers if they offered help. In other words, nothing.

'Lord knows where you'd end up,' whoever it was had said ghoulishly. 'A brothel, perhaps, or enmeshed in the slave trade.'

The girls had giggled at the mere idea — and the warning hadn't stopped Abby and Doreen going into that club with the man outside in the sequinned coat. But now, all alone, the words came back to her.

Her food had arrived on a Bakelite tray laden with a metal teapot, milk jug, two rounds of crusty toast and tiny bowls, one of sugar, one of jam. Her mouth watered.

Abby realised how hungry she was. She'd had nothing to eat since Sunday School the day before. The waitress leaned over the table with the tray. Her eyes caught Abby's and she ever so slightly shook her head.

That was enough for Abby, who'd had no intention of accepting the odd woman's invitation anyway. 'I'm staying with friends,' she announced. 'I'll be getting a taxi there when I've finished my breakfast.'

The woman shrugged and went away.

'Thank you,' Abby said to the waitress, who looked no older than herself, yet was hard at work in a restaurant when it was barely eight o'clock in the morning — Monday morning, Abby recalled. She wondered again if Violet had woken yet and discovered her gone.

She thanked the waitress for her intervention. 'At school, we were warned about people who hung around stations pretending to help young girls when it was actually a trap.'

'That's all right, darlin'. Eat your breakfast now before it goes cold. You've had a long journey, all the way from Liverpool.' The girl returned to her post behind the counter. She must have noticed the address on the label of the suitcase.

Where would she have ended up had she gone with the woman? Abby wondered. Though what she should be concentrating on was where should she go now? She should really be at college, Morgan & Hemmings Commercial College in Bold Street, Liverpool, being taught how to type at sixty words per minute and take shorthand at a hundred and twenty. Abby hadn't been keen, but, as Violet explained, being able to type and take shorthand was an invaluable skill to have. 'It can be useful in all sorts of trades,' she pointed out, so Abby had agreed. Anyroad, it was better than working in a shop or a factory, which was all she was fit for now. But, in truth, it didn't bother her that she was missing college for however long it turned out to be.

Abby had kept a diary since she was six. It was meant to be for the year 1955, though she didn't get it until two years later. Someone had given it to Vi for Christmas, but she'd never used it and it had lain in one of the sideboard drawers for another year before Vi had noticed it and decided to throw it away.

'Though it seems such a shame — I hardly used it.' She flicked through the pages, which were nearly all empty.

Abby was attracted by its smallness and the way the edges of the pages were gold and looked really pretty, like a satin ribbon, when they were closed. 'Can I have it, please, Vi?'

'Or course, pet.'

So it became Abby's diary. From then on, there was always a diary in Abby's Christmas stocking and, although she filled it in religiously every day with events that had happened, these diaries were never as important as the first one. It contained every single bit of information about her.

She took it out of her handbag and opened it at the month of May — the month and the letter M had no significance — it was merely the page she'd reached when she included the personal information about herself, Abigail Holmes. There was her grandmother's address in Exeter, which was the same as the only details she had for the father she'd never met. 'Mrs Catherine Holmes,' Abby had written in her childish scrawl when she was seven, '19 Birch Road, Exeter'. This was whom she was going to see: her grandmother.

She had no warm feelings for Mrs Catherine Holmes, who sent her the broken jewellery, old gloves and discarded library books for presents. She knew only that she wanted to separate her from Will. Violet clearly didn't like the woman and refused to say much about her. But it was something that Violet had said the night before that brought together everything she'd been thinking for the last few months. She didn't have much family and soon she'd have even less. Will was growing up and moving on, and her grandmother must be getting on in years, too. Soon she'd have no one to tell her stories about her mother or father.

She often wondered how her mam coped when her dad fell ill. Then, not long after losing him, Mam herself had died. They were a doomed family. Mam had been widowed years before when Will's dad had been killed in an accident. That meant Mam had been twice widowed. Abby remembered someone saying that. Her name was Mary, she knew that much, but everything else was confusing. It had taken her a long time even to understand how her mam and Violet were related.

So much death! Abby shuddered. Was she also destined to die young?

Edwin Powell had given Abby and Will money on their birthdays and at Christmas. It was to do with the charity, St Jude's something, a legal obligation. Abby had spent little and had nearly fifteen pounds saved. It was in an inside pocket of her suitcase.

She was pouring the last dregs of her tea into the cup when the young waitress reappeared. She no longer wore a pinny and cap, but a navy gabardine mac and a velour hat with a striped band and a badge at the front. She must go to secondary school. She had green eyes and her ringlets were a lovely red. She was extraordinarily thin, and there was a brown leather satchel over her shoulder.

'Oh, hello,' Abby said, surprised. Are you going to school?'

'Yes,' the girl grimaced. 'I'll be back about five, when this place gets crowded again with people going home. They're called commuters.'

'Really?' Abby had never heard the word before.

'Where are you off to now?' the girl asked.

There and then, Abby made up her mind to stay in London overnight and carry on with her journey to Exeter tomorrow. She said, 'I'm going to stay in London, just for now. Do you know where there's a cheap hotel?'

'London's made up of hotels of all different prices and sizes,' she was told. 'If you walk out of here, turn right, you'll find a road which has nothing in it except hotels — there was a time when they were all posh houses. They have the tariff in the window.'

Abby had no idea what a tariff was but took a guess it was list of the hotel's charges. It turned out she was right.

Outside, she left the station, found the road the waitress had described, and knocked on the door of one of the first she came to. It was called Jasmine and the interior was painted mainly lavender with light-flowered wallpaper. It was bright and cheerful, as well as being scrupulously clean and smelling gloriously, presumably of jasmine. She booked a room right away and was shown upstairs.

Abby put the suitcase on the bed and was about to leave when she noticed the sticker. It was paper and looked like a badge. She tried to remove it with her fingernail, but it wouldn't budge — it needed to be done with hot water and a sponge. She decided to do it that night and set off to explore the city of London, not before clicking the case open and taking half the money out.

Although she didn't know it, she mainly followed the route that Violet had taken, along the main streets: Piccadilly Circus, Shaftesbury Avenue, Leicester Square. She passed a theatre where a show called *Firefly* was on and noticed Charles Rice was a member of the cast — she gasped out loud at this sudden reminder of Liverpool. It was Charles Hanley-Rice, Will's friend; he'd dropped the first part of his double-barrelled surname — Will had mentioned it. She hadn't realised he was this famous.

She studied the photographs outside. Charles looked much older than she remembered, but, then, she'd not seen all that much of him.

A man came and stood beside her and also looked at the photos. 'He's my brother's friend,' Abby said shyly, pointing to Charles.

The man looked down at her, an unpleasant expression on his face. 'I'd keep that information under my hat, if I were you,' he sneered, and walked away.

'But I'm not wearing a hat,' Abby said to the empty air. She shrugged, having not the slightest idea what he was talking about.

Since breakfast, Abby, conscious of her limited

supply of funds and the uncertainty of her future, had indulged in only a single cup of tea and a scone, and consequently was starving. She went to the pictures and saw *The Best of Everything* with Louis Jourdan, on whom she had a serious crush that helped dull her appetite.

At half past five, she walked along Tottenham Court Road in the direction of Euston Station and the Jasmine Hotel, wondering what there was for dinner, hoping there would be roast potatoes. She didn't mind what they were served up with. Vi made really gear potatoes. It was because she boiled them first so they were lovely and soft inside and crisp outside. Other people. Abby knew roasted them without boiling them first and they weren't nearly so nice.

'Oh!' Abby clapped her hand over her mouth. She tried to imagine what Vi was doing now. She visualised her sitting, alone, by the kitchen table, crying her eyes out because Abby had left home, secretly, without saying a word. She would be wondering why.

Why?

Why had she left home? She admitted to herself that it wasn't just about going to see who her grandmother really was. It was also something to do with Sunday and Will not coming to see them, but going to see Doreen in Southport instead. Abby had this silly idea in her head that by leaving Liverpool she was punishing Will, but in fact she was punishing herself — and Violet. But, if she'd left a note telling Vi where she was going, she knew she'd have been straight on the phone and Will would have met her at

Euston and put her on the first train back before she could go anywhere, find anything out about her family or even just show them all that *she* was grown up, too now.

And Vi wouldn't be crying alone in the kitchen because she had loads of friends and there could be half a dozen people comforting her right now, saying how ungrateful Abby was. 'Young people today, they don't appreciate not having bombs dropped on them every night or being forced to live in concentration camps or being tortured by the Nazis on a daily basis.'

She had a horrible feeling she'd done the stupidest thing in the world. She tried to think of an easy way of undoing it, but she knew she couldn't go home, not yet. If she went back now, she'd never find out about her family.

'Hello, hello. I don't know your name. Slow down a minute. I'll soon catch up.'

Abby turned. The young waitress from the station restaurant was running after her. 'You work evenings too?' Abby asked when she arrived, panting for breath.

'I told you I did this morning, didn't I? It's only between half-five and seven. It's for when the commuters go home and have a cup of tea or coffee on their way. Some of them hang around in the bar till quite late, but I'm not allowed to work on licensed premises till I'm eighteen. I'm only sixteen now.'

'I'm fifteen,' Abby said. 'What's your name? I'm Abigail, but everyone calls me Abby.'

'Abigail's a lovely name.' To Abby's surprise, the girl linked her arm. 'I'm Reggie and I'm sixteen. Oh, I know that sounds awful, 'Reggie', I mean, but my full name is Regina — my ma's a big fan of the Queen. It's put me off royalty for ever.'

'I'm not surprised.' Abby shuddered. They had arrived at Euston Station entrance, where she stopped. 'I'm booked into a hotel over there,' she told Reggie — it certainly was an odd name. 'And they serve dinner at six.' She remembered there'd been a pile of magazines in the lounge; she'd go to bed really early and take some with her to read.

Being unable to read her thoughts, Reggie said, 'Tell you what, after you've had your dinner, come along to the restaurant. You can read there and I'll give you loads of tea and lemonade. My dad's best mate is the manager, so no one will mind. Oh, and Daphne might be there by now — you can talk to her.'

'Who's Daphne?'

'My friend from school. She's in a different class to me. We have to decide what to do tonight. You can come with us if you want.'

Abby forgot she'd planned to go to bed early. 'I'll see you later,' she promised.

★ ★ ★

There were four couples in the dining room of the Jasmine and two single men. No one spoke to Abby and she reckoned she would have ended up crying her eyes out had she gone to bed by herself with half a dozen magazines. The meal consisted of fish in batter and chips

234

followed by sticky toffee pudding and custard. It was all quite delicious and she felt rather pleased with herself when she left the hotel and ran all the way to Euston Station and into the restaurant.

Daphne turned out to be small, dainty and incredibly clever. 'She wants to be a physicist,' Reggie said when she introduced them. Abby had to confess she didn't know what a physicist was.

'They design bombs,' Reggie went on, 'atom bombs and hydrogen bombs that can blow up entire cities.'

Daphne rolled her gentle blue eyes, which made her look as if she wouldn't hurt a butterfly. She launched into what she said was a description of physics. 'It combines electromagnetism, as well as thermomagnetics and calculus, but some people thought it involved quantum philosophy. Physics is also a force for incredible good as well as bad, such as medical equipment.' She showed Abby a chart of physical phenomena in a book she was clutching. 'See,' she said as if the chart explained everything.

'Oh, yes,' Abby said faintly.

Reggie laughed. 'She didn't understand a word you said, Daph.' She went to serve someone. In the meantime, Daphne made notes from another dusty-looking book that was full of words, figures and diagrams that didn't make any sense at all to Abby, who sat watching.

The older girls had a discussion about where they would go at half-seven when Reggie's hours of duty were over. A badly printed magazine called *Scorn* was produced, which had a 'What's On' column.

'There's a lecture on the relationship between Cuba and the United States,' Reggie pointed out, 'and a poetry reading in that coffee bar with a waterfall opposite Liverpool Street Station.'

Daphne looked over her shoulder. 'That silent film about the Russian Revolution is on in Camden. I've always wanted to see it.' She put the magazine on the table in front of Abby. 'What do you fancy, Ab? I expect you'll be interested in the lecture about Cuba.'

A dazed Abby looked at the list. There were more lectures, more poetry readings, art exhibitions, guitar concerts. 'I quite fancy a poetry reading,' she lied. What made Reggie and Daphne think she'd be interested in this sort of stuff? Was this what teenagers in London did?

Reggie consulted *Scorn* and said there would be a good poetry reading in a coffee bar called Rhyme and Reason by Marble Arch that night at eight o'clock. They could go straight away, have a coffee, and hopefully bagsy some really good seats.

★　★　★

It was like being in a submarine. The coffee shop was deep underground, badly lit, much too hot, and smelled horrible. And the poetry didn't make sense. The poet was a Scot with a deep, echoing voice and a wonderful accent, rolling his *R*s like an engine that was just about to start. It did something to Abby's brain.

After he'd finished he ambled over to the girls, looming over Abby. He leaned in and whispered, 'Will yer sleep with me tonight, darlin'?'

'Yes, oh, yes,' Abby replied, having not understood a word.

'Of course, she won't, you idiot.' Reggie pushed him away. 'She's under age, for one thing, and she doesn't fancy you a bit.'

'How would you know, darlin'?' the poet — his name was Douglas, apparently — asked good-humouredly. He wore a tartan kilt, and a tattered T-shirt. His bare arms were covered with flowered tattoos.

'That she's under age?' Reggie asked.

'No, that she doesn't fancy me.'

'There's not a woman in this room who fancies you.'

'If any one of 'em would like to peep under me kilt a mo, darlin', they'd fancy me something rotten.'

Reggie shrieked and pushed him away. Abby blushed as she realised what they'd been talking about. Reggie pulled her and Daphne closer and shouted. 'We'll have to go soon. If I'm not home by eleven, me dad'll have a fit.'

As they were leaving, she said, 'He's all right, really, is Douglas. He was with us last Easter on the Ban the Bomb march from Alverston to London. His mum and dad were killed during the war when Hitler bombed Glasgow. Did you have a march in Liverpool, Abby?'

'I think so.' Abby's brain scrambled for an answer. 'Is that the one when some old man was sent to prison?'

'They were climbing the stairs, the three girls, when Abby spoke. Reggie and Daphne stopped and stared at her with an expression of horror on their faces. 'Some old man!' Reggie gasped.

Abby badly wanted to cry. 'What have I done wrong?'

Reggie found her voice, a voice taut with passion. 'You have just called one of the most brilliant men who ever lived, a positive giant amongst men, 'some old man'. We're talking about Bertrand Russell, Abby. Have you never heard of him?'

'No,' Abby stuttered. 'Well, yes. He was on that march, last year. I saw a bit of it on the telly. I'd forgotten his name.'

'He was sent to prison after that, six months, for breach of the peace. He was eighty-nine and refused to promise he wouldn't do the same thing again.'

'Why have you got a CND badge on your suitcase if you don't know this already?' Reggie demanded. 'It made me think you were one of us.'

So far, Daphne hadn't said a word, though she looked equally shocked. She spoke now. 'Hold on a minute, Reg. People aren't born knowing all there is to know about the Campaign for Nuclear Disarmament. There was a time when neither of us had heard of it.' She looked kindly at Abby. 'Though why do you have their badge on your suitcase?'

'Someone stuck it there on the station this morning. I tried to scrape it off later, but it wouldn't move. If I'm not allowed it, I'll get it off when I get back to the hotel,' she promised, though now she actively wanted to be a member. She really liked Reggie and Daphne and preferred to be like them rather than herself. And was it really only this morning the CND badge was stuck on her suitcase? One day in London had felt like a lifetime.

'No, don't.' Reggie put her hand on Abby's arm. 'Leave it there in honour of Bertrand Russell. You're a nice person, Ab. I'm sure I'm not wrong in regarding you as one of us. How long are you staying in London? I mean, we don't even know what you're doing here. Shall we have another coffee somewhere and you can tell us?'

'Your dad'll kill you, Reg, if you're really late home,' Daphne warned.

Reggie shrugged. 'Me dad can take a running jump,' she said. 'We've got to take Abby to her hotel, we can't leave her to find her own way back. If we start walking in that direction, we're bound to pass a place where we can have coffee and a talk.' She began to march and the other two girls followed meekly.

★   ★   ★

An hour later, Abby was delivered to the door of her hotel by her new friends, who both now knew more or less everything about her — and Abby knew rather a lot about them. She pressed the bell on the door to the Jasmine while Reggie and Daphne waited nearby to make sure she got safely indoors.

The door was opened by an extremely bad-tempered-looking man who wore striped pyjamas and a dressing gown. He had a distressing squint. At least it distressed Abby. 'Are you Miss Holmes?' he snapped.

'Yes, I am,' Abby agreed.

'Then you should be aware that the door to this hotel is locked at ten thirty. Had I not been told how young you were, then I would not have opened it.'

Abby frowned. 'Are you allowed to do that?'

'It's a rule that applies to this hotel, which is owned by myself and my good wife. Kindly step inside, Miss Holmes, so I can return to bed myself.'

'Thank you.' Abby waved to her friends, who waved back. Reggie shouted, 'See you in the morning.'

She was halfway up the stairs when Abby remembered something. She went back to the owner who was relocking the door. 'I forgot, but I'd like to book for another night, please.'

The man turned on her, his eyes glittering with anger. 'Well, you can't,' he spat. 'My wife told me your suitcase bears a Ban the Bomb badge, the sign of that disgusting antiwar organisation led by that evil jailbird Bertrand Russell. We want you out of here first thing tomorrow. This hotel is not for your sort.'

Abby gasped. 'You have just called one of the most brilliant men who ever lived, a giant among men, evil. You ought to be ashamed of yourself.' If it hadn't been so late, she'd have looked for another hotel there and then.

12

She could see Will, far away across the shop floor, assisting a man trying on a sports coat. It was silly but, from the moment she'd met Reggie, she'd actually forgotten Will was still in London. When he'd telephoned on Sunday, she'd overheard him telling Vi that he was staying in London to work out his notice, then coming back to Bootle to look for a different job — 'more in line with his education', Vi had said in a fake posh voice. She was thrilled. Abby should have been thrilled, too; no doubt Doreen would be thrilled when she found out.

Will's customer was buying the sports coat. Will was preparing the bill, the customer was writing a cheque. They shook hands. Abby was wondering whether to approach him when Will looked across and saw her. She waved and he walked quickly towards her. She expected a warm hug, but instead he grabbed her arm and said angrily, 'What on earth are you playing at, Abby? Vi is distraught, you just disappearing like that. How could you be so cruel and hurtful? Go and find a telephone box this minute and ring and tell her you're all right. I'll give you some coins.'

Abby pulled her arm away. 'I'll do no such thing. I've become a different person since I left Liverpool. I've joined the Campaign for Nuclear Disarmament and made new friends; one is a

241

physicist. Last night a grown-up man, a poet, asked if I would sleep with him.'

'What?' Will looked as if he didn't know whether to laugh or cry. 'Abby, love, there was no need to go all the way to London for that to happen.'

'Well, I've never met a poet in Liverpool.'

'Huh! I've written a few poems myself before now. Not that I go about asking young girls to sleep with me.'

Abby didn't know what to say to that. She noticed a man on the far side of the shop trying to attract Will's attention and felt obliged to point this out.

'I've got to go. I've given in my notice, but I might need a reference from this place one of these days and don't want to blot my copybook at this late stage. Look.' He grabbed Abby's arm again, but this time not so painfully. 'Let's have lunch together. There's a restaurant here on the top floor. We'll meet there at twelve o'clock. Don't be late. I planned on leaving early today. OK, Ab?'

She nodded. 'OK.' She watched him walk away, looking remarkably handsome in his black trousers and brilliant white shirt. It was rare she saw him wear a tie or comb his dark hair so neatly. She uttered a sigh so deep and thorough that it was painful. She had no intention of meeting him for lunch. She knew it would be easy for him to talk her into going back to Liverpool and Vi. Slowly, sadly, she went down the stairs, knowing their lives seemed to be taking them in different directions, wondering when she would see Will again.

★   ★   ★

That morning, Abby had placed her suitcase in the Left Luggage office on Euston Station, transferring the remainder of her money into her bag. She had left Liverpool with the intention of finding out about her real mother's family. She knew a little about her grandmother, but she may have aunts and uncles, even cousins her own age. It wasn't that she wanted to live with them, just meet them. They could stay in touch, send each other Christmas cards.

But the plan had been put on hold in London. She really liked this sort of life, like last night, wandering the streets at nearly midnight looking for a place to have coffee. Today, Reggie had said she was going to arrange her membership of the Campaign for Nuclear Disarmament and Abby would have a proper badge of her own.

She was sitting on a bench in a little square full of trees not far from Selfridges. People were eating sandwiches and drinking coffee bought from a stall in the corner. She thought about Will, turning up at the restaurant and not finding her there. He'd be really angry. She wondered if he would still be waiting if she went back to Selfridges and the restaurant on the fourth floor. Should she do that, or book a different hotel in London and see Reggie and Daphne tonight, or go to Exeter right now?

It frightened her that she couldn't make up her mind, that she seemed to have lost control of her brain — of her life, almost. Another thing she could do would be to go back to Liverpool, where Vi would welcome her with open arms, but she was too ashamed. She felt she shouldn't go back until she'd achieved something, such as having got a marvellous job and earning lots of money. Something to show she wasn't just the baby of the family. Mind you, that might take weeks or months, rather than a couple of days.

Abby bought coffee and a meat pie from the stall in the square. By the time she finished them, she vowed she would have made up her mind.

Half an hour later, she was entering Selfridges and waiting where she had waited earlier and seen Will attending to a customer. It was much too late for lunch, but she wanted to apologise for not going — Will was already fed up with her and she didn't want to make it worse. She'd decided that she had to prove to herself she could stand up to his demand that she return home. Nothing would stop her finding her family, she was determined. But, all the same, she didn't want to leave things with Will on a sour note. And, even if she was too embarrassed to go home, he could at least tell Vi that she was fine. She rehearsed a little speech in her head that she'd come up with while she'd eaten her lunch.

There was different customer there now as well as a different shop assistant. She waited a while for Will to appear, but there was no sign. After a while, she went over to the one there now and asked if she could see William Stein.

'Ah!' The man was as young as Will and

almost as handsome. He smiled at her in a friendly manner. 'I'm afraid he no longer works here, madam.'

'But he was here this morning,' Abby argued. 'Please don't call me madam, I'm his sister.'

'That's because he still worked here this morning, but he doesn't work here this afternoon. I imagine you know he's going back to Liverpool in search of better things.' The man sighed regretfully. 'He was a nice chap, I shall miss him.'

Abby considered things. 'But it's Tuesday. People don't leave work on a Tuesday.'

'In Selfridges, we are employed on a monthly basis,' she was told. 'Mr Stein was due to leave at the end of April.'

'But it's not the end of April,' she argued. 'It's only about the twenty-fifth or -sixth.' She knew she was being excessively irritating.

'Mr Stein had a few days' holiday pay due and wasn't obliged to work until the very end of the month.' His lips twisted into an enticing smile. 'Can I be of assistance, Will's sister? I feel confident that, whatever you wanted of Mr Stein, I would be willing and able to supply myself. My name is Leonard Butler.'

'It's kind of you, Mr Butler, but no thanks.' She turned to leave and couldn't resist saying invitingly, 'Perhaps another time?' After all, she wasn't likely to see him again.

He winked. 'Any time would suit me, Will's sister.'

Will's departure seemed like a sign. An hour later, she had caught an underground train to

Paddington Station and was waiting for the train
to Exeter.

★   ★   ★

The countryside became prettier the further
south she travelled. There really were rolling hills
and little forests with picturesque villages dotted
here and there. She arrived at Exeter St David's
Station where she asked what number bus she
should catch for Birch Road.

It was an attractive city altogether, she
thought, as the bus rattled along the roads of
posh houses — middle class, she decided. Birch
Road turned out to be nothing but detached
residences with garages and beautiful gardens
and a variety of fancy trees.

Number 19 had a glorious chestnut tree on
one side of the lawn and a rockery with a
miniature waterfall on the other. The front door
was half as big again as most front doors and
highly varnished. Abby threw back her shoulders, marched up to it and rang the bell.

A woman wearing a flowered overall opened it.
She must be the housekeeper, Abby guessed.

'Hello, I'm — ' But, before Abby could say her
name, the woman interrupted her.

'Hang on a minute, dear,' and went away,
leaving the door open on a large square hall with
a number of doors off.

There seemed to be a quite a few people in the
house. Voices could be heard coming from
upstairs and down. Most were angry. A man ran
downstairs, shouting, 'You do what you want,

Donald, I'm past caring.' He ignored Abby.

Five minutes later, a woman limped upstairs using a stick, gasping as if she was putting it on a bit. Abby was still ignored. Another woman, much younger than the first, came out of a room actually singing, 'Get me to the church on time . . . ' She stopped when she saw the visitor standing forlornly on the step.

'Hello, love. What can we do for you?'

Abby stepped inside the hall. 'I'm Abigail Holmes. I've come to see my grandmother.'

'Well, you've come to the right place. She's in the parlour. Would you like a drink before you go in? A soft drink or something alcoholic?' She was a pretty woman of about thirty-five with a strong Irish accent.

'A soft one, please.' Abby said, astonished. She had never been offered alcohol before.

The woman laughed. 'Sorry, you're not old enough, are you? Now, if I'd been your age, I'd have jumped at the chance. Come in the kitchen and I'll make you tea or coffee or we can look for lemonade or something. I'm Aileen, by the way.'

She opened a door at the back of the hall and they entered a room into which every example of the very latest kitchen equipment had been fitted, such as an automatic washing machine and a really smart fridge freezer. There was also a coffee machine shaped like a figure 8.

Abby asked for a coffee. She'd acquired a taste for coffee rather than tea since meeting Reggie and Daphne. It was so much more sophisticated.

'I'll have one, too. I'll just use the tinned stuff,

if you don't mind. I've no idea how to use those cafetière things.'

Neither did Abby. She assured Aileen that the tinned stuff was fine.

While it was being made, the woman in the flowered overall who'd answered the door to Abby came in and began to wash dishes. 'Oh, there you are,' she said when she saw the visitor. 'I thought you'd gone away again.'

'What's happening upstairs, Gwen?' Aileen asked.

'Rows,' Gwen replied. 'Rows and more rows. All over money. And things. I think your hubby's bagged the grandfather clock.'

'Jaysus, Mary and Joseph.' Aileen gasped and at the same time laughed. 'It'll never fit in our little house in Dublin.'

'Well, it's his now. It'll have to fit somewhere.'

Aileen had made the coffee. 'Let's take this somewhere quiet where we can chat,' she said to Abby.

'Use the breakfast room,' Gwen suggested. 'It's full of ironing, but that shouldn't bother you. No one'll interrupt you in there.'

Aileen shook her head. 'Before we go, I'd like Abby to see her grandmother. I have a strong feeling she doesn't actually know what's happened here. Leave your drink here a minute, girl.'

Abby followed the woman out of the kitchen, through the hall and into a large, over-furnished room, in the centre of which stood an open coffin. Abby tried to back out of the room, but she was rooted to the spot. Inside the casket she

248

could see an elderly woman wearing what looked like a wedding dress and veil. She was surrounded by lilies, and rosary beads were threaded through her wrinkled fingers.

Abby, shocked to the core, cried out loud, 'Oh, no!' and burst into tears.

Behind her, Aileen said in a hard voice, 'Don't cry for your grandmother, darlin', she was one of the most horrible women who ever lived, and I can say that — she's been my mother-in-law longer than I care to remember.'

A giant tabby cat rose from the foot of the coffin, jumped out, and rubbed itself against Abby's legs.

A man came into the room demanding, 'What on earth's going on?'

'Your mother has just risen again as a cat,' Aileen said with a laugh.

More people appeared, all men. 'Who is it?' 'What's happening?' 'Has the coffin fallen over?' they variously demanded.

'It's Abigail, our Mary's girl,' someone said.

The tone changed. 'Our Mary! I thought the baby died.'

'Well, this one's very much alive.'

The tone changed. 'Is she in the will? Has she been left money? Who is meant to get Oswald's share?'

'Abby, come with me, dear.' Gwen was holding her hand and attempting to pull her out of the room.

Aileen was in the hall and grabbed her other hand. The three women ended up in the kitchen and the door was slammed.

'It's like being in a zoo,' Gwen remarked, 'where the animals are fed with money.'

There was chaos in the house, as if the place had been awoken from a long slumber and was just finding its voice. The kitchen door opened and a man said in an astonished voice, 'Abby, what on earth are you doing here?'

It was Edwin Powell. He had shaved off his moustache, but she would have recognised him anywhere.

★ ★ ★

'Anyway,' said Abby, taking a break from explaining the events of the last few days. They were in Edwin's car on their way to his house. He'd suggested she stay there for the night, and then in the morning he'd put her on the train back to Euston Station, where Abby's suitcase had been left. 'I had no idea my grandmother had died; I was just going to see her, that's all. I've always known I had a grandmother, but had never met her.'

'I was rather hoping you never would,' Edwin told her. 'She badly wanted to keep you when your mother, Mary, passed away, but I made sure she never would.'

'Why?' Abby wondered what it would have been like living in such a posh house. Violet had told her a few things but she felt sure there must be more to the story.

'Well, you know Will had a different father who died?' Abby nodded. 'Mrs Holmes refused to take his son. The poor lad had lost his mother and two fathers and he was only ten.'

'Poor Will,' Abby said tenderly, remembering how cruel she'd been earlier in the day when she hadn't turned up for lunch, despite having promised. And Edwin's story did seem to back up what Violet had always said. 'By the way, if that woman's so awful, what were you doing at her funeral?'

'It's not her funeral till tomorrow. I went to pay my respects, that's all. She contacted me years ago — about you, as it happens. My name was in her solicitor's files and they wrote to me when she died. Oh, and she only wanted you as a little servant, someone to wait on her hand and foot. That was another reason why I wanted Violet to have you and Will. If your grandmother had had her way, the two of you would have been separated and you'd have been stuck being her skivvy.' He glanced at her. 'You were lucky, you and your brother, that Vi was in a position to take you.'

Abby swallowed hard. She'd been horribly cruel to Vi, just walking out without saying goodbye, leaving her to worry all on her own. It was time to swallow her pride. Once she was reunited with the suitcase, she would go straight home. No, she wouldn't. She took her diary out of her bag and scribbled a note to Reggie and Daphne apologising for not going back to say ta-ra. She'd leave it at the station restaurant, along with her address, and hope they'd keep in touch.

For the rest of the journey, they talked about Barbara, Edwin's wife, his beautiful twins and the hopes he had for them. 'I have the same hopes for you and Will, Abby. We must all meet up again one of these days, see how we have all got on.'

Abby nodded. 'Yes, we must,' she agreed. 'We really must.'

★ ★ ★

When Abby got home to Amber Street the next day, Vi had the sound on the television turned low and she was knitting something in pale-blue baby wool, obviously for Doreen's son, Jack.

She looked up. 'Oh, hello, pet.'

'Hello, Vi.' Abby sort of kissed her on the forehead, relieved Vi was so calm. 'I've been to London.'

'I know, Will rang. You didn't turn up for lunch or something.'

'I went late, but he'd gone.'

'That's because he's back here, in Liverpool. He and Doreen have gone to the pictures. Once he's put her on the Southport train, he'll be home.' Violet put her knitting down carefully on the arm of her chair. 'Would you like a cup of tea?'

'I'd love one, Vi.' Abby stretched her arms. 'Gosh, I'm tired. I feel as if I've been away for ages.'

'Three days can feel like for ever.'

'Three days!' Abby could scarcely believe it. She went over her time in London, minute by minute, hour by hour. Gosh, Vi was right. Three days and two nights. Just as some people had a moment of madness, she'd had a whole seventy-two hours.

★　★　★

In the kitchen, Violet buried her face in the tea towel and hid a sob. She was back, all in one piece, and apparently perfectly fine. Between Will and Edwin, they'd filled her in on Abby's reasons and regrets. And it wasn't surprising that she thought she'd been away longer in view of the stuff that arrived as a result of her visit to London. A badge came, confirming that she was a member of the Campaign for Nuclear Disarmament, accompanied by a biography of Bertrand Russell, one of Violet's own favourite people. Then, a day later, a framed photograph turned up with a note from someone called Gwen. It was of a snooty-looking woman whom Violet recognised as Catherine Holmes, who'd come to this very house years ago to tell Violet she had no right to her little granddaughter. Finally, a little parcel arrived containing a pretty silver brooch shaped like a rose. The brooch was accompanied by an invitation to stay in Dublin if she ever felt in the mood for a holiday. There was a PS: 'I'll never get over the shock of that cat jumping out of the coffin! Love, Aileen.'

13

'Would you like a cup of tea, pet?' Violet shouted.

Will blinked himself awake as the words slowly sank in. 'Please,' he shouted back. His voice was hoarse and sleepy. He turned over in bed and eventually shoved himself into a sitting position. He was in the single bed where Abby had slept when they'd first come to live in Violet's house. She'd taken over his room the minute he'd left for university and there was no chance of getting it back.

Downstairs, Violet began to sing, not proper words, but a 'dum-de-dum' sort of thing; pretty senseless. He heard water being run into the kettle. He knew she was in her element having both her children home — him and Abby. As for himself, he was still angry with his half-sister for the way she had behaved: running off to London, failing to turn up for lunch, then turning up later in the day and knocking the socks off his ex-coworker, Leonard, who'd been on the phone since, asking how he could get in touch with her.

'She's a real bobby dazzler,' he'd said with a laugh, 'isn't that what they say in Liverpool? Anyway, Will, don't tell me she's like you and bats for the same side.'

Will had resisted the urge to slam the receiver down, but that might only persuade the guy to ring back just to annoy him.

'She's only sixteen,' he said brusquely. 'I won't let her anywhere near you. Though I might drop in on you one of these days if I'm in London.'

'Oh, yeah!' his supposed friend had sneered. 'Please don't bother or else people might think you and me have something in common.'

There was a knock on the door and Vi came in with his tea. 'Good morning, pet.' She put the tea on the bedside table and produced a letter from her apron pocket. 'A dead posh letter's come for you. It's from somewhere in Manchester.'

'I applied for a position with a school there,' Will said. He could tell by the crest on the flap what was in the envelope.

Violet had noticed the crest, too. She frowned. 'A public school — not one run by the state?'

'Well no, Vi. I have a first-class degree from an excellent university. I think you've pointed that out from time to time. I'll be snapped up by a place like this.' He waved the unopened letter at her. 'It'll be fitted with the most modern equipment in the labs, the library will be full of the very best literature — Malcolm Dennis, the poet, teaches there. Oh, and the gymnasium and sports facilities are — '

Violet interrupted. 'Oh, you don't have to tell me — everything's made of pure gold, and, if it's not gold, then it's silver. Huh! And, while the children born in Bootle where the real workers live, the ones who keep the factories going and drive the buses and trains, they get second-class teachers and second-class schools. This country

255

is tainted by the class system. There's one rule for the rich and one for the poor.'

'I don't think that's true, Vi,' he said gently.

But being gentle with Violet was a waste of time when she was in this sort of mood. She said, 'Huh,' again in an even more contemptuous tone and went downstairs more vigorously than necessary.

Will opened the letter. It was inviting him for an interview the following week. He drank the tea, got dressed and went downstairs with the intention of making Violet see sense, though had a feeling that one of these days she'd manage to do it to him. Anyroad, he was already half convinced she was in the right.

She smiled at him when he appeared, saying, 'Would you like bacon and eggs, pet?'

This was something else that could lead to an argument. 'Have we got any muesli?' he asked.

'I got some in when I knew you were coming,' she said with another smile. He got the impression she was enjoying herself. 'People keep insisting it's more healthy. This muesli has got nuts in it.'

One of the people insisting was himself. 'I'd like that,' Will said casually. He thought all muesli had nuts in it. 'Is there any fruit — fresh, that is?'

'I've got apples, pears and tangerines — and don't forget, Will, that there's always been plenty of fruit in this house since long before you and your sister came to live here. Me mam was always keen on fresh-fruit salad and custard.' She patted the fridge fondly. 'Mam would have loved to have had one of these.'

'I missed your fresh-fruit salad in London,' he said, knowing it would please her.

'It just happens I've got some in here.' She patted the fridge again.

'Maybe I could have some after the muesli?'

'Of course you can, pet.'

They grinned at each other, just as the phone in the parlour rang.

'It's for you,' Vi said.

'How do you know?'

'It sounds different if it's from London.'

Will snorted. 'That cannot possibly be the case.' He went into the parlour and picked up the receiver.

It was Charles. 'Hello, my darling lad. Have you closed the door?'

'Yes.' Will glanced at the door to make sure it was properly shut. It was a fact that other people in the room could hear what people were saying on the phone at the other end.

'Walter Hayes,' Charles said. 'Remember we met him a few times?'

'I do,' Will conceded, a knot forming in his stomach. Walter Hayes was a national institution, a Shakespearean actor of great repute who was presently increasing his reputation on the silver screen. He was also, privately, a homosexual.

'The party he threw in that old cinema?' Charles went on.

'Yes?' Will said tightly.

'There was a reporter there from the *News of the World*. He took an extraordinary number of pictures. Quite a few will be on the front page

257

of the paper this coming Sunday. Oh, and there'll be more inside, rather explicit, I'm afraid.'

'Jaysus!' Will breathed. 'Am I in any?'

'Not that I've seen.' Charles paused. 'You're not likely to be in any, you're not important enough. You know, darling, this isn't the life for you if you're so terrified of being outed.'

'It's not for myself I'm terrified,' Will lied. 'It's Violet. It'd kill her if she knew.' There were times when he felt sure Vi already knew, when she looked at him in a certain way. Not unpleasant — she would never do that — more curious.

Charles said, 'My mother and father have always known, right from when I was a small child, how I would turn out. Father positively refuses to talk about it, Mother acts as if I'm completely normal.'

'If it's the way you — and me — were born, Charles, then it must be completely normal.' As Charles chattered on before bidding him goodbye, Will stared into the ugly china cupboard or cabinet, whatever it was called, that Vi hated, said it was hideous. It had a leaded-glass front that you could scarcely see through and was full of little china ornaments like 'Present from Bournemouth' or some other holiday resort. There was actually one from Paris shaped like the Eiffel Tower, though Vi had no idea who had sent it.

'Mam didn't know either,' she'd told Will. 'It must be really old.'

He'd often urged her to get rid of the cabinet, even agreed it was hideous, but she claimed her mother would turn in her grave if it left the house.

He said goodbye to Charles on the phone and returned to his breakfast.

'It'll be all soggy by now,' Vi warned.

'I quite like it soggy.' Will genuinely did.

'What did Charles want at this time of the morning?' Vi spoke as if it was barely the crack of dawn. How did she know it was Charles? It wasn't possible that it was the ring tone on the phone that had given it away.

What reason could he give Vi for why Charles had called? Will racked his brain. There was no way he could tell her there would be an expose of that great actor Walter Hayes in Sunday's edition of the *News of the World*. You'd think he had a disgusting disease, yet he was a charming gracious man, generous to a fault. He just happened to have different desires from those of most people. Will just shrugged and made a noise that could have meant anything in answer to Vi's question.

'What are you going to do with yourself today?' she asked.

'I thought I might pick Abby up from college and we could have coffee somewhere — lunch, even — then I might get the train to Southport to see Doreen and Jack and be home for tea.' Vi really appreciated having the family there for meals.

'That sounds nice, pet.'

'Why not come with us?' Will urged.

She thought about this, but shook her head. 'I'll come tomorrow,' she said. 'Then I'll have

259

more time to look forward to it.'

He wondered if she was deliberately trying to sound pathetic. If so, it was working.

★ ★ ★

Will got washed and dressed. He enjoyed putting on a pair of jeans, sweatshirt and canvas trainers, rather than the formal outfits he'd worn in the shop in London. He felt relaxed, laid back, 'cool', as people said in the States. He was treated to a dark look from Vi when he went downstairs, who much preferred him in formal clothes.

He smiled, blew her a kiss, and left the house to catch the bus into town and meet Abby.

★ ★ ★

Abby was in the middle of a crowd of girls when she came out of Morgan & Hemmings Commercial College; there didn't seem to be any boys there. She was popular with everyone. As they'd grown older together, Will had come to like her less, though love her just as much. He hoped she'd grow out of this phase, but right now she was spoilt, full of herself and conceited, but she was his sister, his closest relative in the world.

'Hi, Bruv.' She parked herself in front of him and put her face up to be kissed. 'Most of the girls think you're my boyfriend, so make it look romantic.'

'I'll do no such thing.' He pecked her on the

cheek. He thought it was disgraceful the way she'd walked out on Vi a few weeks ago, leaving her scared out of her wits that she'd never come back or come to some terrible harm. 'Do you fancy coffee or lunch?' he asked.

'Lunch, please.' She linked his arm. 'But only in the form of a toasted sarnie from that new coffee place round the corner. I can't remember what it's called.'

They began to stroll in the direction of Bold Street.

★ ★ ★

The air always felt sharper in Southport, where there were no buildings to shield the town from the brisk winds that swept across the Irish Sea. The month of May felt several degrees colder when Will got off the train at Southport Station a couple of hours later.

Doreen was there to meet him with Jack in his pram. She was still living with Sonia Hanley-Rice, Charles's mother; the arrangement seemed to be permanent. The little boy greeted Will with a smile big enough to melt the sun.

'Can I pick him up?' he asked.

Doreen's smile was almost as big. 'Of course you can; you know you can,' she cried.

'Let's have a pot of tea between us in the restaurant,' Will suggested. It had become a popular place with them for snacks and drinks since Mrs Flynn had run off with her grandson some weeks ago and the station restaurant was where they had all ended up. Will liked the

Victorian atmosphere and Vi always said it reminded her of *Brief Encounter*. Will had promised to go and see the film should it ever be shown anywhere nearby.

He ordered the tea. Doreen had lifted Jack out of his pram and handed him to Will to hold. He sat the boy on his knee and gently squeezed his middle. Jack responded with a giant chuckle followed by a fart. He waved his arms in delight.

A feeling swept over Will that at first he could not describe. It was almost familiar, yet he knew for certain he'd never had it before. He sat there, the baby on his knee, Doreen beside him in the blue coat she always wore in winter, at least over the last few years, the knitted scarf and matching hat that Vi had made her for Christmas. He felt as if the picture they made had always been there, that it was inevitable — Doreen, the baby, and Will.

'Doreen,' he said haltingly, 'Will you marry me?'

Doreen's response was to burst into gales of laughter. 'Ha, ha, ha,' she sang in a false voice. 'Shall we do it this weekend, or the next?'

Will was hurt. 'I meant it,' he said. 'You're old enough if you get your mum or dad's permission. You could even say we've started a family.' He ruffled Jack's silky hair.

Her laughter turned to tears in an instant. 'That's not funny, Will. That's a really stupid thing to say.' For some reason, she snatched Jack off his knee and cuddled him against her shoulder, an action that caused Jack to join in the tears and for Will to wish he could cry too.

Even the girl behind the counter of the station café looked tearful.

'But I mean it,' Will insisted. 'I really do.' He surprised himself with the fervour of his words. He stroked Jack's neck. 'Look at me, Doreen.' She sighed deeply, lifted her head and looked at him. He'd never thought her beautiful, but she had a lovely expression of kindness and honesty, as if she would never hurt a soul, though she was almost hurting Jack now by pressing him so hard against her. He loosened her hands and the little boy stopped crying. Will stroked his cheek and he smiled.

'He's a grand little chap,' Will said, smiling himself. He went over to the counter and ordered another pot of tea. Coming back, he said to Doreen, 'I meant what I said before.'

She frowned. 'You're too old.'

Will was hurt. 'Don't be daft. I'm only twenty-two. We're not so far apart in age. After all, there's at least twenty years between Charles's mum and dad.'

'Is there?' She shook her head. 'Anyroad, it's not me that's daft, Will, it's you. I mean, you've been to university; I didn't even finish school.'

'Only because of Jack, and that was hardly your fault. The tea came with more milk and sugar and he filled their cups. 'Tell you what, let me buy you a ring, right now, as soon as we've finished our tea. Not a gold one with a precious stone like a diamond or an emerald, but . . . ' He racked his brain for a stone that wouldn't be expensive. 'Amber,' he said eventually, 'or

263

amethyst on a silver band. I couldn't afford anything expensive.'

★ ★ ★

There were plenty of jewellery shops in the area: the cheap sort selling second-hand stuff where you could pawn the jewellery you already had if you were hard up enough, and larger places with carpets and brilliant lighting that made everything sparkle. He chose the cheap type — he could always get her a more expensive ring in the years to come. He felt a bit foolish trailing round these places looking at trays of rings costing just a couple of quid. In the end, she chose a three-stone garnet ring that cost just five pounds ten shillings. Doreen considered it a joke, though in the nicest possible way, and seemed happy to play along, even if she still didn't believe Will was in earnest.

'I'm not telling people we're engaged,' she warned him. 'People'll think we're off our heads — or at least one of us is, and it's not me.'

She showed it to Sonia when they got back to the house, without mentioning an engagement. Still doubting Will, Doreen had refused to put the ring on yet, instead letting Charles's mother see it in the little box it had come with. Sonia nevertheless eyed Will curiously.

'What does this mean?' she asked. She was well aware that Will and her son had been exceptionally close friends for years.

Will shrugged and said it didn't mean

anything, knowing he still had to win Doreen round before he could tell people the truth. 'But she does need a ring. You know what some people are like, looking for a ring on a young woman if she's seen with a baby. They can be very rude.' Well, he imagined they could be. He wished he didn't sound so prissy.

'Then you should have got her a wedding ring, shouldn't you?'

Will shrugged again and said it was time he went home to Vi. 'I think she's making lamb stew.' He had no idea what she was making.

'I'll come with you to the station,' Doreen offered. Jack was fast asleep and Sonia suggested he be left behind to sleep in peace. 'It's getting chilly out there.'

On the way, Doreen confessed she was in a bit of a dilemma. 'Me mam keeps turning up, but Sonia won't let her in the house. We have to go somewhere for a cup of tea, usually the station — they must be fed up with us there.'

'Don't you mind your mother turning up?' Will asked.

'Not really.' It really was getting chilly and the girl linked his arm. 'Mam loves Jack and I don't mind her picking him up a bit or taking him for a walk. She's all right without me dad around. Do you think Sonia would mind if I moved into a place of me own?'

Will thought Sonia would probably mind a lot. Doreen and her baby had made a huge difference to the woman's life. 'I'll have a word with Vi about it,' he promised. 'See what she thinks.'

★ ★ ★

'Poor Sonia's in a bit of a state,' Vi said later that night when Will explained Doreen's problem to her. 'Her husband's retiring soon and he's looking forward to playing golf every weekend.'

'Doreen and Jack being there won't stop him from doing that,' Will said. 'I doubt very much if Sonia will want to go with him.'

'That's what you know.' Vi made a face. 'He wants her to go everywhere with him: America, Australia, Europe — everywhere. She's dreading it, but she can't refuse, though she'd far sooner spend her time with Doreen and the baby.'

'Gosh!' Will looked mystified. 'Life's full of . . . ' He couldn't think of a suitable word. 'Difficulties,' he said at last.

'You can say that again.' Vi shook her head as if everything about life was quite beyond her. 'Anyroad,' she went on. 'It wouldn't be a bad idea if Doreen and Jack got a place of their own — but only if it's Southport, not Liverpool. It'd be best if she kept well away from that father of hers and the rest of her family, apart from Mrs Flynn, that is.'

Violet was thrilled at the interest Will was taking in Doreen. When he'd told her about the ring, she'd been delighted at the inference that Will and Doreen might become a couple. There must have been a good reason why Will had moved out of Charles's flat and come back to Bootle. She was convinced he would be happier in a conventional relationship with a woman — and he loved Jack.

266

This discussion took place while Violet and Will were having their tea; Abby had arrived home earlier, had her own tea, and gone rushing off to the pictures.

'What's she gone to see?' Will asked.

Vi made a face. '*The Grip of the Strangler*,' she said. 'It's on at the Trocadero. Me, I wouldn't go near it.' She shuddered. 'But half the girls at Morgan & Hemmings went to see it last night and said it was marvellous, so the other half have gone tonight. It's all about Dr Jekyll and Mr Hyde.'

Will thought he might go tomorrow himself. Tonight, he would read the letter again that came this morning from the school in Manchester, as well as the various enclosures they'd sent, and think about how to reply. He helped Vi with the dishes and decamped to the parlour, where there was a decent light bulb.

Before it became a school for boys, according to the brochure, Sir James Woollcott's had been a seminary, teaching only priests. It wasn't until halfway through the nineteenth century that the building became a school, though not an ordinary down-to earth school like Will and his ilk had attended but one, according to the photographs, with leaded windows, some of them of stained glass, elaborately plastered walls, its own chapel, tennis courts, theatre, rugby pitch . . . The list seemed endless. Yet there were dormitories that made him think life wasn't all luxurious there. He hadn't realised it was a boarding school, with just a handful of day boys.

Will stared gloomily at the expensive surroundings in which the boys were educated, not counting the dormitories, that is. In fact, they reminded him of a concentration camp, at least what he imagined a concentration camp would look like: iron beds, sparse bedding, much too close together. He'd like to bet the boys didn't have much fun there. At least when he was at school, Vi made sure he and Abby were warm in bed and decently fed.

She was right: it was wrong to allow yourself to be educated by the state, entirely free of charge, then take a job in a school like this where you taught only the children of the rich, turning your back on the poor.

There was a knock on the door and Vi came in with a cup of tea and three ginger biscuits on a plate. 'Thought you'd like a cuppa, pet.'

She put the things beside him on the table. Will had no idea what happened next, what made him reach for and bury his head in her arms and just hug her, really hug her, very tightly. Just at that moment, he felt he didn't know who he was or where he was going. The one thing he did know was that he'd always have a home with Violet. He managed, with enormous difficulty, not to cry, to cry and cry and cry and never stop.

'There, there, son,' she said softly. 'Everything's going to be all right.' She'd never called him 'son' before. It was a mistake and she probably never would again. Perhaps she hadn't realised that she'd done it. What was the 'everything' that was going to be all right?

He actually managed to make a joke of it. He moved away, saying, 'This always happens when I'm left alone for long with that depressing china cabinet. I get depressed myself. How much will you take to get rid of the damn thing?'

'I'd let it go for nothing,' she said, matching his mood. 'What about all the stuff inside?'

'Second-hand shop for the cabinet and jumble sale for the stuff inside,' he suggested. 'We could replace the cabinet with a bookcase, Vi; put all the books in the same place rather than scattered all over the house.'

'Why not? You've got enough books to sink a battleship after that degree — it's time we sorted out some shelves. This is your home, too — for however long you want.' She went to the door. 'Abby should be back soon and she'll want to tell us about that picture.'

While he'd been talking to Vi, other thoughts had been worming their way into Will's mind. He now dismissed entirely the thought of working with a pile of rich kids in Sir James Woollcott's exclusive school in Manchester. Instead, he'd look for one in Africa, a place built of wood and straw where the pupils used slates and chalk and sat on the floor. It would give him time as well — and hopefully time for Doreen to realise he was serious about his proposal. If he wrote to her every week while he was away, surely she'd see that they could build a future together when he came home. He'd miss everyone — Violet, Abby, Charles. But it felt like the right thing to do. He'd been so lucky to find Violet. It was time to help other children make their own luck. He might even attempt to start a school himself, he thought — though it would be a battle getting the money to fund something, but he'd enjoy it; it would be a challenge. Oh, and Vi would be great at raising the money back in this country. He sometimes forgot how clever Vi was. During the war, the job she'd had had been vitally important, yet she'd put all that behind her, and her life had become the children — him and Abby — who'd taken over.

★ ★ ★

Abby came home. The picture had been good, she'd enjoyed it, but thought Vi would be wise not to go, though it was right up Will's street.

Will said he might see it the next day. Before he knew where he was, he might be working again, possibly abroad, and who knew when he would be able to go to the pictures again during the day?

Without trying to, they turned their chat about the film into a quiz. They asked each other impossibly silly questions about actors and pictures to which no one knew the answers. It was as if they all recognised that days like this, when there were just the three of them, would become fewer and fewer until they hardly ever happened at all. The children could go anywhere in the world — Violet couldn't imagine either of them staying in Liverpool, let alone Bootle. Will was clearly going through some sort of crisis. Abby had decided that commercial college was a good thing as her ambition these days was to be a newspaper reporter, for which shorthand and typing were essential. As for Violet herself, with Will and Abby gone, what would become of her?

'Vi, what's the matter?' Will put his arm around her shoulders. 'You're crying!'

'I'm sorry,' Vi sobbed. 'I didn't mean to.'

Abby welled up, too. 'Everything seems sad all of a sudden.'

'It'll be all right tomorrow,' Will soothed. He had decided — it had only taken a flash — that, at some time in the future, he really would marry Doreen. He just had to hope she didn't meet anyone else if he found a teaching job overseas; he knew she was in love with him, could tell by the way she looked at him, the brilliance of her smile. He was sure he would make her happy and she would do the same for him.

★   ★   ★

The next morning, he tore up the details of the school in Manchester, and began to investigate what was available in South Africa. Violet was delighted.

The last few days had been a time of decisions, one decision leading to the next. His next act was to make an appointment with the South African Embassy in London to discover the rules and regulations pertaining to working there as a teacher. When he travelled down for the meeting he was encouraged. He understood his presence in the country would be welcome, particularly if he was hoping to teach black children. He was given plenty of information

271

regarding vacancies. He put everything in his briefcase to take home.

It had been his intention to call on Charles while in London; he didn't know he was there and Will intended to surprise him. But when he emerged from the Embassy, he realised he'd far sooner go straight back to Liverpool — to Southport — and see Doreen and Jack.

'When I asked you to marry me,' he said to Doreen when he was about to leave Southport that evening, 'I really did mean it.' She started to interrupt, but he put his hand gently on her lips. 'Let me finish, please.' He shook his head. 'You were right: you're much too young. But another two years and things will be different. You'll have had all that time to think about it. When I get back from South Africa, I'll ask you again — and we'll do it.'

Part 3

14

The school wasn't as impoverished as he had first imagined from the details he had acquired from the charity he'd approached. It was in a wooden building, clean and watertight with electricity throughout and decent outside sanitation. The furniture was rough and ready and the sports facilities basic. It catered for more than eighty black children between the ages of eleven and sixteen. It was only recently that they'd started taking girls, so there were roughly four times as many boys.

It was situated on the edge of Johannesburg and was called Father Patrick's after the Catholic priest — coincidentally, from Liverpool — who had established it thirty years before. He had been referred to as 'the boss', rather than 'headmaster'. He had only recently died and, to all intents and purposes, Will had replaced him, though not as 'the boss'. This was an architect called Geoffrey Head, who taught maths and art. Will took English and history. There were five other teachers, two of whom were women, and only one black. None stuck rigidly to their own subjects but filled in with other lessons if they happened to be free. Will, for instance, had taken science more than once, yet he'd been hopeless at it at St Peter's College in Liverpool, receiving only a low-grade O-level.

The attitude of the white population in the city to the black was on the whole disgraceful. Black women seemed to exist only to look after the children of the white. They would leave their own offspring back in their remote villages and travel, sometimes daily, sometimes weekly, into the cities to wash the white families' clothes, clean their houses, cook their food, possibly tend their gardens and clean their cars and, most importantly, look after their children. The white women, with every single household task done for them, played cards, went shopping or filled in their empty days enjoying themselves and doing nothing at all to benefit the rest of humankind.

Will had spent a year there and intended staying another year before returning home and settling down as a teacher. He had made a friend, Tim Waterson, an Irishman ten years older than himself. Tim, a giant of a man, had been a top rugby player at university back home and now covered half a dozen sports: football, rugby, cricket, hockey, rounders, and a limited form of golf played on a field with holes in rather than a genuine golf course. He was also handy at mending things such as cameras and anything electrical. He was married to Tulip, who was of mixed race and incredibly beautiful. She was soon expecting a baby. The union was frowned on by the authorities.

The nearest secondary school was all white, rather similar to Sir James Woollcott's in Manchester. King's Head College was long-established, full of trophies, ancient portraits of

long-dead members of staff, gleaming floors
— highly polished wood seemed to be a feature
of these sorts of places, particularly the stairs
that Will thought looked highly dangerous. He
wondered how many people had fallen down
them over the years?

It would soon be June. Both schools were due
to break up for the summer holiday. It was at
this point in the year that they played each
other at cricket. The match always took place at
King's Head College, whose team invariably
won — they'd lost only twice when the players
had come down with an unexplained, painful
rash and another time with a sort of summer
flu. They had better everything: players,
equipment, a proper ground, a retired cricketer
for their instructor, a smart white hut to serve
tea.

The day — the first Saturday in June
— dawned well but days nearly always did in
Johannesburg. It was early morning and the sun
was cracking the flags, as was said in Bootle,
when an ancient coach drew up in front of
Father Patrick's establishment and the team got
on. The newest member, only temporary, was the
side's secret weapon, a fifteen-year-old black boy
who was six feet five inches tall and a genius at
cricket. His name was Randolph, and he had
been raised in Australia. He was there only for
his great-grandfather's one hundredth birthday,
after which he would return home.

Tim and Will sat at the front of the coach. The
boys were full of excitement, though they fully
expected to lose. It was their role in life, though

they looked like winners today in their brilliant, if shabby, whites and black hair trimmed only the night before.

'Keep an eye on those other buggers,' Tim said to Will. 'They can't stand to lose. It offends their swollen white pride. Last year, they got both umpires totally pissed on some drugged liquor and their decisions were as mad as the proverbial hatters.'

Will laughed. 'I've been told way back Father Patrick put a curse on them — King's Head College, that is.'

'Well, it hasn't worked so far.' Tim shrugged gloomily.

'There's still time.' Will crossed his fingers and waved them in the air. He set up a singsong and they drove through the gates of King's Head College singing, 'My old man's a dustman . . . ' Will was thinking he'd never be able to do that if he belonged to Sir James's Woollcott's or King's Head College.

The match started at midday and Father Patrick's were doing exceptionally well. The other side won the toss and chose to bat first. Randolph, an all-rounder, was a first-class bowler, his long arms making huge perfect circles when he tossed the ball with the accuracy of a bullet towards the King's Head batsmen, who fell like skittles before the power of his assault. His performance was greeted with a chorus of boos and groans each time another batsman was declared out.

Not everyone on the other side greeted Randolph's tremendous performance in such a mean-spirited way. There were genuine cricket-ers there who admired his style and grace, as well as his cheerful smile and obvious good humour.

Four o'clock, and it was time for tea, and by then the King's Head College side were all out, mainly due to Randolph's ruthless bowling. Father Patrick's side ate in the coach, but the others stood in a huddle outside the tea hut clearly planning their method of play for the second half.

Tim was worried. 'I don't like the look of them,' he muttered. 'They were well and truly routed in that innings. There are a couple of chaps from the press over there — this match is an annual event. If our side, in other words, Randolph, are as good at batting as they were at bowling, King's will be a laughing stock.' He snorted. 'And they won't like that.'

'There's not much they can do about it,' Will remarked.

'I wouldn't bank on it.' Tim grabbed Will's arm. 'Let's go and have a coffee. Or would you prefer something alcoholic, like champagne?'

'Oh, the latter. It might help calm my nerves.'

★ ★ ★

Randolph's first six went over the tea hut roof and the ball took a while to find. The bowler, a most unpleasant young man, swore and gazed with hatred at the batsman, who breathed casually on his gloves as if they were his nails and pretended to polish them.

279

The look of hatred intensified when the bowler realised his opponent seemed unaware he was black and it just wasn't done to act in a way that implied he was superior, or even level, to a white man. This black man was acting as if he was every bit as good a cricketer as any white man on earth.

Throughout the first over, Randolph continued to hit sixes in every direction. Before long, Father Patrick's side would have matched the other side's score in half the time they'd taken to score it themselves.

Suddenly — Will wasn't sure if he was merely imagining it — everything seemed to fall quiet. Not a child cried, not a bird sang, not a person spoke, well, not loudly enough to be heard, and the bowler began his run at Randolph waiting casually, bat poised.

But the bat never went near the ball. Instead, the ball smashed into Randolph's young, handsome face in an explosion of blood and bone and he fell to the ground unconscious. With a roar, the giant figure of Tim bounded onto the pitch and punched the bowler so hard on the chin that he must have lifted him at least six inches off the ground.

'You cowardly bugger,' he roared. 'I'd like to do that to your fucking head.'

Pandemonium reigned. Half a dozen policemen had run onto the pitch. Will joined them — why, he had no idea, as there wasn't a chance he'd rescue his friend against such odds. But Tim was shouting at him, anyway, and waving his arms.

'Get back to Father Patrick's,' he yelled. 'And take Tulip home — to England. Christ knows what they'll do to her if I'm not around. And don't forget she's up the stick.'

'Right.' Will turned and made towards the coach. Seconds later he became aware that an open-top car was pulling in beside him, driven by a woman he'd never seen before.

'Get in,' she shouted, slowing down. 'Someone else can drive the lads back to school in the coach while you look after Tulip. And somebody needs to take that charming young cricketing genius to hospital and get his beautiful nose fixed.'

Will managed to get in the car without opening the door, a talent he was unaware he possessed. 'Who are you?' he asked.

'An idiot,' the woman replied with a grin.

* * *

Two days later, Will was in East Finchley with Tulip Waterson while her husband languished in a Johannesburg prison charged with assault and the Irish government demanded his release. Randolph had been flown back to Australia and the country's ambassador was demanding compensation and an official apology for his injuries. There was quite a fuss in the press on two different continents, though Will was hardly mentioned except by a couple of journalists who wanted to know how he had come by the surname 'Stein'.

Once the excitement had died down, Will

began to enjoy himself — he had always been happy in the capital city. Tulip's family seemed to expect him to stay with their daughter until Tim returned, when the couple would go to Ireland and settle down. Her father was from Kenya, an expert meteorologist who worked for the BBC; her mother was Welsh and taught at the local school. They had another daughter, Peony, fifteen, who developed an instant crush on Will and stared at him fixedly whenever they were in the same room.

He went to see all the latest pictures. *Some Like it Hot*, his favourite film of all time, was on at a little cinema in Camden and he saw it three more times.

Charles Rice was still starring in *Firefly* at the same theatre. Will sat in the back row of the upper circle and his heart lurched when Charles came onstage, though he hadn't expected to have such a strong reaction. There would always be a bond between him and Charles, he realised now. But his future was with Doreen, he was convinced. He left in the first interval and went into the nearest bar, where he would have got plastered had he not had to go back to Tulip's family. He thought about Doreen and the children they would have. During his year in Johannesburg he had written to her regularly, at least once a week, sealing his letters with kisses that were truly meant.

Yet his heart was still thumping crazily after seeing Charles on stage. It was just something he would have to get used to. Anyway, he was convinced the day would come when it wouldn't happen any more. He didn't believe most people had only one love in their lives — you could love different people at different times, he decided. But, once you'd promised your life to someone, there was no going back. And he was sure now — more than ever — Doreen was the one for him.

★ ★ ★

That Friday, Will went to Liverpool for the weekend. It was a year since he'd seen everyone. Apart from Doreen, he had also really missed Violet and Abby, who was now working for the *Bootle Herald* and had actually managed a scoop with a local man, her own brother, being involved in the cricket incident in South Africa that had received worldwide publicity. His little sister had grown up while he was away, and he felt proud seeing how hard she'd worked to achieve what she'd set her heart on.

Doreen was so pleased to see him that he felt if he'd asked her she would be overjoyed to marry him there and then.

Violet kept patting his neck when she passed behind him. 'When are you going back? To London or to Johannesburg, luv?' she asked on his first morning.

'I might not go back,' Will said vaguely. He didn't know what to do. He felt as if he had completed his turn with a charity and it was time he got an ordinary everyday job with a future and got on with earning an ordinary wage. After all, he was just an ordinary chap. He didn't need any more adventure, not if he could have Doreen and Jack. There'd been a time, when he was very young, when the people around him had kept dying. But he'd had stability for all these years, broken only when he'd taken off for a different world. Then all hell had broken out at that damn cricket match and here he was back home in Bootle, where he'd had no intention of being for another year.

The decision on what to do next was taken for him on Sunday, when the telephone in the parlour rang and it was Tim Waterson calling from Johannesburg. He'd been released from prison and was about to board a plane for London.

'I don't want to spend another minute in this godforsaken country, Will, old chap,' he said. Will imagined him scowling at the other end of the line. 'Me and Tulip will stay in London till the baby comes, then we'll be off to Ireland as planned. You might have second thoughts about going back yourself in view of what happened.'

'I don't like letting Father Patrick down,' Will said.

'Oh, don't let that worry you. The publicity they got from that damned cricket match has done the school a world of good. Money and sports equipment has poured in from all over the world and teachers have turned up at not quite the same rate, but offering their services for nothing.' He chuckled. 'You're not as precious as you once were, mate.'

Will felt an enormous sense of relief. 'Then I won't be going back to Johannesburg,' he told his friend. 'I brought all my things back with me for the summer, anyway. Good luck for the future to you and Tulip,' he said fervently.

15

Will asked Doreen if she would marry him a few short weeks later. In the past, he had often wondered why couples became engaged and got married sometimes years later. He could see no point in waiting. Doreen had recently turned eighteen. There was no need to ask anyone's permission. It did cross his mind she might turn him down, but he knew now she was in love with him, even though he still had a job convincing her that he felt the same — that he really did want her for his wife. There were only six years between them, so there was nothing odd about their ages. Having Jack, who was three, required an explanation, but, hopefully, no one would be tactless enough to demand one.

Will couldn't believe it when she finally said yes. But there was one condition on Doreen's acceptance. She insisted on getting married in Bootle in St James's Church, only yards from the street where she was born — not that Will cared where the ceremony was held.

'But you've been living in Southport a few years now, luv,' Violet pointed out as if Doreen hadn't noticed this herself. 'It's much prettier.'

'Me mam would prefer I got married in St James's,' Doreen argued. Her lips formed a stubborn line.

Despite her unpleasant upbringing, Doreen

was fond of her mother, whom she seemed to regard as much a victim as she was herself. No one present — other than Doreen, there was only Violet, Abby and Will — was inclined to argue the point. A Bootle wedding would be easier to arrange and thronged with guests. Abby had hugged them both when they'd told her their news. While a small part of her felt sad at watching her big brother prepare to start a family of his own, she'd got over the jealousy of her younger years, when she realised his feelings for Doreen were the a big part of why he came back from South Africa. She'd worried Will might meet someone and settle over there, leaving her and Vi a lonely twosome.

Violet sighed. She'd congratulated them of course. But she felt confused. She knew this marriage would be the best possible course for Will, whom she loved more than anyone else on earth, to take. This way he would be happiest. Still, a part of her feared Will was hiding his real self behind this rather nice young woman and her child. She had to trust him, had to believe that he had chosen Doreen for the right reasons. And she understood why Doreen and her mother wanted the wedding to be local. The Flynn family had always been looked down on. Their house was filthy, as were their children, all boys except for Doreen. The older ones were in and out of prison, and Mr Flynn was hardly ever out of it. And who had fathered that baby? people wanted to know. But now this miracle had happened, or was about to. A young man with an impeccable background — a university graduate, a schoolteacher — wanted to marry Mrs Flynn's Doreen. Probably the most desirable young man in the whole of Bootle would soon become her son-in-law. Her own sons were saving up for new suits and intended having their hair cut in a proper barbers'. Mr Flynn, however, was currently residing in Walton jail and missing all the excitement, much to everyone's relief.

⋆　⋆　⋆

The September day dawned, not quite so brightly nor so warmly as days had done so recently for Will in Johannesburg, but the nearby River Mersey added a sparkle to the fresh, salty air.

Violet set up a pasting table outside her house from where Madge McGann served tea, sarnies and cake as well as lemonade for the children. She wouldn't be surprised if this was the last wedding that included the whole street. Things like that hardly happened nowadays. People were less friendly, though more folk than ever before waited outside the church for the bride and her bridesmaids to arrive. Doreen wore a dress of lily-white organdie, a prim and proper style with a wide satin sash, and Jack was a pageboy in a suit made out of a maroon velvet curtain. He was going on honeymoon with his mother and his new dad afterwards. There were four brides-maids, Abby Holmes at their head, all in pale-blue lace.

The guests had already arrived. Edwin Powell

with his wife, Barbara, and their lovely twin daughters. Peter and Carol Cooper and their four lively children, all named after film stars, who skipped their way into the church. There was beautiful Tulip and her dead tough husband, who looked as if he played rugby for a living or went a few rounds in the ring. There were even guests from Violet's past whom she'd known during the war or she'd worked with at Briggs' Motors. Some she'd invited, others had turned up out of the blue and had come to watch because they'd heard about the wedding. They all came back to Amber Street and danced the day away.

Will blessed the day he'd fallen in love with Doreen Flynn as he watched her happy starry face on the day of their wedding. He thought about making love to her that night and didn't feel frightened at all.

But halfway through the afternoon he went into the house and found Charles Rice sitting in the lounge. He wore a silver-grey suit, a pink satin tie and a pink rose in his lapel.

'How did you get in?' Will gasped. Charles belonged to another life.

'Came in the back way, darling,' Charles said, grinning. 'Past the outside lavatory.'

Will rolled his eyes impatiently. 'Why?'

'Didn't want to be besieged by admirers at the front.' He shrugged nonchalantly. 'Actually, I thought I'd be asked to be your best man.'

'I would have asked, but I knew you wouldn't want to be besieged by admirers,' Will said.

'Touché!' he grinned again.

'Where are your parents?' Will asked. 'They were invited.'

'Daddy's playing golf in Spain and Mummy's there with him. Unfortunately, their invitation must be at home in Southport. Sorry, Will.' He genuinely looked it.

Will was sorry, too. Sonia Hanley-Rice had been like a mother to Doreen and her son over the years. 'Give me their address out there and I'll send a telegram as soon as I can,' he said.

Charles sighed. 'You're the love of my life,' he said softly.

Will wanted to say something like, 'Don't talk daft,' but he wouldn't have meant it. His friend was being serious. He didn't know what to say back. He didn't know how he felt. This wedding, *his* wedding, was all part of the confusion. He was no longer working class. He didn't know what he was any more.

He left the house, unable to remember why he'd gone in, and stood a few doors away, waiting for Charles to leave and catch the train. He'd be due on stage for the evening performance of *Firefly* later — his understudy must have taken on his role for the matinee. To his surprise, Charles came out the front way. He was smiling and no one gave him a second glance, something that he knew very well would happen. He waved to people as if they'd waved to him.

Someone had noticed, though: Abby. These days, his sister always carried a camera in her bag and had just taken Charles's photograph for her Bootle newspaper. WEST END STAR 'STARS'

AT LOCAL WEDDING, Will imagined the headline saying. He wondered if she'd get a bonus for it.

Doreen was wearing the going-away outfit she'd bought from C&A Modes, a dark-blue linen suit, very smart. Her mother looked smart, too, in a cream suit with brown spots. She was crying.

'You'll never go away for good, will you, luv?' she said to Will when he approached.

'No,' he stammered. 'Of course not.' They were about to go away on their honeymoon in Paris. He promised fervently they would come back.

Doreen turned to her mother. 'See, did you hear that, Mam? Now go and get yourself a nice glass of sherry from Vi's kitchen. You can bring me a glass if you like.'

Her mother shuffled away, looking as if she'd already had enough sherry to last a week. Doreen grasped Will's hand. 'Would you like to go soon, luv? I bet this isn't the sort of wedding you really wanted, is it?'

She looked and sounded so sympathetic Will wanted to cry. He laughed instead. 'I can't wait for us to get on the train for Paris,' he said, breathing deeply for some reason.

'I hadn't forgotten about Paris.' Doreen rolled her eyes dramatically. 'I can't wait to throw my bouquet at someone,' she said.

'You *toss* your bouquet *to* someone,' Will told her. 'It's less harmful.'

It was Violet who caught the flowers later. She hadn't even thought to try, but they were heading straight for her and she had no alternative.

'As if I'd be getting married,' she scoffed.

★ ★ ★

Abby was one of the last guests to go home; it was nearly ten o'clock. She had moved out of Amber Street on the assumption a flat in Parliament Square in town made more suitable accommodation for a budding newspaper reporter.

Now, there was only Madge left. The wedding guests had all gone, either home or to various hotels in the area. Many of them would meet tomorrow for lunch. Violet was glad of the chance to make the most of the celebrations. But now she and Madge were tidying up in a desultory way, throwing the rubbish away, putting the dishes in the sink or on the draining board ready to be washed in the morning, along with the washing in the machine. The boiler had been ditched the year before.

'How d'you think you'll get on on your own?' Madge asked. She had perfected the art of smoking with the cigarette dangling from the corner of her mouth and the eye on that side half closed.

'I was on me own for years between Mam dying and Will and Abby coming to live here,' Violet said, swallowing the sudden lump that came to her throat. 'Now they've gone and I'm on me own again. It's the way of the world, Madge. It's happened to you,' she pointed out.

And, now Violet no longer had children to look after, she had plans to extend the small business she had started as a freelance shorthand typist. But before that she had been thinking vaguely about having a holiday. She hadn't discussed it with a soul, but really fancied going somewhere abroad to which she would have to fly.

'Why don't I come and live with you, Vi?' Madge said. Bob had left months ago and was living with another woman. 'It'd save rent, we could share the housework, the groceries would be cheaper, the heating half as much.'

Violet resisted the urge to laugh. 'But you don't do housework,' she pointed out. 'Your house is a tip. And you bring men home. I'm not lying in bed while you're at it in the next room with some chap you've picked up that night in The Butcher's.'

'That's not very nice, Vi,' Madge said sulkily.

Violet yawned. 'There's a limit to my niceness. Anyroad, go home, girl.' She made shooing gestures. 'I'll see you tomorrow. We'll all be having lunch somewhere. Once Sunday's over, everything will go quiet again.'

She wasn't looking forward to it.

★   ★   ★

The man arrived at around six o'clock the evening of the following day. All the far-flung wedding guests had started leaving after lunch and would now be back home. Madge was in her own house having a lie-down, Violet was reading the Sunday paper.

'Mrs Duffy?' The man raised a pale-grey velour hat that she deeply admired. In fact he was a very smartly dressed person altogether, wearing a dark-grey suit and a tasteful striped tie.

'Miss.' She corrected him. '*Miss* Duffy.'

He smiled. 'Miss Duffy. May I come in? I'd like to speak to you about William.'

It reminded her of Edwin Powell's first visit all those years ago. She stood back, as she had done then, to let him pass, and he waited to see where he should go. She went into the living room and he followed.

'It's about William Stein,' he said.

'I know, you just said,' she snapped, without meaning to, but she remained protective about the boy, even now he was grown and wed. She sat down, forgetting to ask him to do the same. 'What about Will?'

'My name is Eric Stein,' he said. 'I'm William's father.'

There was silence, but not a true silence. The clock was ticking unnaturally loudly; the man's breathing could be heard quite clearly, as well as Violet's own.

'Will's father is dead,' she said shakily. 'Long dead.'

He shook his head. 'I thought Will was dead, but I've recently found out he's alive, and I'm alive. Look, have you got something — whisky, brandy, maybe? Tablets? You look pale. We probably both do. Can I fetch a friend for you?'

'No!' Violet said sharply, imagining Madge

being there, listening, taking it all in, and going on and on about it for the next couple of years. 'There's sherry in the kitchen. I wouldn't mind a glass. They're all clean, the glasses.' She and Madge had washed them last night. 'You have some if you like.'

He went into the kitchen and returned with sherry for her and something different for himself. He held up the glass. 'Rum,' he said. 'I prefer rum.'

'I hate it,' Violet told him. It was thick and dark and sticky and she felt drunk after a mere sip. She hadn't known she had any.

He sat down at the table and she looked at him properly for the first time. He was the same size as Will, clean-cut with dark eyes, hair more grey than black, a rather withdrawn expression on his face. Of course, he could be lying and have nothing to do with Will. He could be a conman who'd come to trick her out of her savings — she had least twelve and sixpence saved in a china pig on the kitchen windowsill. Or he may want to sell her life insurance.

The thing was, neither of those was as bad or as serious as telling her he was Will's father if he wasn't.

'He thinks you're dead, Will does. Edwin does. So did I.' She drank too much of the sherry in one go and nearly choked. 'Edwin said you'd died in a motorbike accident,' she said when she'd recovered. 'You were in the army.'

'I was in the Canadian Air Force. Who's Edwin?'

'Edwin Powell. He's a charity worker,' Violet explained. 'Years ago, he came to ask if I'd have the children — your wife was my cousin, but my mother had known nothing about that side of her family.'

He frowned. 'Did you say 'the children'?'

Of course, he mustn't know about Abby. 'Your wife remarried and had a little girl, Abby,' she told him. 'If you've found Will here, you must have heard that Mary died, as did her new husband. As for Edwin Powell, it was his charity who arranged for me to take on the children, which I did. He was the one who tracked me down and told me I'm their aunt. Edwin was here yesterday in fact. At the wedding — '

'Ah, yes, the wedding.'

There was something about the way he'd said it. 'You knew about Will's wedding?' she asked.

'A few months ago, I read in the paper about an incident at a cricket match in Johannesburg and it mentioned a William Stein, aged twenty-three, from Liverpool.' He paused and Violet nodded at him to continue, which he did after a long pause. 'In April, nineteen forty-one, we — that is myself, my wife, and William, who was only a baby — landed in Liverpool. I had joined the air force back in Canada and wanted to do the same thing here. We found accommodation and I left for London to sign up.'

'On a motorbike?' Violet interjected.

He shook his head. 'No, the train. I've never ridden a motor-bike in my life.' He looked slightly irritated.

'You lived in Liverpool.' She shook her head in wonder. 'That's a coincidence.' Actually, it was the place anyone coming from Canada was likely to land. 'D'you know which street?'

'It was named after a poet, I can't remember which one, but, when I came back from London, the house where I'd left Mary and William had been destroyed by a bomb. We'd only lived there a couple of weeks. I searched everywhere, but no luck, I'm afraid.' He shrugged helplessly as if the memory still upset him.

Violet got up without a word and went into the kitchen to make a pot of tea. If she drank the entire bottle of sherry it wouldn't have the same calming effect as a couple of cups of tea.

'Would you like some tea?' she called to the man who claimed to be Will's father.

'Have you got coffee?' he called back.

'Yes.' It was in a bottle and awfully old.

'I'd like that, please. Black, no milk or sugar.'

Violet shuddered at the idea of what that would taste like. Sooner you than me, she wanted to say. But he didn't even wince when she made it and he took the first sip.

'Anyway,' he was saying. 'When I read about the recent cricket match, I did what I imagine most people would do in the same situation and hired a private detective. He came back quite quickly to say it was definitely my son, William, and that he and his mother — in other words my wife Mary — had moved from Liverpool to Devon during the war, assuming I was dead. He told me Mary had remarried, but was now also dead.'

'Did he — the private detective — say what prompted your wife and William to move to Devon?' Violet asked. 'People down there seem to think you died in a motorbike accident.' Perhaps he'd like to look at the streets in Liverpool that were named after poets, see if he recognised the one where he'd left Will with his mother. There was a famous photograph of one street during the raids with a piano at an angle in the middle, thrown there by the force of a bomb, apparently undamaged. People had gone to look at it for days.

'When I returned to collect my family, no one said anything about Devon.' Eric Stein shook his head. 'You can imagine how confused things must have been, air raids every night. I asked in places like the Town Hall and the police station, but no one had information about them.' He shrugged. 'In the end I went back to London. But I didn't give up. Over the years I advertised in the newspapers from time to time.'

'The May Blitz went on for a week, hour after hour of bombing, day after day.' Violet could clearly remember the unremitting chaos. For its size, Bootle had been one of the most heavily bombed areas in the country.

'Where do you live now?' she asked and was surprised by his reply.

'Germany,' he replied. 'West Berlin. I own a factory manufacturing refrigerators, washing machines, stuff like that.'

He spoke with the suggestion of an accent, a touch harsh, and she had been wondering where it came from. Now she realised it was German.

She was surprised and wondered was it he or his family who'd decided to leave Germany for Canada in the years before the war began? And who had then made the decision to return to the family roots in Germany when it was over? 'Are you staying in Liverpool?' she enquired.

'Yes, at the Adelphi,' he told her. 'I hadn't known about the wedding until after I'd arrived. When the detective told me, I thought it was the perfect way of seeing if I was right about Will. I stood outside the church yesterday and knew it was him.'

He smiled, not noticing Violet's consternation over the fact that this man had blended into the crowds yesterday. He carried on blithely. 'Would you like to have dinner at my hotel tonight? We have so much to talk about.'

She had never been inside the Adelphi, which was the poshest and most exclusive hotel in Liverpool. Having dinner there required weeks just thinking about it. People like Violet didn't go there on impulse or unprepared. It was a really big deal. She patted her head. 'I haven't had my hair done,' she said plaintively.

'It looks very nice. Didn't you have it done for the wedding?'

Of course she had. She nodded. And she had a new costume: tan boucle with a velvet collar, shoes to match, a new handbag, new hat.

'Why don't I go for a stroll around Bootle while you get ready?' Eric Stein said in a tone of voice you'd use when speaking to a child.

Violet pulled herself together and hoped it wasn't noticeable. 'That's a good idea,' she said firmly. 'I'll see you in about half an hour.' She finished off her sherry, saw her visitor out and went upstairs, where she sat on the bed. The front door closed.

'Oh, my God!' she said aloud.

It wasn't just his news about Will that she needed to come to terms with. As she sat there with her pulse galloping, she realised she was attracted to him. She was attracted to him more than she'd ever been to a man before. How old was he? He looked about fifty but was more likely to be sixty. She wanted him to be as old as she was — or at least nearly as old. 'You stupid old woman,' she whispered. 'You're acting like a teenager.'

She stared at her new costume hanging on the wardrobe door in front of the mirror. The hat was a tan velvet beret, but she wouldn't wear it tonight for dinner. She would have worn it if they'd been having lunch. But dinner . . .

Violet sighed. She had been looking forward to a couple of restful weeks after the wedding, and then, when the honeymooners returned, helping Will and Doreen move into a temporary place to live in Southport while looking for a house to rent or even buy. Buying your own house was a popular thing to do nowadays, though it meant taking on a mortgage.

She put on the costume she'd bought for the wedding, followed by the shoes that hurt a bit. She powdered her nose, combed her hair, sat on the bed again and thought about Will's father. Gosh, Will would be astonished when he found out.

There was a knock on the door and Violet went downstairs to let her visitor in. She was about to tell him what number bus to take to the Adelphi, but he pointed to a car waiting at the pavement.

'I have a taxi,' he said.

* * *

Violet didn't doubt that there were hotel dining rooms all over the country that were grander than the Adelphi, Liverpool, but, apart from that one anxious meal at the Ritz when Abby was missing with Doreen, she had never been in one and was therefore hugely impressed when she was faced with half a dozen dazzling chandeliers, equally dazzling white linen tablecloths and cutlery. The tables were round and a silver vase containing red roses adorned each one.

'It's beautiful,' she breathed.

'Have you never been here before?' Eric Stein asked.

Violet shook her head. 'I could never afford it,' she said.

A waiter came and seated them. Another waiter came to take their order for wine and there was a long discussion between the two men as to what sort to order.

Violet was asked what she would like to eat: fish or meat.

'Meat,' she replied.

'What sort of meat, madam?' the waiter enquired.

'Beef,' she said timidly. At least there was no

chance here that the food would come wrapped in newspaper.

The perfect wine was chosen to drink with the beef, along with a variety of vegetables, and minutes later a glass was standing on the table in front of her waiting to be drunk.

'Your very good health.' Eric Stein held up his glass.

Violet touched it with her own. 'And yours.'

She'd had sherry at home, now she was having wine. She wasn't used to drinking. Her head began to swim. She felt as if she could sleep for a week.

'How long are you staying in Bootle?' she asked.

'I don't know.' He shrugged. 'I need to see if I can find the street where I left Mary and Will. I remember going in a public house once. The manager was called Larkin — Tom Larkin. I might look out for him.'

'Don't forget there was a blackout,' Violet reminded him. 'In winter, the entire country was as black as night for over half the day. Though, come to think of it, the raid you're investigating occurred in May.' What with double summer time, it hadn't got dark until nearly midnight.

'Those were truly awful times. So much death!' He shuddered.

She wondered where he had spent the rest of the war. Did he join the Royal Air Force as he'd set out to do? Had he married again? Did he have more children? Her head was spinning. She'd better not eat much or she'd be sick.

She'd ask him questions another time, when she felt sober and had experienced a good night's sleep.

⋆ ⋆ ⋆

She was relieved to get back to her own house a couple of hours later, having managed not to disgrace herself in any way. Eric Stein had invited her back for lunch at the Adelphi the following day. She had accepted, but impressed upon him that there really was no need for a taxi, that she was perfectly capable of catching a bus all on her own — had been doing it since she was fourteen and had started work with Briggs' Motors before the war. They shook hands when they said good night.

Violet couldn't wait to get out of her formal clothes and the tight shoes, intending to go straight to bed. She was therefore extremely annoyed to find Madge McGann in Mam's chair finishing off the sherry. What was even more annoying was the fact that Madge was annoyed with her.

'Where have you been?' she said indignantly. 'I thought you intended to read the Sunday paper.'

'I thought you intended having a sleep,' Violet retorted.

'I had a sleep — I had to wake up some time.'

Violet didn't bother with the obvious reply. 'Kindly go home, Madge,' she said coldly. 'I'm very tired and anxious to go to bed.'

'Did you just arrive home in a car?' was her friend's response.

Violet headed for the stairs. 'Goodnight. Don't forget to put the light out when you leave.' Perhaps it was time she stopped leaving the front-door key so easily available.

★   ★   ★

The following morning, she telephoned Edwin Powell in Exeter to tell him about Eric Stein's arrival, but was told he was on a plane on his way to America. 'He's going to a conference in Washington,' Barbara said proudly.

'But he was only here, in this house, the other day,' Violet protested, 'at our Will's wedding.'

'It only takes hours to fly from here to the States,' Barbara told her. 'The conference is all to do with adoption versus fostering,' she went on to explain. 'Which is best: to adopt children, or foster them? Experts from all over the world are gathered there to discuss it. Despite being relatives, you probably wouldn't have been allowed to adopt Will and Abby because of your age and being unmarried, but the fostering rules aren't nearly so strict; there aren't so many rules. You've been fostering Will and Abby all these years without a single hitch. It's been the best thing that ever happened to those children. Anyway, Vi, did you want to speak to Edwin about anything important?'

'Very important, actually. Please ask him to get in touch as soon as he gets home.'

'I will,' Barbara promised. 'Oh look, here are the twins. Come and say hello to your Auntie Violet, girls.'

She had barely put down the phone when Abby arrived. 'Shouldn't you be at work?' Violet commented. 'Aren't you supposed to start at nine o'clock?' She was rather hoping Abby would say she'd decided to move back home — she was living with three of the girls she'd gone to commercial college with and sometimes complained it was mayhem — but Abby said no such thing.

'I've brought you a present,' she said instead, putting a basket with a lid on the table. She opened the lid and lifted out a tiny grey kitten.

'Oh!' Violet wanted to cry. 'Oh, let me hold him.' She sat down. Abby put the kitten in her hands and she could feel its tiny heart beating madly. 'What's his name? Is he a he?'

'Yes, he's a he, but he hasn't got a name. That's up to you, Vi. He's probably scared after a journey in that basket.'

'Poor little mite.' Violet had always wanted another cat, though none could replace her beloved Sammy. Even now, she felt slightly traitorous nursing this furry little creature in place of her dear old pet. But one look at his face and she knew she would keep him. What should she call him? 'What about Smokey for his name?' she suggested.

'That's too predictable.' Abby made a face. 'It shows no imagination at all.'

'You think of something then.' What with weddings, Eric Stein returning from the dead and Madge behaving more irritatingly than usual, Violet had lost the power to think.

'What about Grey?' Abby suggested. 'It's really classy.'

'It's also really daft.' Violet had a brainwave. 'How about Dusty, after the singer Dusty Springfield?'

'Perfect,' Abby decided on the spot. 'She's my favourite singer. What do you think about being called Dusty, Dusty?' The kitten responded with a yawn and promptly fell asleep.

Violet had remembered that Eric Stein was taking her to lunch. She would like Abby to have gone by the time she needed to get ready for the Adelphi. 'Aren't you going to be late for work?' she said to the girl.

'I've already been into work. I took in an article that I wrote yesterday and some photographs I developed myself. I went in early so I'd have time to nip out and pick up Dusty and bring him here. I've been planning it for days. I thought you'd need something to distract you after the wedding was over. I've got to go back after but there's time for a cup of tea. I'll just put the kettle on.' She disappeared into the kitchen.

Violet put Dusty on a cushion, where he sighed deeply and continued to sleep. She didn't want to tell Abby about Eric Stein until she'd spoken to Edwin Powell. Edwin might think it best that they didn't tell Will yet that his father was still alive, which meant Abby mustn't know, either.

She went into the kitchen to help make the tea in the hope Abby would be gone quickly. What had become of Will's father for all these years was a mystery that she would quite like to have solved as soon as possible.

★ ★ ★

By the time Abby left for work, it was almost time to leave herself, when Vi remembered Dusty couldn't be left on his own, for what might be hours, not when he was only a sad little baby just separated from his mother — who was bound to be feeling sad herself. She was still annoyed with Madge, but she was the only person Violet knew whom she could leave the kitten with. Abby had left behind the basket he'd arrived in and Violet carried him round to Madge's house.

'Who are you having lunch with?' Madge inevitably wanted to know after she'd almost kissed Dusty to death.

'Just some woman I knew at Briggs' Motors,' Violet told her. Fortunately, Madge didn't ask the woman's name, so there was no need for another lie.

★ ★ ★

She met Eric Stein in the Adelphi, where the dining room was rather less brilliantly lit for lunch than it had been the night before. He was curious to know why his wife and son had ended up in Exeter. 'How on earth did they get down there?' he asked.

Violet confessed she had no idea. 'I'm waiting for a phone call from Edwin Powell, the man I

307

mentioned yesterday. When we first met, he spoke as if you'd been living in Exeter with Mary and Will for some time. Will tells people you were killed in a motorbike accident, says you were very brave. But in reality he wasn't old enough to remember much about that time. I expect he was building a picture in his head of what might have happened.'

'And did you know Mary, my wife, well?' He looked upset.

'She was my cousin, yet neither of us knew of the other. It's even stranger when you think that, for a few short weeks in nineteen forty-one, we were living less than a mile apart; my mother too.' Violet would never cease to regret that they had missed each other. 'What are you going to do now?' she asked. She couldn't for the life of her imagine what Will's reaction would be to finding out his father was still alive. 'Will's due home from his honeymoon in less than a fortnight,' she said. 'Do you intend to wait for him in Liverpool?'

He looked a bit lost. 'I'm not sure what to do.'

'If you don't mind me asking, did you get married again?'

'No'. He shook his head.

It seemed to Violet that he looked at her a bit warily. 'Once I realised Will was still alive I wondered if I could spend some time with him.' He looked at her again. 'Or at least in the vicinity — in the same town, perhaps. What do you think, Violet?'

Violet didn't know what to say. Thinking about it, she couldn't guess what Will would say.

Would he be delighted — or baffled as to why it had taken his father so long to find him? Over all these years he'd had little to say about either of his parents. As she'd just told Eric Stein, he'd once or twice remarked his father had been brave because he'd died on a motorbike, as if he had been involved in something dangerous. Yet, according to Eric himself, he hadn't played any part in his son's, or wife's, life in Exeter, having left them both in Liverpool. Will spoke even less about his mother, yet they'd been together for four or five more years before she died. She had always assumed it was too painful for him to look back on those days.

'What are you thinking about?' Eric Stein asked. 'You've been quiet for a long time.'

'Sorry.' Violet had forgotten he was there. 'Your appearance has taken the wind out me sails.' That was one of her mother's favourite sayings.

She told him it was Will's intention to live with his new wife in Southport while looking for a teaching job in the vicinity, 'That is, in Lancashire or Cheshire.' Once he had done this, he would start looking for somewhere to live permanently; in other words, buy a house.

'What's Southport like?' Eric asked.

'It's a lovely seaside town,' Violet told him. 'Very classy — and very healthy.'

'Is it far from Bootle?'

Violet shrugged. 'I'm no good at distances,' she told him. 'It's about ten stops on the train from Bootle — it's an electrified line. Marsh Lane Station is only five minutes away from where I live in Bootle. You could get there from here in half an hour. Why don't you go this afternoon, see what it's like — Southport, that is?' she suggested.

Eric Stein smiled. 'Why don't you come with me?' he said. 'We could have afternoon tea there.'

'I'm sorry, but I have things to do.' She felt she was getting too involved with this man; his charm suddenly felt a bit too free and easy. Will didn't even know his father was alive, let alone had turned up all these years later in search of him. She regretted having told him anything about his son's future plans — she couldn't even be one hundred per cent sure he was related to Will. She tried not to let her sudden doubts show.

'We'll get the Bootle train together,' she suggested. 'I'll get off at Marsh Lane and you stay on as far as Southport.'

'When will I see you again?'

Violet was lost for words. His keenness felt almost oppressive. What did he want? He couldn't expect her to drop everything and meet him every day until Will came home. She wanted to slow things down — at least wait until she'd spoken to Edwin. At the same time, she couldn't just abandon him mid-air, as it were. 'Perhaps we could have lunch together again this weekend?'

At this, he looked extremely disappointed.

Sometimes, telling a lie can be preferable to hurting people's feelings. 'I'm sorry, but I have work to do,' she told him. 'I run my own business, and Abby, Will's half-sister, is a newspaper reporter and I frequently help with typing her articles.' In fact she really had helped Abby a few times when she was overloaded with work — not that she got paid for it. 'She was there this morning and left work for me to do.'

They parted at Bootle Station — he stayed on the train, she got off. She sensed he wasn't all that pleased with the way things had gone, but she couldn't devote all her time to him over the next few weeks till Will came home.

It was a shame, but, since he'd become a bit of a nuisance, he had also become less attractive, even a bit off putting. Actually, it wasn't really a shame, but a bit of a relief that she'd gone off him. She giggled. What had she been thinking earlier, checking her appearance repeatedly before she set out to meet this man whom she'd known for only twenty-four hours? Oh, she had to talk to someone. Instead of going home, she went round to Pearl Street and knocked on the door of Madge's house. She wouldn't dream of mentioning Eric Stein, but Madge was sure to have some gossip she could share that would take her mind off things.

But Madge was out. Violet let herself in and found Dusty asleep in his basket behind the settee. She thought about taking him home with her, but Madge might think he'd been stolen when she came in herself.

Anyway, returning the kitten would give Madge a good excuse to come and see Violet.

Violet went home. As she pulled the key through the letterbox, she could hear the telephone ringing inside.

'Hello,' she gasped, grabbing the receiver before she fell on top of it.

'Violet, it's Edwin. Is something the matter? Barbara said you called sounding worried.'

'Oh, Edwin! You didn't stay long in Washington.' It was a relief to hear his voice.

'I'm still in Washington, Vi. What's wrong?'

The call must be costing the earth. 'It's Will's dad, Edwin. He arrived the day after the wedding. He's still alive.'

There was a long pause before Edwin answered. Violet rested her face against the receiver, waiting for him to continue. When he did, she could scarcely believe her ears.

'I've often worried something like this would happen, that the bastard might well turn up like a dirty penny one of these days.'

16

'Edwin!' Had he been within reach, rather than on a different continent altogether, she would have shaken him till his teeth fell out. 'You told me he was dead, the father — Will's father. You're meant to be a charity worker, doing the Lord's work, and yet you've lied to me all these years, and now you're blaspheming about it.'

'I'm sorry, Vi. And for my language. It's just a shock. I thought he was almost certainly dead,' he said rather lamely. 'But there wasn't any proof either way.'

'You just this minute said you worried he might turn up like a bad penny,' Violet reminded him. 'At least now Will is old enough to make up his own mind how he wants to react to his arrival.'

'What does he want?'

'I assume you mean the father, not the son?' Edwin agreed. 'First of all, tell me how Mary and Will, only a baby, got from Bootle to Netton in nineteen forty-one?' Violet demanded.

Thousands of miles away in America, Violet heard Edwin groan. 'There was some chap,' he said. 'He'd been posted from Netton to Bootle to work in a munitions factory, the one in Kirkby. He lived in lodgings in Chaucer Street. One day, in the middle of April, nineteen forty-one, this other chap — Eric Stein — turned up. After a few days, he left his wife and son in the their shared lodgings and took off for London to join the RAF — which the chap thought pretty odd because there's no reason to go all the way to London to do that when you could do it anywhere. There was a series of pretty horrendous air raids and the lodgings were bombed. Our chap, Mary Stein, and the baby survived several nights in an air-raid shelter, but there was no sign of the husband coming back and nowhere for them to live when the raids stopped. The house they'd lived in was badly damaged. I gather they tried to track him down but there was no trace of her husband.'

Somehow, having heard this story before from the lips of another of the participants in this tale, the husband, Violet wasn't surprised. She'd met this person and realised, underneath the sharp suits and gleaming smile, she didn't like him one bit. It seemed just the way that Eric Stein would act, to leave his wife stranded in a strange city and a strange country and not bother coming back to collect them.

'So, what did the chap from Netton do?' she asked. 'The nice one.'

'He found somewhere for them to live, and, as soon as he could get a few days off from the factory, he caught a series of trains and buses and took them down to Netton and left them with his mother, whose name was . . . ?' He paused.

'Jessie Arnett!' Violet finished for him.

'Precisely.' He groaned. 'Jaysus, Violet. This phone call's going to cost more than my hotel room. I'll have to ring off. If you have any more questions they're going to have to wait until I get home.'

The line went dead, despite Violet having loads more questions. She went to make a pot of tea, but found herself completely out of it, and there was hardly any milk left, either. She put her coat back on and went out to do a bit of shopping.

★   ★   ★

That morning, when she'd called at home, Abby could tell that Violet had wanted her out of the way, but wasn't prepared to tell her why. It wasn't a bit like Vi to have secrets — though, if she was so good at keeping them, then no one would know if she'd had any! The logic of that was confusing.

She'd called in on her way home from work on the pretence of checking how Dusty was settling in, and found the house in Amber Street empty. It meant Violet had gone out and hadn't yet come back, been out, come back and gone out again, had a visitor who'd left and . . . Oh! Abby gave up.

'Drat!' she said aloud. There were hundreds of permutations. She decided to go and see Madge in Pearl Street.

Madge had no idea where Violet was, but was eager to find out. 'She's got a new feller,' she told Abby.

'But she didn't have an old feller,' Abby pointed out.

'Oh, you know what I mean,' Madge said

irritably, though Abby didn't. 'There's taxis been seen calling at the house.'

'Taxis!'

'And she goes out wearing that posh gear she bought for your Will's wedding. Her neighbours are keeping an eye on her.'

'And what's this chap's name?' Abby enquired.

'Well, I had a feeling she didn't tell me everything, but I think she said the chap's name is Crocker. He's a Yank, apparently — she met him during the war.'

'So, he's not a new chap? And Vi has never been to America.'

'No.' Madge looked bemused. 'I think your mam's been having me on, girl,' she said.

A tiny grey kitten peeped nervously from behind the settee. 'Oh, she brought Dusty round for you to look after,' Abby commented.

Both women paused to admire the baby cat and tell him how beautiful he was. Abby offered to take him back to Vi's house, but Madge insisted he be left with her. 'She'll probably want to tell me how she got on today,' she said hopefully.

'OK.' Abby shrugged. She couldn't understand old people. She went back to Vi's house and found her in the kitchen putting groceries away.

'Hello, pet.' She kissed Abby's cheek. 'I suddenly found I'd run out of virtually everything. Do you fancy a cuppa?'

'I always fancy a cuppa, Vi. Where have you been?' she asked, having only just noticed she was wearing her tan wedding outfit, but with a new dark-brown jumper underneath instead of the frilly cream blouse she'd bought with it.

'I just went into town,' Vi replied vaguely.

'What for?' Abby demanded.

Violet's calm expression gave no sign of her inner turmoil as she desperately tried to think of someone she could have met in town that day. She was relieved when the telephone in the parlour rang and was about to answer it, but Abby said crossly, 'I'll see who that is,' and shot out of the room.

There followed a long period of silence. Violet tiptoed into the parlour. An open-mouthed Abby was listening to whoever was on the telephone. The person was speaking very quickly and, although it was only faint, as she got closer it was easy to recognise the voice as belonging to Edwin Powell. She heard him say, 'Bye, Violet.'

'Goodbye,' Abby said before replacing the receiver.

'What did he want?' Violet asked.

'It was Edwin.' Abby was staring at the telephone suspiciously as if she was worried it might jump up and hit her.

'I know it was Edwin. And he thought you were me, I could tell. Out of interest,' Violet asked sarcastically, 'what did he have to say to me?

'He said he couldn't talk for long but was calling to say that Eric Stein was most likely a spy, a traitor, during the war, which he apparently spent in London.' Abby looked at her curiously. 'What's going on, Vi? Is this Eric Stein anything to do with our Will?'

'He's his father.' Violet felt as if she was about to choke. She went into the kitchen, where she'd been making tea when the phone had rung. Abby followed. She took two cups and saucers off the shelf, while Violet poured hot water into the pot and stirred it. Minutes later, the two women were drinking the tea. Violet let out a long, slow breath.

'How did you find out?' Abby asked. 'Was it through Edwin?'

'No, he came here,' Violet told her. 'Eric Stein. He'd read that article you wrote mentioning Will and the cricket match in South Africa.'

'Will's father has been in this house?' Abby's voice was a squeak. 'And you didn't tell anyone? Does Will know?'

'I told Edwin, didn't I? What else could I have done?' Violet couldn't think of anything. 'Will's on his honeymoon. Should I spoil it by ringing the hotel in Paris and telling him about his father, or leave it till he got back? Or,' she went on, 'perhaps not tell him at all?'

'You couldn't not tell him at all, Vi.' Abby shook her head vigorously.

'But what about what Edwin just said? That his father was a spy or a traitor? Did he give any more detail?'

'It's awful,' said Abby. 'Edwin said Eric Stein intended joining the British Army and supplying Germany with any useful information that he happened to come across.'

Violet took a long, deep breath. 'I don't half wish I smoked,' she said. 'I bet it'd really help in this situation.'

'It might make you feel calmer, but it wouldn't help you make a decision.'

'Feeling calmer would do for now.' Violet took Abby's cup and her own into the kitchen for more tea. 'What do you suggest I do now?' she shouted.

'Where is this Eric Stein?' Abby shouted back.

'He's staying at the Adelphi. I've just had lunch with him. This afternoon, he went to see what Southport was like. He called on his way back and said he liked it very much, and would like to buy a property there. If that was all right with Will, he said when he phoned. Said they'd got so many years to catch up on and was looking forward to seeing him again. So I said, 'I'm sure you are.''

Violet had said that sympathetically, but it was before Edwin had told her that during the war this man had not been a genuine soldier. He'd joined the army in Canada because then it would be easier to join the army in Britain. Rather than a man with a distinctly German name, instead he'd just have been seen as a Canadian soldier wanting to settle here with his British wife.

★   ★   ★

They never saw Eric Stein again. Violet waited for a call from him, even a visit, but what came was a bouquet of chrysanthemums — beautiful, brilliant, gold. There was a card attached that said, 'Farewell, Violet. Love, Eric.'

Violet wondered if somehow he'd learned that the truth had become known and he was no longer welcome in England. When she told Edwin about the flowers and the note, he admitted he'd made some calls to various places in London to get permission to tell her what was in files about Eric Stein. He felt sure word had got back to him. But, now he knew his son was alive, perhaps he'd turn up again one of these days. It was only fair that Will should know the truth about this most confusing and mysterious episode.

★   ★   ★

Will came home and was straightaway employed as a supply teacher in Ormskirk. He and Doreen seemed extremely happy after their honeymoon. It had clearly been a success, while Violet had been worrying it might have been the opposite. In fact, it was a secret for now, but Doreen was almost certainly pregnant. Only little Jack had failed to enjoy himself, pronouncing Paris 'dead boring'. 'They sold tea in little paper bags,' he complained. 'It was really silly.'

Shortly after the newlyweds returned, Edwin came to Liverpool with the intention of telling Will about his father's reappearance. Violet thought the news better coming from him. She'd spent so many years protecting Abby from Mrs Holmes, she'd never thought she'd need to do the same for Will.

'He just shrugged,' Edwin told Vi later. 'You and I had built ourselves up for this, and, after all that, he didn't seem too shocked by the news, not really. He's got a wise head on his shoulders,

320

that boy. He's been through so much that I think it takes a lot to ruffle him now. He said he wasn't going to brood on the past when he should be looking to the future. He even said it mattered less to him what kind of man his father was than what kind of father he was going to be to his own children. I suppose to the younger generation, it's so long ago. It hardly seems to matter any more, not even the stuff that happened during the war. Don't you think, Vi?'

Violet nodded, but she thought nothing of the sort. She thought it mattered very much and had no wish to see Eric Stein again, stirring up their lives. Anything that seemed to threaten her children, even now they were grown, and she was on the defensive. Perhaps Will was basically a much nicer person than she was.

Eric Stein's visit had unsettled her, upset the calm rhythm of her life that she'd expected to lead after the wedding — or was it the 'dull' rhythm? She was suddenly left looking for something more. Perhaps it happened to everyone, mainly to women with children. They lived the rest of their lives through these children. They organised their weddings, helped with grandchildren, listened to their complaints about their jobs, their girlfriends and boyfriends, husbands and wives. Violet wouldn't have changed her children one iota. She loved them totally and yet she wanted to have her own life as well as helping with theirs. Was she too late or too damn stupid to have ambition?

She still had her home typing business, and soon any spare time was taken up helping

Doreen, who was having a tiring pregnancy. Will had bought a washing machine and an automatic clothes dryer and so Violet went to their flat in Southport on Monday mornings and did the family laundry. She didn't mind, but would rather have done something more inspiring.

★ ★ ★

Ben Smith's phone call came three days after a lovely Christmas. 'Oh, hello,' a man's voice said in a friendly tone when Violet answered.

'Violet Duffy speaking,' she said primly.

'Hi, this is Ben Smith,' continued the voice. 'I'm ringing on behalf of my pop. He's not so well at the moment.'

Who the hell was Ben Smith? 'I'm sorry,' Violet said, still primly, 'but I don't know who you are.'

'Ben — Christopher's son.' There was a sound, as if Ben Smith had hit the wall, hopefully not with his head. 'Jeez! What did he call himself during the war?'

Violet smiled, as an idea dawned on her. 'Crocker?'

'That's it. Crocker!'

'Did you say he wasn't well?'

'Yeah. I wondered if you could write to him or something, give him a call. He's on about you all the time lately, about the things you did together in the war. Jaysus, you must have had one helluva time.'

There's no doubt about it, they'd enjoyed themselves, but it sounded as if Crocker had

322

been exaggerating just a bit. And she wondered how he'd explained to his son that, while his family were back home, he was spending the war living it up in Liverpool, carousing with folks like the Larkins and Violet. Had he told Ben theirs was just a platonic friendship? Or was he old enough to realise that, during the war, it felt as if the normal rules didn't apply — not when you knew every day might be your last.

'What's wrong with him?' Violet asked.

'Well, he's getting on for seventy,' Crocker's son told her, 'and, while he looks more or less OK, he's becoming a bit vague, slowing down, though he still plays a few rounds of golf once or twice a week, does the crossword.'

'I'll write to him tonight,' Violet promised.

'Great, ma'am. Do you have our address in Boston?'

'No, I'm afraid I haven't.'

The call finished. Violet decided to write to Crocker straightaway. She kept the stationery in the parlour in one of the sideboard drawers. She took the writing pad out, placed it in front of her, screwed the top off her pen and wrote, 'Dear Crocker,' then sat for ages trying to think of how to start the letter to her old friend and lover with whom she'd shared the strange, tragic and occasionally beautiful years of the last war.

'How are you?' she wrote. But she'd just been told he wasn't well. 'Sorry to hear you're not feeling so well.' That was no way to start a letter to someone you haven't spoken to since roundly rejecting their proposal of marriage.

She made several more attempts but nothing

sounded right. Her mind went back not just to their last awkward meeting, but back to the war years, dancing with Crocker, the music. The wonderful songs: 'We'll Meet Again', 'Goodnight Sweetheart', 'Yours till the stars lose their glory . . . '.

Violet closed her eyes and began to sway from side to side. For the first time in many years, she forgot about the children and all she could think of was herself — herself and Crocker dancing, but not really dancing, more shuffling around a dimly lit ballroom locked in each other's arms.

She wouldn't write to him. She picked up the telephone and dialled the number Crocker's son had just given her. Ben answered at once, as she had expected him to do.

'Would it be all right if I came to see him?' she asked.

Of course it was all right. In fact, it was the greatest idea ever. Could she come straightaway? If not this week, then the next?

She needed to buy a plane ticket, clothes, a new suitcase, but, most importantly, she needed a passport for what would be her first trip abroad.

'I'll come as soon as I can,' Violet promised.

17

Just over three weeks later, on a freezing cold day in January, Violet took off from Manchester and landed in Logan Airport in Boston, where it felt even colder. She was met by Ben, a hefty young man of about thirty with a big laugh and a big car — a navy-blue Lincoln convertible, he told her, with plaid upholstery. He had brought his cousin, Hector, with him, and both had been waiting when she had alighted from the plane, holding a placard saying 'VIOLET', making her feel rather special.

'Does Crocker know I'm coming?' she asked.

She was assured that he did. 'He's really excited,' Ben said. 'He wanted to come with us to collect you, but we wouldn't let him, not in this cold weather. He lives in the games room, you know. It's really warm and cosy out there.'

'The games room?' she queried. It didn't sound warm and cosy.

'He had it built when I was a kid. It was mainly for me — to play games in, obviously — but he's since bought a billiard table for himself and his pals. They used to play after Mass on Sundays.' He laughed. 'You wouldn't believe the noise they made. It drove Mom wild. After she died and my wife and I moved in, Dad chose to stay living out there, said he didn't want to be under our feet — but I think he likes his freedom, really.'

Violet was looking out of the window. It was after midnight when the plane had landed and Boston was deserted, the streets touched with frost. There was little traffic and the rain in the air was flecked with snow. It looked alien and so completely strange that it made her shiver. What was she doing here, on an entirely different continent, coming to see a man she'd known more than twenty years ago? She wished with all her heart she were back in her own house in Bootle. Abby and Will had thought she was barmy to go halfway round the world because of one phone call, but they'd told her it was high time she did something for herself, so she'd gone with their blessing. Except now she wished she'd stayed put.

The car turned sharply right and stopped suddenly. Violet was thrown forward in her seat, surprised to find she'd been asleep. They were outside a detached miniature mansion with about twelve windows and a white pillar on each side of the front door. Most of the windows were lit and the front door was wide open. A woman stood there wearing a fur coat.

'Here we are,' Ben sang. He leapt out of the car, opened Violet's door and helped her out.

The woman in the fur coat came racing across and flung her arms around the new arrival. The fur felt damp. Violet wondered what animal it had come from.

'Violet,' the woman panted, 'come indoors this minute and get warm.'

Where was Crocker? Violet wondered.

'Take her out to Pop first,' Ben yelled. 'He'll

get mad if we keep her in the house.'

Once they were inside the house, children appeared: two boys of about ten, both with curly brown hair and wearing pyjamas, red furry dressing gowns and matching slippers.

'Hiya, Violet,' they said together.

'Hello,' Violet stammered.

They were hardly in the house a minute when they all went out the back — Violet, Ben, the fur-coated woman, the children, and the young man who'd come to the airport with Ben whose name Violet had forgotten. There was a single-storey building decorated with fairy lights. She could hear music, a woman was singing, 'I'll be seeing you in all the old familiar places . . . '

Violet gasped. Her head was suddenly crowded with memories. Her doubts evaporated and she felt dizzy and superbly happy. She took a few steps towards the vividly lit building when the door opened, and there he stood, Crocker, wearing his army uniform, a bit loose on him now. When he saw her, he held out his arms. She paused, but only for a moment, before running into them. He lifted her up and she felt as light as a feather and remembered it was something he used to do during the war. It was a wonderful sensation.

From somewhere behind, a voice shouted that they would be fetching food very soon. Crocker's arm reached over her shoulder and slammed the door shut.

* * *

327

Violet opened her eyes. She was fully dressed and had no idea where she was, but appeared to be half sitting, half lying on a giant settee in a room big enough to hold a dance in. Music was being played somewhere, very low: Glenn Miller's 'In the Mood'. She and Crocker had danced to it during the war.

Crocker! This was his room. 'He lives in the games room,' his son had said. There was a billiard table at the far end, but no sign of Crocker. Violet got shakily to her feet. A door behind was slightly ajar. She crept towards it and he was fast asleep on a bed inside. He had changed out of his uniform into a flannel shirt and cord trousers. Half of the blanket covering him was on the floor. Asleep, he looked ill, his face pale and drawn, the skin on his neck like a rope of cords. The music was coming from a small wireless on a chest of drawers.

Violet tiptoed into the room, picked up the blanket, and spread it over him. He opened his eyes. 'Hi, kid,' he said. He lifted the blanket and patted the mattress. 'Join me.'

Without a word, she got into bed with him and he tucked the blanket over her, left his arm across her chest, and immediately fell asleep again. She was overcome with the strangeness of it all and very soon she fell asleep herself.

★   ★   ★

It was the children who woke them: twins, aged twelve, Daniel and Adam, they told her. They burst into the bedroom, stopping, open-mouthed, when they found the woman who had arrived the night before in bed with their grandpa.

'Hi,' they said together.

They were quickly followed by the woman who'd worn the fur coat, now in jeans and a polo-necked sweater. She was lovely, with dark eyes and glossy black hair.

She turned on the children. 'Get indoors immediately. Tell your father to make a pot of coffee for grandpa. I'll make Violet a drink when I come in.'

'Good morning!' she said to the occupants of the bed. 'Violet, I'm so sorry, but your luggage is still in the house. I only found it this morning. Your arrival was just a bit chaotic.' She seemed neither embarrassed nor shocked to find them in bed together. 'And I prepared you a room in the house, if you'd sooner sleep there.'

'She's OK here, Laura.' Crocker put a protective arm around his partner in the bed, as if to protect her from capture.

'I'm fine,' Violet said meekly, thereby consigning herself to sleeping with Crocker for the length of her stay, however long that might be. She wondered what Madge would think about it.

Breakfast was eaten in the house: French toast, pancakes, gallons of coffee and orange juice. The family ate together and the twins cross-questioned Violet about English football. Surprisingly, one of their favourite teams was Liverpool and Violet, who had only once in her life gone to a match, was asked to describe it, kick by kick, and goal by goal. She had tried to introduce Will to the game, but he told her it was the most boring couple of hours he'd ever known. He liked playing football, but not watching it. Nether he nor she had ever gone again.

Once the boys had finished with Liverpool Football Club, they started on the Beatles. How could she possibly live in Liverpool and not have met any of them? She explained that her son and daughter had both seen them at The Cavern before they became world-famous, but that was all.

Ben was arguing with his father about his decision to take Violet to a shop called Macy's for coffee. 'Later on we can have lunch somewhere.'

'But Pop,' Ben said patiently, 'you haven't been outside for weeks. You're seriously ill. You're taking tons of medication and need to stay where it's warm.'

'Poppycock!' Crocker said colourfully. 'We're going, and that's all there is to it.'

'I hope you don't intend going by car. Don't forget the doctor ordered you not to drive.'

'We'll go by taxi.'

'Well, that's a relief,' Ben said crossly.

Laura showed Violet the room that had been prepared for her. It was pretty with rose-patterned bedding and cream lamps. She would have enjoyed sleeping there had she not already slept with Crocker in the games room.

'I think you'd be very comfortable here,' Laura said.

'Oh, I would,' Violet assured her. 'But I've promised Crocker, haven't I? I don't want to let him down.'

In the games room, Crocker was having a shave. This wasn't easy, as his hand was shaking badly. Violet watched, heart racing, fully expecting him to cut himself.

'Why don't you use an electric razor?' she asked.

'Don't like 'em,' he mumbled. 'Never shave close enough in my opinion.'

'Can I do it for you?'

'Have you ever shaved anyone before?'

'No,' Violet confessed.

'Then what makes you think you can do it now?'

'Well, my hands aren't shaking like yours.'

He picked up a towel and wiped the lather off his chin. 'You can do it next time. I've finished now.'

⋆   ⋆   ⋆

Macy's was crowded. When Violet remarked on this, Crocker said, 'It always is. Whatever time you come here it's packed with people. My mom used to bring me on Saturdays for an ice cream. It's where I got my school uniform.'

Violet couldn't for the life of her imagine a tiny Crocker wearing a cap and blazer. She told him so and he half closed his eyes and said he could see her in a gymslip and white socks. 'I bet you were as cute as a button.'

She'd been a plain, frumpy little girl, but

didn't tell him that.

They found the coffee parlour, which had moved into the basement since he was last there. As they chatted, she noticed a film of perspiration on his forehead. She touched it with her finger. He felt much too hot.

'Would you like to go home?' she asked him. 'I think you're running a temperature.'

'I probably am. But I don't want to go home. I'm OK, Violet. Let me tell you something.' He took her hand, squeezed it, and tucked it against him. 'I want to die on my feet, not in my bed, literally bored to death from lack of action. Ben and Laura, they treat me like a hothouse flower.' He grinned briefly at the idea of referring to himself as a flower. 'The kids come and see me in the games room; all the family do. I have the occasional visitor from the old days, I watch TV, listen to music, particularly stuff from the war, but it's not enough. Nothing is compared to coming to places like this where there's people and noise and I know I'm still alive. But,' he added with a grin, 'now I have a beautiful woman on my arm and it's perfect.'

Violet nodded gravely. 'OK, Crocker. So you want me to back you up when you say you want to go out?' In other words, help him to die more quickly than his family wanted him to.

'Yes please, sweetheart.'

She didn't think anybody had ever called her that before.

It wasn't until after three o'clock that he asked if she minded if they went home. She said of course she didn't mind and he hailed a taxi — he called it a 'cab'. The house turned out to be empty. Ben had gone to work, the twins were at school, and Laura could be anywhere: shopping, at lunch with friends, gone to the movies, at the hairdressers . . .

Crocker made coffee in the games room. He also produced a tin of chocolate biscuits. Violet ate them until she felt sick and then they both lay on the bed and fell asleep. They woke up at the same time. Crocker turned on the music and they danced to 'We'll Meet Again' and 'The White Cliffs of Dover'.

★　★　★

The following day they went to a cinema that screened old movies to see *The Band Wagon* with Fred Astaire and Cyd Charisse. Violet had seen it before and it was one of her favourite films. She caught her breath when Cyd Charisse began to move her long willowy body to the music of 'Dancing in the Dark'. It was so beautiful she wanted to cry. She squeezed Crocker's arm, but he was fast asleep, which he hotly denied when he woke up. She didn't argue. Let him think that if he wanted to.

They went home and made coffee in the games room. Crocker had his along with a large bourbon and a medicine box on his knee.

'What's really wrong with you?' she asked when they were having coffee afterwards and she had sung 'Dancing in the Dark' to him to show him what he had missed.

'Nothing,' he said with a grin.

'Then why are you taking so much medicine?' There was an assortment of tablets and bottles in the box and he was taking one or more of them all.

'They're tonics.'

Violet snorted. 'No one needs ten different tonics.'

'Nine,' he argued.

'Nine different tonics then.'

He sighed. 'I suppose you have a right to know. I have lung cancer and something wrong with my heart: one of the valves is misbehaving. There's also a couple of minor things that don't really matter.'

'Really?' Violet said sarcastically. She suggested he lie down. He looked chronically tired.

'I'll give you a hand,' she argued.

He turned down her offer. 'Just now, I need a stronger hand than yours, sweetheart.'

She tut-tutted, but wanted to cry. During the war, he'd been a genuine tough guy, smoking like a chimney and drinking like a fish. He'd joined the army as a teenager in the First World War, won medals in the Second. He was still smoking and drinking — there was evidence in the games room of both. As if he knew what she was thinking, he said, 'It's all my own fault. I did this to myself.'

Perhaps he wouldn't have smoked so much or drunk so much if she hadn't turned him away so abruptly the time he'd come to see her in Liverpool, she wondered. They could have at least made some plans for the future, arranged holidays, written to each other, telephoned. But she'd cruelly shut him out of her life. She was just about to apologise for the way she'd dismissed him back then, when he looked at her, as if he understood exactly what she'd been thinking.

'But I don't want to spend time on regrets. Life's too short for 'if only'.' He pulled her towards him and she laid her head on his shoulder. They stayed that way until the twins burst in a moment later and announced that food was on the table. Violet didn't know whether it was dinner or tea. When they got back to the games room, Crocker went into the bedroom to take his coat off, but didn't come back. When she looked, he was in bed, fast asleep.

★　★　★

Next day, he told her a little about the house. It was where he had lived with his wife, and where Ben had been born. The garden wasn't all that big, he said, only a couple of acres. It seemed huge to Violet, like a private park, when he showed her around. It had a tennis court, looking sad because it was full of dead leaves.

He complained to Ben about it at dinner time. 'It looks untidy,' he said. 'Will you please get someone in to clean it up?'

'Why, do you feel like a game, Pop?' Ben asked with a grin.

'It's too windy,' Crocker said, as if he would have enjoyed a game if it hadn't been for the wind.

'Where did you go today?' Laura asked.

'The military museum,' Crocker said. 'It was really interesting.'

'You're wearing yourself out, Pop,' Ben said. He looked worryingly at his father. 'You've lost more weight.'

'I feel fine, son.' He slapped the table. 'Come on, Vi. I'm teaching her to play pool,' he told his family.

'And I want to watch *The Dick Van Dyke Show* later,' Violet said. It was on in England and the funniest programme she had ever seen.

'Can we watch, too?' the twins chorused. They really loved their grandpa.

'Sure thing, kids.' Crocker smiled at their eager faces. He really loved them back.

Violet was hopeless at pool. She gave up after a while, worried she would tear the felt covering with the stick, she told him.

'Stick!' Crocker hooted. 'It's called a cue.'

Daniel and Adam shrieked with laughter. They were getting overexcited. And Crocker was drinking whisky. Any minute now he'd light up a cigar. The room would smell like most public rooms had during the war when men and women smoked and drank themselves to death because very soon they would be going off to face death, anyway.

Violet wondered if she should have a word with Crocker, advise him to remember he was a sick man — a dying man, in fact. But that was exactly what he didn't want. He was enjoying the raucous atmosphere.

Dick Van Dyke would be on soon. She

decided to make coffee and they could all sit down and watch. After it was over, she'd suggest the twins go back up to the house and Crocker go to bed.

This arrangement seemed to work. They sat in a row on the giant settee: the boys, Crocker and herself. As well as Violet, the others laughed loudly. Crocker's laugh came from deep inside his stomach, a loud rumbling sound. All of a sudden, his head fell heavily onto her shoulder and she had a terrifying thought.

She said to the boys, 'Go in the house, will you, and watch the rest of the programme there.'

'But it's right in the middle,' one of them complained — she couldn't tell them apart.

'You'll only miss a minute or two.' They left, but most unwillingly.

Violet turned to Crocker. He was grinning widely, in the middle of one of his big enthusiastic laughs. She turned the television off and he opened his eyes.

'I was watching that,' he said accusingly. 'Turn it back on, if you don't mind.'

'I thought you were dead.'

'I don't think so.' He felt the pulse on his left hand with his right thumb and cocked his head as if he were listening to it. 'No,' he said triumphantly. 'I'm still alive!'

18

'Where are we going?' Violet asked next morning when the taxi he had called, much earlier than last time, appeared to be taking them out of the city on a route that looked vaguely familiar. She frowned. 'Isn't this the way to Logan Airport?' she asked Crocker, who was smiling impishly.

'It is indeed,' he said. He was better dressed than usual. Apart from church on Sundays, when he wore a smart suit and overcoat, he usually went round in corduroys and a logging jacket.

Perhaps her suitcase was in the boot and she was being sent home — expelled. She was having a bad influence on the invalid, Ben and Laura might claim.

'New York,' Crocker cried triumphantly, as if he'd just discovered the place. 'We're going to good old New York.'

She was more than surprised. 'How long for?' she gasped.

'However long it takes, Violet, me darlin'.' He cackled in an evil manner and pretended to twist the moustache he didn't have.

It took around four hours to fly from Boston to New York, where the atmosphere was perhaps a degree warmer. It was also so brilliantly sunny that it hurt her eyes to look at the sky, which was full of soaring buildings. Everything in America had been overwhelming — the people, the cars, the shops and houses, they all seemed big and shiny and new.

Crocker hailed a cab and asked to be taken to Worth Street. 'The Office of the City Clerk,' he explained to the driver.

'What's there?' Violet asked after they'd climbed into the vehicle.

'I'll tell you when we get there,' he promised.

The cab stopped and they alighted in a busy, colourful street. Crocker led her straight into a self-service restaurant, where he sat her at a table and then queued for coffee and a beer for himself.

He returned with the drinks, plonked them on the table, sat opposite her and said in a broad New York accent, 'Marry me, kid, and I'll give you a part in my next movie.'

'Oh, Crocker,' she groaned and it turned into a laugh. He'd never lost his wicked sense of humour.

He nodded. 'This place is special to me. Farther down the road is the Office of the City Clerk, where we will find the Marriage Bureau and for a few dollars obtain a marriage licence. Once obtained, twenty-four hours and one minute has to elapse and we can get married. Tomorrow, we shall return to this hallowed place and tie the knot. Now let's go and buy a ring.'

'Crocker!' she snorted. 'I thought you were joking. Of course I won't marry you, for God's sake.'

'I can't think of a better reason than the bridegroom is likely to kick the bucket in a very short space of time.' He spread his arms, shrugging, as if he didn't understand. 'You're rescuing a dying man, sweetheart.'

'It's a totally daft reason.' Violet started to laugh again. 'C'mon, let's go somewhere.' Back to Boston, for example.

'Not until we're married,' Crocker said stubbornly. 'And we can't do that until I've bought a ring and got a licence. There's a ring shop around the corner.'

'You mean a jeweller's?'

'I mean a ring shop.'

A young man on the next table with bright-red hair butted in. 'For Chrissakes, lady, put the poor guy out of his misery and marry him. It's obvious he hasn't got long to go.'

The man was right. Crocker was right. What possible harm would it do?

'Promise me something,' she said.

'Anything, my love.' He genuflected in front of her and she had to help him up.

'You're not to change your will.' She didn't want him leaving her money when his family might claim he wasn't in full possession of his senses.

He claimed not to know where his will was, while the young man offered to physically help him as far as the jeweller's.

The shop assistant there seemed to blanch when Violet requested just a narrow silver wedding band and so persuasive was he that she emerged with a fat gold one.

Their Good Samaritan, whose name was Joe, showed them into the room in the Office of the City Clerk, where they were to wait. It took more than an hour to be attended to.

It was dead on two o'clock when they emerged with their newly acquired marriage licence. 'What happens now?' Violet asked Joe.

'As you're obviously in a hurry, come back tomorrow at the same time,' he advised them. 'The licence is timed for one fifty-five p.m. and at one fifty-six tomorrow you're entitled to get married. Would you like me to be your best man?'

Joe and Crocker shook hands on it and Crocker hailed a cab that took them to the Plaza Hotel — 'the ritziest and most beautiful hotel in the whole of New York,' he said — where he had reserved a room.

He called Ben from their room and explained where they were. It was impossible not to hear Ben shriek at the other end of the line, 'Did you say 'New York'?'

'We'll be back home late tomorrow, son.' He rang off, chuckling, and saying to Violet, 'Thought it best not to mention the wedding or the poor guy might have a heart attack.' He grinned. 'This is the best time I've had since the war.'

Five minutes later he was fast asleep. Violet went for a wander around the hotel. She discovered there was a hair-dresser's and a beauty parlour, so booked a wash and blow dry and a facial for the morning of her wedding — the beautician remarked that she had lovely skin. She went outside and bought her wedding dress from the nearest boutique — a violet wool two-piece seemed apt.

Around eight o'clock, Crocker woke up. He

had a shower and they went down to dinner, where an orchestra was playing. The meal over, the diners danced to all the old songs. It was as if they'd chosen them especially for Violet and Crocker.

Violet knew, with utter certainty, that this was the last time she would dance with Crocker. She pressed her face against his. 'I'm sorry I turned you away when you came to Bootle,' she whispered. 'We could have been doing this for years.'

'You had your kids,' he whispered back. 'It was crazy of me to think you'd drop everything just for me.'

The music stopped and he led her back to the table. When they were seated he held her hands in his. 'These last few days have been magic, Vi. I love you. Did I tell you that in the old days?'

She kissed his hands. 'I can't remember. Did I tell you?'

'I can't remember either. I used to wish the war had never ended.' He sighed. 'How selfish can you get? But we're luckier than most people, Violet. Right now, I feel like the happiest, luckiest guy who ever lived. Let's go to bed so I can hold you in my arms.'

They leaned forward so their foreheads were touching and they were the only two people in the world.

★   ★   ★

The day after was a dream day, hardly real. Violet felt as if she were floating around New

York and Crocker were floating with her. He looked so well, so much younger. She clung to his arm. Joe, their best man, wore a black velvet suit and a red rose in his lapel. He was an actor, he told them, unemployed. Yesterday he'd been in the area auditioning for a part in an off-Broadway theatre.

The wedding ceremony took less than two minutes. Violet and Crocker emerged, man and wife, and she remembered something incredible. The day Will got married, Doreen had thrown her bouquet over her shoulder and Violet had caught it. It had seemed utterly ridiculous at the time, but it had been true, it had happened, she was now Mrs Christopher Smith, though she would always think of him as Crocker.

Joe even came with them to Logan Airport. He had become a friend and had given her his address. She had promised to write to him.

Crocker slept soundly during the flight home. Ben was waiting to meet them at Logan Airport. He punched his father lightly in the ribs. 'You old idiot,' he said, close to tears. 'You look as sick as a dog and the happiest man alive. How'd'ya manage that, eh?'

'Dunno, son, but I've never felt better.' Crocker grinned and came clean about the wedding. Violet even showed them the gold band, which she kept glancing at, scarcely believing it was real.

Back at the house, Laura hugged him warmly and showered kisses on his thin cheeks. 'Congratulations,' she sobbed, 'but I wish you'd got married in Boston and we could have come to your wedding.'

'And have that son of mine glowering at my back the whole way through, thinking I'm too old for a second chance at happiness? No, thank you.' He shook his head. 'Now I think I'll lie down for a while. You stay here, honey,' he said to Violet, 'and have cup of tea or coffee. I'll be back in an hour.'

She knew full well he wouldn't be back in an hour. Once he fell asleep it would be for ages.

When she'd been in the house for almost two hours, she went to wake him, but she felt the stillness in the room as soon she entered. Crocker was dead on his bed. He had died in his sleep, all alone, when she'd wanted to be with him when he'd breathed his last breath. She put her hand through his shirt and stroked his chest, which was still warm, but there was no heartbeat.

Violet kissed him for the last time, then went to tell his family.

★ ★ ★

She didn't know what to do with herself. She could hear activity outside: cars arriving and departing, voices. After a while, the twins came in when she'd thought all along they were asleep upstairs. They were as pleased to see her as she was them. Both had been crying. They asked dozens of questions about their grandpa during the war, though there wasn't much to tell them that hadn't happened on the dance floor or in a smoky bar.

'He didn't do any fighting in England,' she explained. 'It wasn't until he left that he had the opportunity to be brave and he won the Purple Heart.'

She wished she could go home. There was no need for her presence any more. She would only be in the way and she could imagine Ben and Laura thinking that Crocker was dead only because of her, all this reckless activity when he was a sick man.

Laura came in. 'I'm sorry. We forgot about you,' she said. 'Would you like to sleep in the bedroom I showed you when you first came?'

'Yes, please.' She hadn't unpacked from the trip to New York. Laura took the small bag that had gone with Violet to New York upstairs and switched on the cream-shaded lamps. The room looked particularly lovely, but Violet was too numb to feel anything.

'Thank you,' she said to Laura. 'I'm sorry about Crocker.'

Laura sighed. 'We knew he was dying,' she said. 'He just went sooner than we all expected.' She left the room.

Violet put on her nightdress, got into bed, but didn't lie down. She wished with all her heart that she could go home, but it seemed rude and uncaring. Crocker's family would expect her stay for his funeral, which wasn't likely to be for at least a week. She dreaded it. She knew no one outside the house.

She slid down the bed, convinced she would

never sleep, but when she woke it was daylight and time to get up.

★ ★ ★

Violet spent the days before the funeral helping in the house. There were scores of callers, there to pay their respects. She made endless pots of tea and coffee, sandwiches and even several trays of fairy cakes and shortbread, her speciality. She was introduced to all the visitors and was convinced Laura appreciated her presence — Ben was out most of the time.

More than fifty people turned up for Crocker's funeral. Amazingly, there were three army veterans who remembered Violet from the war, having been in Lancashire with 'Good Old Crocker', as they referred to him. They were delighted to see her there, and even more so when they heard about the wedding in New York. 'You've got to snatch your chance at happiness when you can,' one of the old servicemen said to her, and, even in the midst of the funeral, Violet thought about Crocker's face as they'd said their vows, and smiled.

★ ★ ★

The strangest thing happened on the flight home. Violet, whose eyes had remained dry ever since Crocker had died, began to cry and didn't stop until they were about halfway across the Atlantic.

She didn't know why she cried; it wasn't for

Crocker, but for the world, for herself, for everything and everybody. And it wasn't a loud wailing, just a quiet snuffling that didn't bother the other passengers, though one of the stewardesses must have noticed and placed a large whisky in front of her.

'Here we are, honey, drown your sorrows with that,' she said cheerfully.

The whisky worked. Violet moved into a different world, cushioned against grief and full of cheer. She began to think about tomorrow rather than yesterday. After all, she was soon to be a grandmother. Doreen was due soon and another chapter would begin with the new life. And Violet was travelling home with a secret of her own. She rubbed the wedding band, which still felt out of place on her finger. Crocker had left her a thousand pounds in his will. Should she share it with Will and Abby or perhaps have something done on the house? Maybe, she thought, she should do something exciting like going on holiday? After all, she had a passport now. She could take Madge — she'd be nicer to Madge in future, she vowed.

'There but for the grace of God go I,' a familiar voice chanted in her head. Oh, it was ages since she'd heard from her mother! Your family never really leave you, she thought. She couldn't wait to get back to hers and tell them everything. Abby and Will wouldn't believe it — Violet, married, gadding around New York.

Stewardesses appeared, they began to collect trash, put things away, close cupboards. A queue formed for the toilets. People put on their coats.

A voice told them to fasten their seatbelts.

They were nearly home.

She walked with the other passengers through customs, through passport control, and came to the exit. Violet looked around at the sea of faces. She thought of the people she'd never see again, like Crocker, or Mary, whom she'd never even got the chance to meet. But now wasn't a time for goodbyes. There, right at the front of the small crowd, were Will and Abby, her children, waiting for her.